CHASING
Castles
FINDING FOCUS BOOK 2

JIFFY KATE

She was the purest beauty
But not the common kind
She had a way about her
That made you feel alive
And for a moment
We made the world stand still

~ Lady Antebellum

CHAPTER One

Camille

Present

S ITTING IN FRONT OF A half-painted easel in the middle of my little studio with the window shades drawn for the perfect lighting, I stop painting and lay my brush to the side. As I wipe my hands on my smock, I listen closely as a siren from an emergency vehicle draws near.

Any sort of action is noticed in a town the size of French Settlement. If Ms. Becky burns a cake, the whole town knows about it. And the day Mr. Johnson's truck got stuck in the pond, practically every person was there to witness the fire department getting it unstuck.

Yes, the fire department, because, generally, they don't have a lot to keep them busy.

So, sirens this close to town, especially on a Saturday morning, are a rare thing.

I watch out the window and listen for a minute or two as the sirens seem to get closer. Unable to curb my curiosity, I walk from the back of the studio, through the gallery, and out onto the sidewalk.

No one is around. My SUV is the only vehicle on the street. So, it doesn't surprise me when the sirens get further away. There must be something going on out on the highway.

My heart skips a beat because I hate thinking about anyone being in a wreck or anything like that. As I walk back into the gallery, I say a quick prayer for whoever it is. Normally, that's enough to help me relax. I always pray when I drive by a wreck or see an ambulance fly by.

But, as I sit back down at my easel and pick my paint brush back up, my heart still feels like it's in my throat.

As I wait for another minute, still hearing sirens off in the distance, I decide to calm my nerves with a call to Annie. Carter is staying out there with her and Sam this morning because my daddy and Kay went into Baton Rouge to buy a new sofa.

"Hey, honey." Annie's voice sounds calm and chipper, so I try to make my stomach take a cue from her.

"Hey, Annie."

"How's it going this morning? Everything alright?"

"I was calling to ask you the same," I say, laughing at my paranoia. Since Carter came into my life, I have a tendency to be a bit over-protective. I now understand why my daddy was always keeping a tight rein on me when I was little. It would kill me when he wouldn't let me do everything the boys did. But now I get it. I don't know how I'd feel if Carter had been a girl. Being the mom of a boy is bad enough. It might be worse on some levels because boys can be such little dare devils.

"Everything is right as rain out here," she says, with a clang of a pot in the background. "Me and Carter are whippin' up some banana nut muffins."

"Sounds delicious."

"We'll be sure to save you some."

"Don't let Deke eat them all."

"You're in luck. He went into the restaurant to finish up some paperwork."

"I thought he was takin' the day off."

"Well, he said if you were gonna be busy all day at the gallery, he might as well get ahead on some ordering."

"Okay," I say, the nervous ball back in my stomach. "Did Micah go in with him?"

"No, Micah's in Baton Rouge this mornin'. He must've stayed at the apartment last night."

"Okay."

"I think these muffins are ready to go in the oven. What do you think, Carter?" I can hear Carter telling her they're ready. He loves being in the kitchen with Annie. I think he takes after his Uncle Micah in that sense. "Will we see ya for lunch?"

"Yeah, I should be done by then."

After I hang up with Annie, I still can't get the worry to go away. I think about taking a drive out to the highway just to check things out myself, but that would be silly. I'm not sure what's going on, but whatever it is, I doubt they need an extra rubber-necker.

So instead, I sit back down on my stool and hit send on Deacon's number, smiling as his handsome face comes up on the screen of my phone.

"It's Deacon Landry. Sorry I missed your call. Please leave a message."

I pull the phone away from my ear and frown at the screen, hitting end and immediately hitting the button to call again.

Voicemail.

Maybe he left his phone in his truck?

He does that sometimes.

Taking a deep breath as I try to stay calm, I begin to pace around the room as I call the restaurant. Normally, if Deacon's doing paperwork, he won't answer the phone, but if he's at his desk and sees it's me, he will.

After five rings, the long message for Pockets comes over the phone.

"Thank you for calling Pockets, Home of the Gator Pocket. Our hours are Monday through Thursday, eleven to eleven. Friday and Saturday, two to two. We're located on Highway 16. You can't miss us. Hope to see you soon!"

I don't know why I listen to the entire message. It's not like Deacon can answer once the voicemail picks up.

Staring at the phone, I hit redial for the restaurant, letting it ring until the message starts over.

Hang up.

Redial.

After three more tries, I call Deacon's phone again.

Still no answer.

I can't ignore the feeling in the pit of my stomach. There's no way I can paint like this, so I might as well drive out to the restaurant and see for myself. I'm sure everything is fine, and I'll have wasted fifteen minutes of my day, but I can't relax until I know he's okay.

As I pick up my purse and keys, my phone rings in my hand. I let out a relieved sigh until I see that it's not Deacon who's calling.

"Hello?"

"Cami." Sam's voice comes over the phone, and he sounds worried, which makes my heart beat even faster, and my knees feel weak. I don't even need him to tell me something's wrong. I know it. I can feel it deep in my bones.

"What's wrong?" I ask, already having to force the emotions out of my voice.

"There's a fire at the restaurant. I'm on my way there now. Where's Deacon and Micah?"

"Deacon's there," I tell him as I try to convince myself that everything's fine. He's fine.

Maybe he's the one who called the fire into the fire department?

Maybe that's why he didn't answer?

It could be something small.

"The Chief said he got a call from some guy driving down the highway. He called me on his way out because he couldn't get ahold of the boys."

"Yeah, I heard them . . . the sirens." My voice sounds foreign to my ears, like it's far away. For whatever reason, I'm still standing in the middle of the gallery, holding my phone tightly to my ear with one hand and gripping my keys so hard with the other that they're leaving an indentation. "I called Deacon," I tell him. "No answer."

"Everything's fine, Cam." Sam's reassuring voice reaches out, but my mind is all over the place. "I'm sure everything's fine. I'll call you once I get there."

"No," I practically scream over the phone as the haze I've been under lifts a little. "I'm coming. I'll be there." Without a second thought, I run out the door.

I've been chasing after Deacon Landry for practically my entire life. With our wedding one week from today, I refuse to lose him now.

Chapter Two

Camille

Past

"GIRL, YOU'RE LOOKIN' HOT TONIGHT," Stacey gushes. "All the boys are gonna be stuck on you like glue."

Stacey Guidry is my best friend. Well, she's my best *girl* friend. We've been close since the first day of kindergarten, and she knows almost everything about me.

What she doesn't know is that I don't care if the boys like how I look tonight; I only care about how one boy looks at me. That one boy who is truly my best friend and has been my entire life. The one boy who'll never feel for me the way I feel about him because he's my brother's best friend and only thinks of me as a little sister.

Deacon Samuel Landry.

The Deacon Samuel Landry, first son of the wealthy lawyer Sam Landry and his wife, Annie. Deacon lives in a gorgeous plantation home that's been in his family for generations and is a star football player at our high school. Girls want to screw him, and boys want to be him. He's perfect in every way, but the best thing about him is that he doesn't think of himself that way. To most people, he's the life of the party but, when he's with me, he's quiet and thoughtful. He has a good head on his shoulders, and he already knows what he wants in life. I consider myself very fortunate to be able to see both sides of Deacon. I just wish he could see the real me, as well.

"Hello! Earth to Cami!" Stacey waves her hand in front of my face, bringing me out of my thoughts. "Good grief, girl. Daydreamin' again? You always have your head in the clouds." Stacey is teasing me, but she's right—I often have my head in the clouds, so to speak. I sometimes find it's easier to deal with life by escaping into a fantasy from time to time.

A fantasy where my mom is still alive.

A fantasy where I'm not constantly under the watchful eye of my brother.

A fantasy where I can spread my wings and be free.

A fantasy where Deacon Landry sees me for more than just a little sister.

"I wasn't daydreamin'; I was thinkin'. There's a difference, you know."

"Uh huh. Which boy were you *thinkin'* about? Jared? Connor? Henry? You know they all like you."

"Well, I don't like them. They're so immature and dumb," I say, scowling.

"Of course, they are, silly! They're barely fifteen years old, which is the prime age for teaching them how to treat a girl, if you know what I mean. They'll mature in no time." Stacey giggles and turns her attention to her reflection, fluffing out her curly hair.

Sure, I know what she means. I've kissed a few boys, but Stacey has gone as far as second base. That certainly makes her more of an expert on boys than I am, and I'm okay with that.

Because I just want one boy.

IT'S BEEN SAID THAT HIGH school football is everything in Texas, but I think it must be that way everywhere in the south. I learned from my dad, here in Louisiana, that Friday nights are for high school football, Saturdays are for college football—SEC only, please and thank you—and Sundays are for watching the pros play. All weekend activities center around those three things in the fall, and we are to say an extra prayer of thanks for the invention of TiVo for the rare occasion when we have no other choice but to miss a game.

Naturally, the stands are almost full when my dad drops Stacey and me off at the gate so that he can find a parking spot. He doesn't have to worry about finding a seat because he'll be standing with his buddies against the fence. They're the real referees of the game. If you want to know the true score, ask them.

Before squeezing through the crowd and making our trek up the bleachers, we stop at the concession stand to buy a few snacks to tide us over until halftime. And that's when I hear her.

"See that spot right over there under the bleachers?" she asks. "That's where Deacon kissed me yesterday after football practice."

If there's one girl I hate in life, it's Marcy Bernard. Marcy is a senior, and she thinks she's better than everybody. She's also a stuck-up busy-body, and now she's a liar too. Normally, I can channel the voice of Deacon's mom, Annie, and simply 'bless her heart' and walk away, but there's no way I can let her get away with spreading lies, especially when I know they're not true.

"Get me a Coke and popcorn," I tell Stacey, handing her two dollars. "I'll be right back."

I walk closer to where Marcy and her group of simple-minded followers are standing.

"What do you want, Camille? You want in on the details of my love life, too?" She smiles, brushing her hair over her shoulder, and her friends laugh. But I play it cool, barely managing to contain my eye roll.

"Yeah, no. I'm just here to let your friends know that you're full of shit."

Marcy gasps. "You can't talk to me like that, you stupid little sophomore. What do you know anyway?"

"What I know is that, after practice yesterday, Deacon drove *me* home." I don't add that my brother, Tucker, and Deacon's brother,

Micah, were with us, because . . . well, because it isn't important. "I was waiting for him at his truck and watched him leave the field house and walk straight to me." That part is true. Deacon had obviously showered after practice because his dark, wavy hair was still wet when he waved goodbye to his teammates and headed to his truck. He was beautiful, and I couldn't keep my eyes off him.

Hands on her hips, Marcy glares at me. "Just because Deacon was nice enough to give you a ride home doesn't mean you're his girlfriend or anything." She snorts, like that's the farthest thing from the truth. "You're just a little girl with a crush. Deacon doesn't want *you*; he wants a real woman."

Her words go straight to my gut as she plays on my insecurities, but I'll be damned if I let her know. "Well, when he finds a *real woman*, I'll be sure to tell you because another thing I know about Deacon is that he has taste. He can spot bullshit a mile away, and he would never be seen with a tramp like you."

Before Marcy can speak again, I feel an arm wrap around my shoulders and pull me back. Unfortunately, it's not the arm I want to be wrapped around me. That arm is getting ready to throw the first snap of the game. And I'm gonna miss it because I'm down here getting ready to engage in my first-ever fist fight with Marcy. My blood is still boiling when Tucker's smooth voice comes on the scene. I love him, and I love that he always wants to come to my defense and be my protector, but he is always sticking his nose in my business.

"Now, now, ladies. What seems to be the trouble here?" he asks.

Marcy huffs and crosses her arms over her chest, pushing her boobs up. "Your sister thinks she knows everything about Deacon Landry and can't accept the fact that he wants me instead of her," Marcy tells him.

Shaking off Tucker's arm, I turn and face him. "Marcy was telling her gaggle of groupies here that Deacon kissed her yesterday after practice, and I simply explained that she was lying through her teeth."

"Is that right?" Tucker's grin grows wider. I know he loves this. He loves putting Marcy in her place and calling her out on her bullshit. There's no love lost between my brother and Marcy Bernard. She can't stand that he won't worship at her feet like the majority of boys at French

Settlement High School. She's never been able to weasel her way in with Micah or Tucker, and she sure as hell has never succeeded with Deacon, which is why I feel the need to put her in her place.

"Well, ladies," he starts, focusing his attention on Marcy's friends. "I'm sorry to say that your leader is, in fact, pullin' your legs. You see, Deacon went home with us yesterday. And there was no kissin' of any sort, except for when Micah and I were makin' out with the Johnson sisters against the fence before we left."

"But—" Marcy tries to argue, but Tucker shuts her up by covering her mouth. I watch in satisfaction as her face turns six shades of red behind his hand and her eyes practically bug out of her head.

"And, as for your insinuation that Cami likes Deacon as anything other than a friend, you couldn't be more wrong. My little sister is way too good for a dumbass like Deacon Landry, and he knows he'd better stay away from her." His eyes turn from the girls to me, and I watch as his stare turns into a glare. "Otherwise, I'll have to kick his ass."

I *really* hate my brother sometimes, but I keep my expression even, not giving him one twitch of my lips or quirk of an eyebrow, because I'd never want him to know how I really feel about Deacon.

"Whatever, Tucker!" Marcy screeches, completely losing her composure. She yanks on one of the girls' arms as she starts to walk off, flipping her hair over her shoulder and then flipping us the bird. Pausing, she turns back and yells, "I'd stay away from those Johnson sisters if I were you. They're walking STDs!"

Tucker chuckles and I take the opportunity to push him away from me, hoping he'll fall flat on his ass. No such luck, though. He catches himself and runs his fingers through his hair before looking at me like I'm crazy.

"What the hell was that for?"

"For being a jackass, that's what."

"All I did was stand up for you to Marcy Bernard. What did you expect me to do, stand around and let you two fight over Deacon?"

"You didn't have to do anything, Tucker. Stop trying to protect me and fight my battles. I can take care of myself!"

"As long as I'm around, I'll always come to your defense. I'm your big brother. It's my job," he says, throwing an arm around my shoulder, but I shrug it off.

"I gotta go find Stacey."

"Fine," he says, still smirking at me and my lack of appreciation. "I'll see you after the game. Try to rein it in, Mohammad Ali."

I groan and roll my eyes before walking away.

When I get closer to the steps leading up to the bleachers, I see Stacey still standing by the concessions stand with our snacks, talking to some boys, so I motion to her that I'm going to our seats. She quickly says her goodbyes and catches up to me.

"You okay?"

"Fine. I'm just annoyed at Tucker."

She raises her eyebrows and takes a drink of her Coke as we start making our way through the crowd.

We find seats close to the top of the bleachers, right by the press box, that aren't very crowded yet and sit down. I like watching the game from up here. It's far away from gossiping girls who only come to the game to talk about which player has the biggest package and who's seen it in person.

"Well, I think it's sweet that Tucker stepped in and helped you. He's such a great brother," Stacey says.

She's never been subtle about her crush on Tucker.

"I know he means well. I just wish he'd mind his own business."

The truth is, he *is* a great brother, but it's like he tries to be a second parent to me just because we don't have a mom anymore, and it pisses me off.

And hearing how he feels about the idea of Deacon and me liking each other makes my stomach hurt. I can't wait to graduate and get out of here. I want to live my life for me, not for my dad or my brother or anyone else.

Even if that means being away from Deacon.

That's how badly I want just to be Cami. Not Tucker's little sister or the late Jessie Benoit's daughter.

Just Cami.

I watch in rapt attention as Deacon commands the field. He makes solid passes, and his offensive line is doing a great job of keeping him protected. The only part I hate about watching Deacon play football is the worry that creeps in from time to time. Those boys are out for blood. I've watched some nasty sacks over the years, but Deacon always brushes them off and gets back in there, ready to make them pay.

After another solid victory by the French Settlement Wildcats, Stacey and I meet Tucker and Micah in the parking lot so we can catch a ride to the after-game party at the Crawford's. I wish Deacon were riding with us, but he has all that post-game wrap-up stuff and his truck to drive.

"So, Micah, does it suck being on the junior varsity team while your big brother is a star on varsity?" Stacey asks as we make our way out of the crowded gravel parking lot and onto the country road that leads to Byron's house.

Micah is a sophomore like me, and I know he hates when people compare him to his brother; not because he hates his brother, but because as much as people try to create a competition between the two of them, there's never been anything but love. I think everyone in town expected Micah to follow in Deacon's footsteps and play varsity right off the bat. He's certainly good enough, but he didn't want Deacon breathing down his neck all season. So instead, he'll bide his time and wait for Deke to graduate in the spring. Then he'll try out for varsity in the fall.

I've always loved that about Micah. He never lets his last name go to his head, and he doesn't care what people think he should or shouldn't do.

"Nope, doesn't suck at all. I get to play on Thursday nights and leave my Fridays open for the babes," Micah replies, earning him a high-five from Tucker.

Idiots.

Did I forget to mention that Micah is well on his way to being a man-whore like my brother?

In that sense, Micah is *nothing* like Deacon.

Deacon is a lot more subtle in his endeavors. He's dated, but he's never been one to be attached to a different girl's hips or lips every other week. Or every other day, as in Tucker's case. Even though girls like

Marcy are always making it sound like he's playing the field, the only field Deacon plays is the football field.

Tucker pulls into the grassy field that's already filling up with vehicles as everyone filters in from the game. After he finds a spot, he parks his truck, and we all head inside.

Once we're in the house, Stacey and I take a few minutes to look around for familiar faces while the boys go straight to the back porch, where I'm sure the keg resides. No one here is legally old enough to drink, but that doesn't stop it from happening after every home football game. Living out in the country has many advantages, and one of them is that just about everyone has huge yards that people can pass out in for a while before driving themselves home in the morning. All the parents here grew up together and did the same things their kids do. So, everyone pretty much turns a blind eye. Don't ask, don't tell.

We've been exchanging small talk with various people for over an hour when I reach my limit.

"This is boring," I whisper to Stacey. "I'm gonna walk around for a while."

Walking into the kitchen, I grab a red cup that everyone is filling up with booze and get some water out of the tap before stepping out on the back porch. The first voice I hear is Tucker's, of course, and I inwardly cringe.

"Baby, I can't play football and risk hurting these magical fingers." He holds up both hands and wiggles his fingers. "I'm a musician. I gotta keep these safe and sound for playing my guitar."

Amanda, the girl he's talking to, flirts back. "I bet that's not all you need your fingers for."

"You would be correct, my dear," Tucker murmurs before kissing her cheek.

I'm about to say something, but before I can get a word out, Deacon pipes up.

"Don't be fooled, honey. Tucker only needs his fingers for one thing and, because his *thing* is so small, he only needs to use two of them to get the job done." Deacon slaps my brother on his back while laughing at his own joke, and even though he's referring to the size of my brother's penis, I can't help but chuckle.

Deacon walks past Tucker and Amanda into the kitchen, giving me a playful shoulder check on his way by.

"Laugh it up, Landry," Tucker calls after him. "You're just jealous I get more play off the field than you do."

It has always been like this with Tucker and Deacon. They've been the best of friends since before kindergarten, and they show their love for one another through teasing and put-downs. The only difference now is that their jokes are much dirtier.

I find a seat on one of the patio couches and, to my surprise, Deacon walks back out and sits down next to me.

"You're not drinking the Jungle Juice, are you?" He points to the cup in my hand.

"No, just water. What about you? Looks like you've been nursing that beer for a while. There's not a drop of condensation left on the bottle. You need a nipple for it?"

I don't even realize what I'm saying until I hear the words leave my mouth, and then I just want to die of embarrassment. I have no problem teasing like that with the boys in my life, but the fact I just asked my crush if he needs a nipple is pretty mortifying. My face is burning up in humiliation, but when I see the blush on Deacon's cheeks, I relax a little. Normally, he'd fire back with a witty retort, but he can't even look me in the eyes right now.

Interesting.

"Relax, Deke. It was just a joke," I assure him.

He clears his throat before replying. "I know. You just caught me off guard; that's all. Besides, you know I don't really drink at these parties. Not when I have to drive home anyway. This," he holds up his beer, "is just for show."

And there he goes, showing me the real Deacon that not many other people get to see.

"You played a great game tonight," I tell him, nudging his shoulder with my own.

"Thanks, Cam. I love knowing you're in the stands watching me play. You're my good luck charm. You know that." He quirks a smile up at me and winks. He's told me that since the first game I ever watched him play back when he was in fifth grade. It was his first time to run the ball into the end zone. He told his mom and dad that I had to come to every game after that. And I haven't missed many. The one time I had strep throat in eighth grade and missed his opening game for varsity, he fumbled the ball twice. Later that night, he brought me soup his mom had made for me and informed me I wasn't allowed to miss any more games.

But I don't think he has any idea what those familiar words do to my insides now—now that we're older, and my feelings for him go way beyond backyard football and bike rides down dirt roads. And I can't decide whether I want to kiss him or punch him for making me feel the way he does.

Before I get the chance to make up my mind, someone yells at him from inside the house, saying they need him for a game of beer pong.

"Duty calls," he says, slapping my knee with his large palm as he gets up from the wicker loveseat.

I smile but hate the warmth he takes with him as he leaves.

"Oh," he says, making me jump. "Don't let Tucker drive home. He's been drinking the Kool-Aid."

I tip my cup to him and nod. Then I gulp the last of my water, hoping it'll put out the fire in my belly.

CHAPTER Three

Camille

Present

FIRE.

Pockets is on fire.

I can see the smoke billowing from the restaurant as I turn out onto the highway, and my heart stutters in my chest.

No.

This can't be.

Deacon and Micah have worked so hard on getting this restaurant off the ground. They've poured their blood, sweat, and tears into it, not to mention most of their life savings.

I clutch my chest as I drive faster.

As I get closer, I can see the flames as they edge out of the door that's partially open on the side of the building. It's the door that leads down the hallway where the bathrooms and offices are, and my heart squeezes in my chest like someone has it in a death grip.

I see Sam's truck parked beside the fire chief's. Then, I see Sam.

He's pacing in the gravel parking lot. A fireman comes up to him and takes him by the shoulders, forcing him to take a few steps back.

When I pull up, I barely remember to put my SUV in park before jumping out and running to him.

"Where's Deacon?" I yell.

Sam's hands grab my shoulders, and he looks at me for a second before hugging me to his chest. "He's gonna be fine."

He says these words like he's trying to convince himself, like he's assuring himself as much as he's assuring me.

"Where is he?" I ask, tears pricking my eyes. I'm not sure if they're from the smoke that's taking over the air around me or if it's from the emotions that are squeezing their way up my throat.

"He's gonna be fine," he says, smoothing down the back of my hair.

When I pull away from him and make eye contact, I see the tears in his eyes too. And something else, something that Sam Landry never shows.

Fear.

"I can't lose him," I tell him.

He nods and bites his lip as he squeezes my shoulders. "I know."

I can't.

I know what it feels like to lose the person your world revolves around.

When I was six, I barely knew what it meant to lose someone.

But today, I know what it means. I know it by heart. And I'm not sure if I can live through it.

Four

Camille

Past

ORMALLY, IF I HAVE A bad day, I'll grab a canvas and some paints and use that as an outlet. If that doesn't work, I often walk to the Landry's house, and either find Annie in the kitchen or her greenhouse out back. Today, though, I don't feel up to any of that. My mood is hanging over me like a black cloud. Instead of spreading it around like the flu, I find a spot close to the pond that separates the Landry property from my family's land and settle there on the soft grass, hoping that some fresh air and good ol' Louisiana sunshine will do me some good.

It's so warm out today; it's hard for me to believe it's already January.

Fall was a flurry of events. Deacon's last football season was the best in school history. He led them straight to the state playoffs. They didn't win, but the way our small town rallied around them, you would've thought they won the Super Bowl. Deacon was happy with the success, and everyone thought he would for sure sign with one of the colleges who've been scouting him, but he didn't. He's sticking with his dream of attending LSU in the fall.

I'm happy for him. I really am. I'm happy he's staying true to what he wants in life and blazing his own path. But I can't help the melancholy that's settled over me the last week or so. Ever since New Year's Eve, all I can think about is that this is the last semester Deacon and I will be in school together. It's the last few months that things will be like this, with him living just down an old beaten path.

In August, he'll move into the dorms at LSU, and everything will change.

It never fails, when I start thinking about change, I think about my mama, because change is a reminder that life goes on, and she's not here.

I was six when she died.

What started off as the flu quickly became pneumonia and within a week, she was gone. I don't remember much about that week, but I do remember being in the hospital and holding my mama's hand. The adults whispered while Tucker and I played quietly in the next room.

And I remember seeing my daddy cry for the first time.

He loved my mama. Even at the young age of six, I knew that much. We all loved her.

And with every passing year, I forget details of the little time I had with her. My greatest fear in life is waking up one morning and not being able to remember anything about her—the way her eyes and nose crinkled when she laughed or the way her hair hung down her back when she was standing at the stove cooking . . . or the sound of her humming while doing things around the house.

I wish I could bottle it all up and keep it with me forever, pouring a little out each time I miss her. I'd need an endless supply.

I thank the Lord on a daily basis that Annie Landry was my mama's best friend. She's always been there for me when I needed a woman's perspective and saw to it that I had a female influence in my life. My daddy has always done the best he can. He's been there for me, held me when I cried myself to sleep . . . cried with me. He's done a good job. My mama would be so proud of him, but sometimes a girl needs someone to talk to about girl stuff. Annie's always been that someone for me. She doesn't have daughters of her own, so I think I fill a missing role in her life, too.

The most important thing is she's never tried to replace my mama. She reminds me of her in a lot of ways—her gentleness and the way she smells so sweet all the time. She told me one time it's because she and my mama always used the same lotion. She even told me she'd change it if I wanted her to, but I didn't. It's little things like that that have kept my mama's memory alive for me. And ten years down the road, I'll take all the help I can get. I think Annie needs it too.

I lost my mama and she lost her best friend.

Lying back, I close my eyes and let my mind wander. I let the sad memories go and let the familiar sounds from the pond soothe me. The crickets chirping in the distance, the cool breeze blowing over me, carrying the combined smells of water and earth. They all do their part to help me find a bit of the peace I'm seeking. Eventually, my mind clears enough that my body relaxes, and I drift somewhere between conscious and unconscious.

It's not until something blocks my warmth coming from the sun that I realize I've drifted off to sleep.

"What are you doing out here by yourself, Cami Benoit?"

I should've known he'd find me. He's always had a sixth sense when it comes to me, much like his mama.

"Sleeping, Deacon Landry," I reply back in a groggy voice. There might be a little annoyance there too because my body was so warm and relaxed, and it was the first time today I haven't felt like a black cloud was following me around.

"Why?"

Slowly, I open my eyes and see Deacon in all of his six-foot-three glory standing above me. He looks beautiful with his tanned skin that lingers from the long days of summer and fall and those bright blue-green eyes that remind me of tropical waters. My heart races, but I ignore it like I always do. He has no clue what he does to me.

"I just wanted to be alone for a while."

"Anything you want to talk about?" he asks, sitting down next to me, letting the sun shine down on me again.

The question is genuine and caring, so much like his mama and so different from the cocky Deacon on the football field or the life of the party Deacon from Friday night.

This is *my* Deacon.

"Just had a crappy day."

"Anyone's ass I need to kick?" he asks, leaning forward with his long arms resting on his knees.

This is what drives me crazy. Him, Tucker, Micah—they're all three like that. Always wanting to kick someone's ass in my honor. It's sweet. I get it. I know I should be grateful, but sometimes I just want to be able to stand up for myself.

"There's no one's ass to kick," I mutter. "My mood has nothing to do with anyone else, just me."

He exhales and stretches out beside me on the grass.

I glance over at him, still amazed sometimes at the man he's becoming. I know that sounds cheesy, but it's weird and crazy to think that this mammoth lying next to me is the same kid who was only a head taller than me at one point.

We lie there in silence for a while, just watching the clouds pass by, something we've done a hundred times, but something about this time feels different. I'm acutely aware of every move he makes—his leg grazing mine, his hand twitching next to me. I can hear his breaths and when he swallows.

"There's a turtle," he says, pointing up toward the sky, pulling me out of my thoughts and back to reality.

I relax and let out a pent up breath. This is just Deacon. This is no different from any other time I've laid beside him. I mean, we've spent the night at each other's houses for goodness sake.

Get a freakin' grip, Cami.

"There's a frog," I tell him, joining in our game and pointing up and to the right. "Like, if you're looking at him from the front . . . see his big ol' eyes?"

"Yeah, I see it."

And just like that, all my worries and troubles drift away like the big puffy white clouds we're watching overhead.

"There's a steamboat," he says, reaching his arm across my body to point to something in the distance and making my skin tingle at the contact.

"A steamboat, huh?" I ask, trying to play it cool and like his touch doesn't affect me.

"Yeah, see the smoke coming out of the stack?"

I shake my head, stretching my neck up as I try to see what he's pointing to and also putting us a few inches closer. "No, I don't see it."

"Right there," he says, leaning up on his elbow and putting his hand lightly on my cheek, forcing me to take a closer look. "See it?"

I want to lean into his touch, but I try not to as I strain my eyes to see what he sees. Finally, it comes into focus, and I practically jump up with excitement. "Oh, yeah . . . and it kinda looks like water beneath it," I add.

"Yeah."

It's amazing what you can see when you want to.

"Hey, there's a castle," I tell him. This isn't the first time I've pointed out a castle. It's my unicorn—the thing I'm always looking for. When I was little, I dreamed that my mama lived in a castle in the clouds.

"You're right," Deacon says, playing along. "It's got two big towers."

"Yeah, and I think it has a drawbridge."

"And probably a moat."

"Definitely a moat."

"To keep out all the bad guys."

"Yeah."

Deacon knows all about my fantasies. Well, *most* of my fantasies, anyway.

When Micah and Tucker used to make fun of me for always day-dreaming and having my head in the clouds, Deacon would stick up for me and tell them they just wished they had an imagination as good as mine.

He gets me.

He's exactly what I needed today.

"Your birthday is coming up," he mentions nonchalantly.

"Not for another few months."

"Yeah, but it's the big sixteen. You've gotta think this one through . . . what do you want? How will you celebrate?" he asks, his voice rising as he gives me a wide-eyed expression, disbelieving that I'm not as excited about this milestone as I should be, and it makes me laugh.

"It's not *that* big," I tell him. Most kids are excited about turning sixteen because that means they'll have a license and freedom. I've been driving a farm truck since I was twelve. And freedom, I doubt that'll come with a change in my age.

"Sure it is. Your sixteenth birthday is a huge deal." He turns back on his side and faces me, leaning on his elbow, giving me his undivided attention and it makes me feel like the luckiest girl in the world. I wish I could tell him that this is all I want for my birthday, just time with him, but that would sound stupid and cross whatever imaginary boundary we have between us.

My sixteenth birthday probably should be a big deal, and I probably should be excited about it, but I can't help but think about the fact that me turning sixteen means Deacon is turning eighteen. And Deacon turning eighteen means he'll be leaving soon. And no birthday can make me happy about that.

"What's that frown for?" he asks.

"Nothing," I tell him, shaking my head. Usually, I'm transparent when it comes to my feelings in front of Deacon, but not with this. My sadness over his impending departure has to stay with me. I can't tell him. Regardless of my feelings, I'd never want to ruin what we have.

"What do you want for your birthday?"

I smile, loving the way his face lights up when he thinks about presents or gift-giving occasions. Deacon Landry loves gifts. His favorite kind of gifts are souvenirs. Like when his dad goes away on business, if he doesn't bring back a T-shirt or a snow globe, Deacon is crushed. You'd think someone ran over his dog or forgot *his* birthday.

"I want a big pink cake."

"A cake?" Deacon asks, frowning.

"Yeah, every year since . . . well, since I was little . . ." I don't have to be specific with Deacon. He knows. "My dad has always made me a chocolate cake for my birthday. Which is great," I preface. "Don't get me wrong; I love his chocolate cakes. But . . ."

"You always wanted a pink one," Deacon interjects, finishing my thought for me.

"Yeah." I shake my head and laugh, knowing it sounds completely ridiculous. I mean, what sixteen-year-old wants a pink cake for their birthday?

I do have one more thing I want, but I can't say that out loud. Just thinking it makes my stomach flip like a fish out of water.

A kiss from Deacon is what I've wished for my last two birthdays. But now, being older, I want more than that. I can't even explain exactly what I want or why, but I want it—him and whatever he'd give me. But I could never say that, not to his face anyway. I just say it in my head. It's my most vivid fantasy these days. It's all I can think about sometimes.

"I better get up to the house," Deacon says, jumping up off the ground. "Mama will have dinner ready, and you know how pissed she gets if we're late."

"Yeah, I gotta go, too. My daddy will be in from the fields soon and expect somethin' on the table."

"You wanna eat with us? You can take him a plate. I bet Tucker's still up at the house. Him and Micah were messin' around out in the garage when I took off to find you."

He stretches his long arm down to me and offers his hand to help me up. I take it, loving the feel of his skin against mine.

I think about his offer, but I really just want to walk home and be there when my daddy gets in. Besides, I have a canvas I started on over the weekend, and I want to work on it a little more. Being out here this afternoon has cleared my head and inspired me. The painting is actually of this pond. I've painted it before, but this time, I'm trying out a sunset, kind of like what we're experiencing, and the lighting is perfect. I want to work on it while it's fresh on my mind.

"I think I'll head home," I tell Deacon after we walk a little way down the path. "Tell Tucker I'll see him at the house later, and I'll have dinner ready if he wants to come home."

"You sure?"

I nod and sigh, taking him in one last time before we part ways. "Yeah, tell your mama I said hi and that I'll be over tomorrow after school."

"Okay," he says slowly, eyeing me cautiously, and there's something different in the way he looks at me. "You sure you're okay?"

I start to walk backward down the path, needing to put a little distance between us before I say something I shouldn't. "I'm fine. Thanks for the talk."

"Anytime, Camille." He smiles mischievously, using my full name. He hardly ever does that. Usually, only when he wants to tease me or get my attention. I wonder what makes him use it now.

Smiling, I shake my head and laugh lightly, turning to take the path that leads me back home.

CHAPTER Five

Camille

Present

"LET'S GO, CAMI," SAM SAYS, gently pulling me away from the back of the ambulance. "We'll follow them to the hospital."

I can't.

I can't walk away from him.

I can't leave him.

He looked so beautiful, but so . . . gone?

He wasn't awake and had smudges of dark soot on his face. The leg of his jeans was covered in blood, and they had his neck in a brace.

He was my Deacon, but not.

And they won't let me ride with him in the back of the ambulance.

"Cami," Sam's voice carries more authority and his hold on my arm is tighter. "We'll follow them, honey. I'll drive you. He's gonna be fine."

I turn to look at him, tears streaking my face. "You keep saying that, but I don't think even you believe it."

"I do." He squares me with a look, one that is a lot more Sam than the fear I saw in his eyes earlier. As a lawyer, he always has a good poker face, so who's to say he's not using that with me now.

"I need to go with him." My words come out somewhere between a plea and a full-on cry. I just need Deacon. I need to touch him and feel that he's still breathing. I need to be close to him, there for him. "What if he wakes up on the way over? I don't want him to be alone."

"He's not alone. The paramedics are working on him. Let's let them do their job."

I allow him to guide me to his truck, and I let him help me into the passenger's seat. I stare out the window at the departing ambulance as he pulls the seatbelt around my shoulder and fastens it at my hip. When he hops in the driver's side, my eyes go back to the restaurant. It's still smoldering. From the outside, it doesn't look like a complete loss, but who knows what it looks like on the inside. But it's just a building. Buildings can be replaced.

The man in the ambulance cannot.

He's wrapped up in every fiber of my being and my life.

He's in every memory.

He's everything.

CHAPTER Six

Camille

Past

"HAPPY BIRTHDAY, CAMI!" EVERYONE CHEERS as I walk into the Landry's house on a normal Tuesday night.

I feel the heat on my cheeks, and I try to hide the ridiculous smile on my face. I don't do surprises. This is totally out of my comfort zone.

"What are y'all doin' here?" I ask, looking around the room, noticing that Deacon is the only person missing.

"Well, we couldn't let a monumental day like today go unnoticed." Annie walks toward me and pulls me into one of her famous hugs. "Your mama would be so proud of you," she whispers against my hair. "I'm proud of you, too. Happy birthday, sweetheart."

"Thank you," I reply, squeezing her back equally hard.

After Annie lets me go, it's my daddy's turn to tell me how proud he is of me and how much my mama would love to see the young lady I've grown into. It makes me tear up, and I have to breathe deep to keep from crying.

We all move from the kitchen to the outdoors, where Annie's

beautiful garden is blooming, and Sam has meat on the smoker. I love his barbecue ribs. I love all of these people. I even love my stupid brother who bought me a pair of Jimmy Buffett tickets *and* talked my daddy into letting him take me when he's in Baton Rouge this summer.

When the food's done, we all make a plate and eat. The crowd is silenced under the hypnotic powers of Sam Landry's barbecue.

I'm close to asking where Deacon is, when the back doors of the house open and he walks out with a huge white box and a gigantic smile on his face.

"Did y'all start this party without me?" he asks, sounding genuinely offended.

"Well, Cami got here, and we couldn't tell her to go back outside until you showed up," Annie says, walking toward him.

"Happy Birthday," Deacon calls over the top of his mama's head. "Sorry I'm late."

Forgiven.

"Thanks, Deke." I play it off like it's no big deal and like I haven't been sitting here wondering where he's at or if he was coming. Or if he had a hot date. Or if he ran off and joined a traveling gypsy band. My mind is a scary place when I start wondering.

Micah nudges me and pulls something from his pocket. It's a folded note, like something we'd pass in the halls during junior high, and I look at him funny. "What's this?"

"Open it."

"Okay." I take it from him, but turn it over a couple of times. Knowing Micah, it's going to be some practical joke or something he and my brother cooked up, but I open it anyway.

When the paper is unfolded, I notice that it's a printed flyer. Pressing the crinkles out, I read it. A craft show? At the Catholic Church? I look up at him confused, and he smiles. "I rented you a booth so you can sell your paintings."

The lump in my throat shows up out of nowhere. Micah Landry, the one person who's never missed a chance to make fun of me—the same Micah Landry who told me the tower on the castle I painted in the barn looks like a penis—*that* Micah Landry rented me a booth to sell my art.

I shouldn't be such a girl about this, but I'm touched.

"That's so thoughtful," I tell him, throwing my arms around his neck. "Thank you." I probably haven't hugged him in five years, since the last time we were fighting in the house and Annie made us hug it out on the front porch before we could come back inside. But him buying me a booth to sell my paintings merits a hug. I've been working on several pieces for a while now, and this is just the motivation I need to finish them. Plus, I've wanted to start putting back money for college and selling my paintings might be a good way to do that.

"Happy Birthday, Cam."

"Thank you."

"It was just fifteen bucks," he says after a while when I'm still hugging him.

Fifteen bucks or not, it was the thought that counts. The thought that he might not think my paintings are stupid after all.

"Who's ready for some cake?" Deacon calls out from the back door.

I wipe a tear that slipped out, and Micah rolls his eyes.

"You're supposed to be happy. It's your birthday."

"I am." I sniff once to make sure the tears are all dried up before walking inside the house. "I'm happy. Thank you."

"Don't go gettin' all soft on me."

"Sorry. Won't happen again."

The next thing I know, Micah has me in a headlock and is giving me a noogie. Nothing like a noogie on your sixteenth birthday.

"Quit," I yell, trying to escape his firm hold on my head.

"I think it's time for birthday spankin's," Tucker calls, coming up behind me.

The squeal that leaves my mouth rivals that of a stuck pig.

"Micah Paul Landry, cut it out!" Annie calls from somewhere to my right. "It's the poor girl's birthday. Can't y'all leave her be for at least one day. Good Lord, you'd think I raised a bunch of heathens . . ." Annie continues her rant as she walks into the kitchen ahead of us.

Micah finally releases his hold, but Tucker gets one good swat in before running ahead of us. I try to catch my breath and smooth my hair, but when I see Deacon holding the huge pink cake with pretty lit candles, what little breath I had gets stuck in my throat. It's beautiful and just like a fairy tale.

It's my cake.

The cake I've always wanted.

It's like the one my mama made me on my sixth birthday. The last cake she made me. The one I told Deacon about months ago. He remembered.

And here he stands, holding it with a big smile on his face. It's perfect. He's perfect.

I don't get a chance to speak, but it's a good thing because I don't think I can. The chorus erupts around me and everyone's singing, some off-key, but they're still singing. Loudly. But somehow, they all fade into the background, and my eyes are on Deacon as he mouths the words to the song. When it ends, he winks at me over the glow of the candles.

"Make a wish," he says, holding it closer to me.

I brush my hair to the side and lean down, taking a second to think about what I want to wish for. I mean, this is my sixteenth birthday. As Annie said earlier, it's monumental. I should wish for something grand— something I'll remember ten years from now.

I take one last look up at him and then I close my eyes and blow.

The cheers let me know I managed to extinguish all the flames. Typically, that's supposed to mean your wish will come true, but this is a big one. One that is as far-fetched as they come, but if you're gonna wish, you might as well make it big, right?

"What'dya wish for?" Deacon asks.

"I can't tell you because then it won't come true." I take one of the candles out of the cake and pop the end in my mouth, sucking off the icing.

The crooked smile he gives me makes my knees feel weak.

"You remembered."

He sets the cake down on the table and taps his temple. "Like a vault."

I laugh and shake my head.

"Let's cut this beautiful cake and have some," Annie says as she walks up with a stack of plates. "Did Miss Becky choose the pink icing?"

"No," Deacon says, smiling at me.

"Well," Annie scoffs, "I *know* you didn't pick pink." She laughs, and I bite my lip to hide my smile.

"No."

"Then who picked pink?" she asks again.

"Cami."

Annie turns to look at me as she pauses cutting the cake. We stare back at each other as seconds pass, but inside those seconds are days and years, as memories register with us both. "Your mama used to make you pink cakes," she says as realization hits and there might be a hint of sadness, or regret, like she should've remembered, but it's not necessary.

"Yeah," I reply with a small smile. "She did."

"She made the best cakes," my dad says, wrapping an arm around my shoulder. "Much better than me."

"Yours are great, Daddy," I tell him, leaning into his hug. I'd hate for him to feel bad or think I don't appreciate all he's done for me. He's always done the best he can to fill the gaps. I love my daddy for so many reasons, but one of the biggest is that he's always kept her memory alive, never letting us forget how much she loved us or how amazing she was.

"You're just sayin' that because you're sweet."

"Nope, it's the truth."

"And, you're sweet," he says quietly, kissing my temple. "Just like your mama."

After the cake comes Deacon's favorite part: presents. But it's not really mine. I love giving gifts, but getting them has always made me feel weird, like, what did I do to deserve them. Plus, even though I don't have a lot, I don't feel like I need anything. Just some paints and a canvas, wide open spaces, and room to roam free—those are things that make me happy.

And Deacon Landry, but that's my little secret.

"Open this one first," Annie says, passing a blue box with white ribbon my way.

"It looks too fancy to open," I tell her, admiring the wrapping.

"Oh, shush. Open it."

Slipping the white ribbon off, I look up and feel the heat on my cheeks flare as everyone's eyes are on me.

This is why I hate gift giving.

So much pressure.

I smile awkwardly and continue opening the box, lifting the lid, and my eyes fill with tears when I realize what's inside. It's not something Annie and Sam spent their hard-earned money on, nor did Annie shop for hours looking for the perfect gift. No, it's something that's been mine all along. It's just been waiting for me to be old enough to have it.

My mother's locket.

She gave it to Annie when she was in the hospital. She made her promise to keep it for me. I've heard the story over and over. Every time Annie let me play in her jewelry when I was little, she'd tell it to me. And every time, I'd ask if I could keep it, and she'd tell me not until I was old enough.

Apparently, sixteen is the magic age.

I don't think it's normal to cry this much on your birthday. I'm not normally a sappy girl, but when I look up, everyone is blurry. It's hard to see them past the tears. I try not to blink and will the tears to dry up and disappear, but one slips out.

It's in moments like this that I know my mama is here, and she's with me, and she's watching. It makes me feel good and like she's not so far away. Running my fingers over the delicate chain and the locket, I remember. I can see her hold onto it when she would bend down to kiss me at night. She's so clear in my mind, and it's the best present anyone could've given me.

"Thank you."

Annie smiles, and Sam wraps an arm around her shoulder. I can see she's battling the tears too.

Maybe turning sixteen isn't so bad after all.

Seven

Camille

Present

EVERY DAY OF MY LIFE has been better because of Deacon Landry, even the days when we weren't together. Just knowing he was there, and that I could call him at any moment, gave me a sense of comfort that I think I've always taken for granted.

As we follow behind the ambulance, my mind races with possible scenarios. I'm usually a positive person, thinking the best of situations, but I can't get the picture of him lying lifeless on that gurney out of my head. I try to shake it and picture him the way he was this morning when he kissed me before rolling out of my bed to make our coffee.

My throat hurts as I try to keep the sob that's threatening its way up to stay down.

"I need to call Annie." The words come out of Sam's mouth like a realization, and they sit in my stomach like weight.

Oh, my God.

Annie.

I shake my head because I don't know how she's going to handle this.

And Carter. Deacon is his world.

And Micah.

And Tucker.

And my daddy.

And Kay.

Deacon is such a pivotal part of all of our lives. I just can't imagine life without him. I refuse to imagine that life. I wipe the tears from my cheeks and suck up the emotion lodged in my throat.

"I'll call her," I tell him, pulling my phone out of my pocket and hitting send once I've found her number.

I glance over at Sam, and I see the worry in his eyes. I know what he's thinking. I know that if he could, he would save Annie from this grief. He would save her from the worry. Because that's the kind of man he is. It's the kind of man he's raised Micah and Deacon to be. But he can't shield her from this. She'll be pissed we haven't called her until now.

"Hey, muffins just came out of the oven," Annie says, the same chipper tone from earlier still present. "Did you smell 'em all the way in town?"

She doesn't know.

I'm surprised because news spreads like wildfire in this town.

"Hey, uh," I start, but I don't know how to say it. I don't know if I've ever had to tell someone bad news before. I look to Sam for guidance. He wipes a hand down his face and then back up into his hair, and I know I'm on my own. If he were the one holding the phone, he'd be lost for words too. "There was a fire at Pockets."

"Oh, my God." I hear the gasp, and the instant worry and my stomach drops even further.

As much as I love Deacon, Annie loves him more. She's everyone's caregiver, their number one fan. She's been there for every moment of his life. I know this kind of love. It's the kind I have for my son. The one I can hear in the background, asking his Nannie what's wrong, and my heart breaks a little more.

CHAPTER Eight

Camille

Past

THERE'S RARELY AN EVENT OR milestone that's celebrated in these parts that doesn't include a bonfire on the Landry's property. Deacon's send-off to college is no exception. It doesn't matter that it's hotter than forty hells here in August; if Deacon wants a bonfire, that's what he'll get.

This summer has been equal parts amazing and awful for me as I've watched Deacon prepare to leave home. There were days when he was too busy to hang out because he was registering for classes, buying his books, or getting his dorm room ready. And, although he's not playing football anymore, he's still been going to the gym with his old teammates who will be trying out for Louisiana State University's second-string team.

Then there were days when he'd be home, and all he wanted to do was be with me, Tucker and Micah. The four of us would either fish at the pond all day or ride dirt bikes around the property before building a fire and staying up late, even if it meant we were getting eaten up by mosquitoes.

All hail the Louisiana state bird.

Those were my favorite moments. Especially the nights Tucker and Micah would either fall asleep in their lawn chairs or go to bed, leaving Deacon and me alone. We had some of the best talks during those summer nights, and I found myself falling deeper for him.

We mostly talked about the future—Deacon's plans for opening a restaurant with Micah and my dream of being an artist.

"You don't just *become* an artist, Cami. It's something you're born to do," he told me one night a couple of weeks ago. His dark hair was wind-blown up and away from his face after a long day of boating with some of his buddies and his lightly sunburned cheeks only made his eyes that much brighter as he looked at me. I hadn't expected to hear from him at all that day and had just turned my bedroom light out for the night when I heard the familiar sound of rocks hitting my window. Occasionally, Deacon comes to my window at night. I guess I should be used to it by now, but every time he does, it fills me with an excitement that's nearly impossible to contain. Somehow, I do, though, because the last thing Deacon Landry needs is another girl squealing over him.

That night, we walked to the pond. When my feet became tangled in the tall grass, he quickly grabbed me by the waist to keep me from falling. There was no doubt in my mind that he could hear and feel my heart beating out of my chest as he held me to him for a second too long, but I didn't care. I could've played it off as a reaction to my tripping, but something told me he knew the truth. It was in the way he kept his arm around me as we made our way to the dock and it was in the way he kept looking at me even when we weren't talking.

Something changed between us that night. I felt it, and I'm willing to bet Deacon felt it, too. Unfortunately, we haven't been alone together since then. So, I don't know if the change was fleeting or not.

I'll find out tonight.

I've made it my mission to tell Deacon how I feel about him before he leaves. Since he's leaving tomorrow, tonight is my last chance.

No more sweet and quiet Cami Benoit. Tonight I'm gonna be confident and sexy and get my man. All I need are my cut-off shorts, a top that shows off my boobs, and some lip gloss. I also need some major liquid courage.

Boone's Farm Strawberry Hill, here I come.

TWO CUPS IN AND I'M already in need of something to eat. I wasn't prepared for how sweet this crap is and I need some chips and dip to even out the taste in my mouth. Plus, my head is feeling a little funny. Outside of swiping a few sips of my daddy's beers growing up, this is my first time drinking alcohol, and I'm praying I don't get sick. That would ruin everything.

The Landry's don't normally condone underage drinking, but they're making an exception tonight with one condition: if you drink, you stay the night, unless you have a Landry-approved designated driver. No exceptions. With two cottages on the property, in addition to their humongous home, they have plenty of room. This pretty much ensures everyone here will be shit-faced within the next hour or so.

Even though drinking is accepted and practically expected tonight, I don't want to do it out in the open. There's no telling what Deacon, Tucker, and Micah would say if they saw me with a drink, and it'd break my heart if Sam or Annie were disappointed in me for doing it. I don't need a lot of alcohol, I'm sure, just enough to loosen me up before I talk to Deacon.

I take one last swig of my wine before screwing the lid back on and hiding the bottle in the cabinet under the sink of the Landry's guest bathroom. I check my reflection in the mirror and give my hair a little fluff before heading back outside.

The party has picked up quite a bit since my bathroom booze visit, and it takes me a few minutes to find Stacey. Of course, she's chatting with Tucker by the bonfire, which means I have to be careful not to act tipsy.

I should've grabbed a mint from inside the house.

"Hey, little sis," Tucker greets me, slurring the *s* sound longer than necessary. He and Micah have obviously been pre-gaming. "Havin' fun?"

"Yeah, of course. Landry bonfires are always the best," I tell him.

"Y'all are so lucky to be neighbors with them," Stacey says.

I shrug but don't disagree, because she's right. I can't imagine my life without any of the Landry's and living so close to them only made my life better. Still, it always gets my hackles up when someone makes a comment like Stacey just did.

The Landry's have money. That's no secret. My family, on the other hand, does not. My daddy inherited his piece of land from my grandparents; as well as the responsibility of running a sugar cane farm. It's not easy. Daddy earns every penny he makes, and he only spends money on necessities and the rare splurge. There's a big difference between our modest home and the mansion the Landry's own.

When I was little, kids would always ask if they could play at my house when, really, they just wanted to go to the plantation. Some kids even accused Tucker and me of being a charity case, but Deacon put a stop to that. I learned to ignore the whispers behind my back and be leary of anyone who wanted to come to my house and possibly use me to get to Deacon or Micah.

I know Stacey didn't mean what she said in the same way those kids did back then, so I decide to leave it alone and change the subject.

"How many people are here do you think? The entire school?"

Tucker answers, "Nah, it's mostly seniors and juniors, but I see a few from your grade. You know everyone loves Deke and wants to party with him."

I do know that.

It's funny when I think about it because he's only moving about thirty miles away. It's not like he's joining the military or going off to Harvard. Half the people here will be starting LSU with him in a few days, but there's no way they'd miss this party.

After discreetly scanning the area for Deacon, I finally find him across the yard playing a game of corn hole. It's a game similar to horseshoes that only gets more fun as the participants have more to drink.

"I'm gonna check out the game over there. Stacey, you comin'?"

"Sure, I'll go. See you later, Tucker," she yells as we walk off. He gives her a sloppy salute and a wink before heading to a keg.

Deacon is about to take his turn at the game but stops when he sees me. "There's my good luck charm! Cami, come over here and give my bag a blow."

The crowd watching the game erupts in laughter while my face heats up, causing them to laugh even more. But his innuendo regarding the corn bag that is tossed in the game doesn't offend me; it turns me on. I'd totally blow him if he asked me to. You know, if I knew what the hell I was doing and wasn't a big chicken.

"I ain't blowin' anything of yours, you big jerk," I tell him, playing it off, as the people around us laugh louder. I walk up to him, and he smiles. "That's my girl, always puttin' me in my place."

My heart flips inside my chest at his words, but I just roll my eyes at him. "Just how much have you had to drink tonight? It's still early, you know. It'd be a shame for the guest of honor to pass out before everyone else."

Deacon takes his turn and tosses the canvas bag onto the game board, earning three points for making it land directly in the hole and winning the game, only to be challenged to a rematch. *Does the bastard have to be good at everything?*

"I've had a few beers, but I'm pacin' myself," he answers.

"Oh, really? Why's that?"

"I made a bet with Micah and Tucker: the first one of us to puke has to run around the bonfire buck naked."

"Of course, you three would make a bet like that," I laugh.

"The thing is, though," he continues, "those two idiots actually want to lose. I think they're just lookin' for an excuse to take their clothes off."

"You're probably right. What a pair of dumbasses."

I get lost in Deacon's face as he laughs. His eyes crinkle so much they're almost hidden, making room for his wide grin. His Adam's apple mesmerizes me as it moves in time with his chuckles. It should be a sin to be so beautiful.

He eventually stops laughing and clears his throat. "You look really pretty tonight." His voice is lower and softer than it was a few seconds ago, and I know his words are just for my ears.

"Thank you," I say, dipping my head so he doesn't notice my blush. I want to tell him what I came here to say, but it's too early in the evening, and neither one of us is buzzed enough yet. Instead, I kiss two of my fingertips and touch the top of his hand.

"For luck," I say, before leaving him and his game. I can feel his stare following me as I walk in search of Stacey, but I don't let myself turn around.

A couple of hours later and the atmosphere of the party has changed again. The crowd has dwindled down with only those that are drunk remaining. It's not as loud as it was earlier, but there's still the occasional sound of laughter ringing across the yard. Stacey's brother picked her up a few minutes ago, so I've been wandering around, moving from group to group, socializing more than I normally do. Boone's Farm will do that to you, I guess. I finished my first bottle about an hour ago, but there's another one still in the bathroom in case I need it.

I've seen Deacon from time to time being the usual life of the party. He seems to handle his liquor well, even though I know he's pretty drunk right now. The opposite is true for our brothers, though.

They decided to forget about the bet and go ahead and strip for everyone. Tucker claimed it was a "win-win" for everyone before he and Micah started strutting around the fire. They eventually realized they were putting their manhood at risk of being burned to a crisp and declared it was more important to protect their "goods" than to show them off. They're now both passed out on the porch swings, wearing each other's underwear because they were too drunk to tell which pair was which.

A high-pitched giggle carries across the lawn, and when I see that it's Lacy Monroe, the girl Deacon took to prom, my stomach twists.

I'd heard that she's been crushing on Deacon pretty hard all summer, but if they've been dating, I've seen no evidence of it. Of course, Deacon could be dating her and not telling me about it, but I'd like to think he wouldn't keep something like that from me, even though it'd hurt like hell to hear it.

I watch the two of them interact, and I don't know how to feel.

Deacon doesn't seem to be very interested, but he's not pushing her away either. She keeps touching him, and it's making me want to claw her face off. Her hands are in his hair and on his chest, and I swear I'll lose my shit if she touches his ass. His resolve is crumbling; I can see it. I have to act fast. I run into the house and straight for the guest bathroom. Thankfully, it's empty, so I go inside and pull out my second bottle of Strawberry Hill. This time, before leaving, I don't just fluff my hair. I also pinch my cheeks, lick my lips, and pull the neck of my shirt down a bit to reveal a little bit of cleavage.

I don't care anymore if someone sees me drinking or what they might think or say. I only care about one thing: getting Deacon away from that skank.

When I find them again, they're still playing the same game. Lacy is trying to lure him away from the party and Deacon's trying to placate her, not wanting to hurt her feelings. He's too nice. He needs to tell her to back the hell off before I do it. She grabs his hand and tries to pull him toward the cottages, but he doesn't budge. Even after being turned down, she doesn't give up. Instead, she giggles and tries to tickle his side. She calls him "silly", but really, she's the silly one. If she knew anything about him, she'd know he's only ticklish on the bottoms of his feet.

Why do girls act like this just because of a boy? I want to scream at her to have some dignity before I remember how I've been sneaking cheap wine from a bathroom all night.

Deciding enough is enough, I call out to Deacon. "Hey, Deke! Can you come over here for a second?"

He looks over at me and his eyes go wide briefly before he notices the bottle in my hand. "Sure, Cami. Whatcha need?"

Shit, what do I say? "You, inside me" always works in the romance novels I read, but I have a feeling Deacon would have a stroke if I said that. Against my better judgment, I say the first thing that pops into my mind.

Okay, the second thing.

"Can you open this bottle for me? Apparently, booze makes me weak."

He walks over to me, and I can tell he's trying not to look at my boobs. He frowns when I hand him the bottle. "Have you been drinkin' this shit all night?" he asks.

"Yeah, pretty much. This is my second bottle. Why?"

"I wish you would've told me; I'd have done a better job keeping an eye on you."

My temper starts to flare. "I don't need you to keep an eye on me. You're not my daddy or my brother."

Before he can respond, Lacy starts cackling. "How cute! She has a crush on you, Deacon. Be gentle when you break her heart, okay?"

I'm mortified, but Deacon just looks confused, as if he's just now realizing her words could be true.

"Shut up," he snaps. It's not the first harsh word I've ever heard him speak, but it's a first toward Lacy. I can tell she's shocked, too. Her eyes widen and her head tilts as she tries to register what he just said. "Gosh, Deacon. I was just kidding."

Normally, at those words and the butt-hurt look on her face, Deacon would soften and apologize, but his eyes never leave my face as he dismisses her with his nonresponse. A second later, she stomps off in the direction of the bonfire, looking for someone else to latch onto, I'm sure.

He takes a step toward me and twists the bottle open without taking his eyes off me. "I know I'm not your daddy . . . or your brother."

His words and the tone he's using make my stomach flip. I swallow hard, searching for something to say, willing myself to be the strong, confident girl I know is inside me somewhere.

"Is this what you wanted?" he asks.

I can hear the double meaning in his words as he stands less than a foot away with the open bottle of Boone's between us.

I nod, watching his lips as he wets them with his tongue.

My eyes go from those lips to his eyes and then back to his lips. I want to kiss them, and I want them to kiss me back. I want them to want me as much as I want them.

A slight frown forms between Deacon's eyes as we stand there letting the electricity between us speak for itself.

"Can we go somewhere?" I ask quietly, mustering all of the courage I can find for those four words.

Deacon doesn't answer. He merely sets the bottle down on the ground by his feet and takes my hand, leading me away from the dwindling crowd.

Away from the glow of the fire.

Away from the house.

We walk in silence into the dark shadows down the side of the house until we reach his truck. He opens the passenger side door and lifts me by my waist, placing me in the seat.

I want to protest. I know he's been drinking. I know he shouldn't drive. But I want this, whatever it is. If it means being alone with Deacon, I want it.

A moment later, he climbs in behind the wheel and sits there, his hand on the keys, staring at me. As if something on my face gives him the answer he's looking for, he nods his head once and turns the key over. The engine purrs to life, and I pray to God no one notices.

"Are you sure you should be driving?" I ask, not able to keep my mouth shut.

"I'm fine. We're just driving down the lane," he says, motioning in front of us. It's not far, close enough to walk, so I wonder why we're driving, but I don't ask. I listen to the quiet . . . to the crunch of the gravel under the tires and the soft rumble of the engine. I glance back to see if any new lights are on in the house or if anyone is following us. When all seems clear, I sigh in relief.

Deacon turns the truck slowly down the lane and drives until we're completely out of sight from the house before putting the truck in park and turning off the headlights. No one else uses this road. It's part of the Landry property and is only used to get to the back sugarcane fields, which aren't even being used right now. So, we're alone.

"Is this what you wanted?" he asks for the second time.

I nod, and I can't help the smile that forces its way onto my face, because this is *exactly* what I wanted. The lingering wine in my body makes my cheeks feel warm, and the nerves I'd normally be feeling are a mere hum, just enough to let me know I'm doing something I wouldn't normally do, but not enough to keep me from doing it.

His eyes are still on me, and I can tell by the way his chest is quickly moving up and down that he's breathing heavily. I honestly can't tell if he's pissed or nervous or what, but I need to know before we go any farther.

"Deke—"

"Was she right?" he interrupts, motioning with his thumb over his shoulder.

Confused, I tilt my head to the side and furrow my brows. "Was who right about what?"

"Lacy. She said you have a crush on me. Was she right?"

There's no reason to lie or play it off like it's no big deal. Having this conversation was my goal tonight, and I can't chicken out now.

"Yes," I breathe out. It's a simple word to say, but the power it holds is incredible. This moment will either rock my world or devastate me completely.

After a few seconds, Deacon still hasn't responded, so I try to lighten the moment. "I'm surprised you hadn't figured it out sooner. I pretty much follow you around like a lost puppy dog every chance I get."

His intense expression softens, and he smiles. It's small, and his eyes don't crinkle at the edges like I like them to, but it's enough to get me breathing again. Until his warm hand cradles my cheek, that is.

I'm frozen in place as I watch his eyes take in every inch of my face. It reminds me of how I feel when I look at a painting for the first time. It's like he's seeing *me* for the first time and doesn't want to forget even the tiniest detail. It also reminds me that he's leaving tomorrow, but I don't want to think about that right now. I can't.

He glances from my lips to my eyes and back, just like I did to him earlier, and he slowly leans forward. He's so close I can feel his warm breath on me like we're sharing the air, and that's a good thing because I'm pretty sure I've forgotten how to breathe on my own.

Deacon leans even closer and whispers my name before placing his mouth on mine. His lips are firm but soft, and he pulls away much too soon. It can't be over yet; I refuse to accept that. To my relief, his mouth is back where it belongs before I can protest. This time, his kiss has more force, and he takes his time sucking on my top lip, then my bottom, before sliding his tongue inside my mouth.

I've been kissed before, but I've never been tasted—explored. It's like he's memorizing me again, but I don't allow myself to think about why he'd need to do that. I refuse to think about what happens tomorrow when this moment right here is what I've wanted for so long.

We eventually separate, both of us gasping for air. Something comes over me, and I have to have him again. With speed and agility I didn't know I had, I'm over the stick shift and straddling his lap within seconds. I slide my fingers through his thick hair and pull him to me. He tastes like beer and mint gum, and he smells so freaking good.

Why didn't this happen sooner?

My train of thought flies out the window when I feel Deacon's hands grab my butt and pull me closer. The movement causes a deep moan to escape, and I desperately want to hear that sound from him again. I grind my hips lower and am momentarily shocked at what I feel. I knew boys . . . *men* . . . became hard when aroused, but I had no idea it was like *that*. He's thick, solid between my legs and he fits perfectly, hitting exactly where I need him to. He continues to move my body over his, and his grunts and heavy breaths make me feel powerful. I can't believe I'm making him feel this way, having this effect on him, and I never want it to stop.

But it does.

Too soon, Deacon halts my movements and pulls his mouth away, but his eyes stay locked on mine. I can see the struggle. The fight he's having with how he's feeling in this moment and what he thinks we should or shouldn't do.

"Cami, we can't do this." His voice sounds pained, but it's nothing compared to how I'm feeling right now. Not only is my heart pounding in my chest, but there's also an intense ache between my legs. I want him so bad.

"Why not?" I demand.

I give him a chance to answer but, when he silently begs me with his eyes to be reasonable, I give him another command.

"Ask me what I wished for at my sixteenth birthday party."

"What? Why?"

"Just do it."

He runs his hands through his hair then over his face before finally giving in.

"What did you wish for at your sixteenth birthday party?"

I don't hesitate. "You."

His brows furrow and I hate that he's struggling to understand. I thought I was so obvious even when I tried to hide my feelings. I guess I was better than I realized.

"I wished for *you*, Deacon. I want *you*. Tonight. Right *now*."

His head falls back against his seat, and he closes his eyes. This is it. This is when he breaks my heart. I remind myself that I knew this was a possibility, and I refuse to cry in front of him.

His hands move from my butt to my hips, and he squeezes. When he opens his eyes and looks at me, I see resolution. And want.

"Fuck, Cami, I want you. I do, but—"

"No," I stop him. "I'm not stupid, Deacon. I know you're leaving tomorrow, and you can't promise me anything. I don't want you to. I just want to be with you."

He slides me off his lap and opens his door. I watch as he steps out, opens the back door, grabs a blanket, and takes it to the bed of the truck. He quickly returns and slips his arms under me, picking me up, and carrying me to where he laid out the blanket. He climbs in after me and pulls the tailgate shut, blocking us from everything but the stars.

Deacon pulls his T-shirt up and over his head and tosses it aside. I watch every movement, unable to take my eyes off of him, feeling like this has to be a dream. If it is, I don't want to wake up, ever. When he lays down beside me and begins to kiss me again, my hands grip his bare arms, needing to touch him, feel him, anchor myself to him, so I don't float away.

"Are you sure this is what you want?" he asks, his breaths coming out in hot, heavy bursts.

"You keep asking me that. Why?"

"Because this is serious, Cami. I don't want you to have any regrets."

"I told you this is what I want. I'm ready," I promise him. And I am. I've never wanted anything more.

To show him how serious I am, I slowly remove my shirt and shorts, leaving my bra and panties on, and lay back down. That must be enough for him because he doesn't waste any more time. He settles between my legs and kisses me again. I take advantage of my position and run my hands over his chest and back, feeling the strength in his muscles, the warmth of his skin.

Soon, we're both completely naked, and he's touching me, preparing me for what's about to happen. I thought I'd be shy or embarrassed to have Deacon see me like this, to touch me, but I couldn't have been more wrong. This is the most intense—the most *intimate* experience—I've ever had, and Deacon is the only person I want to share it with.

He gives me one last glance, making sure I want to continue, before rolling the condom down his length. When I nod my head, he enters me, his eyes never leaving mine. He moves slowly, and I hold onto his shoulders as I feel the expected twinge of pain. I let out a deep breath as it subsides, relaxing when he reaches as far as he can.

The rest of the evening is spent kissing, touching, *loving* until we're completely exhausted. Being like this with Deacon under *our* sky couldn't have been more perfect, and I'll never regret it.

We watch the sun begin to rise, wrapped up together in his blanket before we get dressed and he drives me home.

Careful not to wake my dad, he drives to the dirt road that leads to my house and leaves the truck there, walking me the rest of the way to my front porch. "I'll be home in two weeks. I'll see you then, okay?" he asks softly, kissing the side of my head and letting his lips linger. For whatever reason, that makes my stomach drop. It's like he's inhaling me in, giving himself something to remember and it feels a lot like a goodbye.

"Okay." I give, putting on a brave face, before letting go. "Last night was perfect, Deacon."

He smiles the smile I love most and nods. "It was." Slowly, he walks backward toward his truck. "Two weeks, Cami. I promise." He holds up two fingers and gives me another smile, but I see the uncertainty on his face.

Neither of us knows what to expect next. And the unknown is always scary, but I won't regret my choice to be with Deacon. I'll cherish it forever, no matter what happens.

I watch him leave and immediately start counting the minutes until I'll see him again.

CHAPTER Nine

Camille

Present

HANGING UP THE PHONE WITH Annie, I exhale and stare straight ahead, watching the back of the ambulance.

Normally, the drive to Baton Rouge seems like a hop, skip, and a jump. Today, it feels like we're ascending Mount Everest.

"What did she say?" Sam asks. There's a mixture of worry and sadness and regret in his voice that matches the look on his face.

"She's taking Carter to Ms. Becky and heading up to the hospital."

"Did she tell Carter?" Sam asks as even more worry seeps in.

"She told him that there was an accident at Pockets," I tell him, replaying the sound of his voice from the background. "She told him everything is fine, but she has to go to check on Deke."

I can't say anything else because I know I won't be able to hide the tears. If I open my mouth to say another word, the gates will open and there won't be any stopping the flood of emotion.

"I'll call Micah," he says, reaching for his phone on the dash.

Sam's tone with Micah was a lot like mine, direct and to the point.

I could hear Micah's voice, but couldn't make out what he was saying, only the replies from Sam, which again were direct and to the point. I could tell he was trying to keep from saying anything that he thought would upset me, but he doesn't have to do that. If it's a possibility, I've already thought it.

The worst-case scenario is that Deacon doesn't make it.

Anything else, I can handle. As long as he comes back to me.

CHAPTER *Ten*

Camille

Past

DEACON DIDN'T COME HOME THE next weekend or the weekend after that. On the fourth weekend, I talked Stacey into going shopping in Baton Rouge under the guise that I needed new paint brushes. Unfortunately, there is nowhere in French Settlement to buy brushes, but the truth of the matter is that thanks to Annie, I was stocked up for a year, at least. But Stacey didn't need to know that.

We shopped and I bought unneeded paint brushes and a few new tubes of paint. After shopping, I asked Stacey if she'd like to go to a restaurant Annie had suggested. I left out the part about it being where Deacon works. But when she said no, because it's "too expensive" and "she doesn't like seafood anyway," I had to spill the beans.

First of all, who doesn't like seafood?

Second of all, she had already caught on. I didn't even have to say much. She said when she saw my face drop when she didn't want to go to the restaurant, she knew it had something to do with Deacon.

So, I told her. Not all of it, but I told her what I wanted her to know.

I told her that I missed Deacon, which she already knew, and I told her that I just wanted to see if he was working, because I needed to talk to him. She was satisfied with that answer. So, we went to the restaurant. Stacey settled for mac and cheese, and I had a seafood salad. The food was not a disappointment and well worth the money I took out of my savings to pay for it. The disappointment came when there was no Deacon working that day. Our waiter said he had the day off and wanted to know if I needed him to pass on a message.

No. No message.

'I want to talk about the night we had sex' is not a message you leave with a stranger or with anyone at all.

This is probably why I haven't heard from Deacon. I don't think he'd ever call me to talk about it or write me a letter. He's more of a face-to-face talker. I know that about him, but it doesn't make the disappointment any less painful.

I should be feeling relieved that this weekend is Sam and Annie Landry's 25th wedding anniversary because it means that Deacon will be home. He'll be forced to talk to me, but I realize there's a chance it might not go like I hope.

Part of me wants to forget all about it and go on like nothing happened. It wants to spare my feelings and embarrassment. But the other part of me wants to slap its counterpart and say "what the hell are you talking about? Of course, you're going to talk to him."

Before anything happened between us, back when we were just Cami and Deacon—good friends, confidants, quasi-family—I promised myself that if anything ever happened between us, I wouldn't let it get in the way of our friendship. So, I'm holding myself to that.

"You ready?" my dad asks from the doorway of my bedroom.

I glance back at him through my mirror, and the smile on my face grows.

"Daddy, you look *so* handsome."

The blush on his cheeks makes him look younger, and it makes his blue eyes shine, so much like Tucker. Well, I guess it's the other way around. I'm so used to seeing my dad in overalls or work clothes, and his skin is usually dusty from the fields. This clean-cut guy in the nice button-down shirt is a rare sight, but welcome, all the same.

"I can't pay you for those compliments," he says, his eyes bouncing down to the floor and back up to me. A sly, crooked smile that doesn't make an appearance often enough takes center stage.

He's so handsome, and I'm not just saying that because I'm his daughter. He's a looker.

I remember when I was little, right after my mama died, there were several women who were interested in my dad. Ada Dupuis was one of them. She had major hots for my dad. She was always trying to sit beside us at mass, and she'd make extra food and bring it by the house. After a while, he finally had to tell her that he wasn't interested . . . that he might never be interested. And that was the end of the that.

"You shouldn't waste this," I say, motioning to his shirt and boots. "I better see you dancin' with someone tonight."

"What do you know about this?" he asks, looking down at himself and then smiling up at me.

"Enough." I smile back and kiss his cheek.

He shakes his head. "You're growing up on me."

I give him a sad smile and shrug my shoulders. "That's life, right?"

"You know, Cam, I probably don't tell you this enough, but I'm really proud of the beautiful young woman you're becomin'. It's like you grew up overnight."

I don't know where this is coming from, but his sweet words make my eyes tear up. He hugs me to him, and I squeeze a little tighter than I normally would. Thinking about the day that Tucker and I are both out of the house and my dad is on his own always makes me feel sad.

"Aren't we going to a party?" my dad asks, pulling away and squeezing my shoulders.

"Yes," I laugh lightly, sniffling up the tears that were trying to leak out of my eyes.

"Well, let's go party," he says, taking my hand.

We walk to the Landry's, enjoying the early fall breeze. When we make it to their property, the sound of people and music fill the night air. As we round the corner, I can see that the patio is full of people, and there are tiny lights hanging from the house to the trees, creating a canopy of white. There's also a large pit with a pig cooking over to one side. No, make that two pigs because you can't have a party this big and only have one pig. And there's a live band on the other side of the yard with a dance floor that takes up space beneath the largest oak tree. Tables are set with beautiful flowers in the center. Servers are walking around with platters of shrimp and tiny toasts with stuff on them. I'll stick to the shrimp. I know shrimp. I love shrimp.

My dad takes several of the toasts and a glass of wine and then bids me farewell as he walks off to visit with people.

Everyone is here.

I see Micah talking to some girl over by the greenhouse. Tucker is flirting with another girl on the patio.

And there's Deacon.

He's leaning against the trunk of a tree, arms crossed, legs crossed, head tilted back laughing. He looks like he's from one of those photo shoots for Gap. He's beautiful. The pain in my chest—the one I've felt since he was supposed to come home six weekends ago and didn't—multiplies.

As if on cue, his focus turns to me, and he levels me with his stare.

At first, there's a look of recognition, like he knows—he knows he should've kept his promise, he knows my feelings are hurt; he knows we need to talk. And then, the sweet smile I've always loved creeps onto his face. He leans forward and says something to the person he's talking to and then makes his way over to me.

We don't speak. He just wraps his arms around me and pulls me to him. And it feels like heaven. I know I've been missing him, but I didn't know to what extent until now.

"I've missed you," he whispers.

"I've missed you too," I reply, feeling relieved that this isn't weird. I'm still pissed at him for not coming home, and I'd still like an explanation and to know whether or not he's been avoiding me, but I'm glad we can still be Cami and Deacon, in spite of it all.

I'm about to tell him that we need to talk when the boisterous voice of my annoying brother interrupts us, and Deacon pulls away almost instantly.

"Deke, dude. You better get over here and defend your title. Micah and Everett are tryin' to say you've gone soft since you've been at college."

Deacon chuckles but turns to give me an apologetic look that's only for me. "I'll be there in a second," he calls out over his shoulder.

I try to put on a brave face and pretend like none of this bothers me. I don't regret for one second what happened between Deacon and me, but at this moment, I wish we didn't have a big elephant standing between us.

"Go," I tell him, pushing gently, feeling his tight abs under his shirt, which instantly reminds me of our night together. My eyes flicker to his and his scan my face, looking for answers. I don't miss the way he pauses when his gaze falls on my lips. It makes my insides hum and hope starts to swell inside me. Maybe he hasn't been avoiding me. Maybe he still wants to kiss me as bad as I want to kiss him.

"Go," I repeat, giving him a smile so he'll go because I know we can't do what I want to do here. Not in front of his family and my family and everyone else in town.

"Are you okay?" he asks, his eyes taking on a seriousness I haven't seen in a while.

"Yeah," I say, trying to sound convincing. "I'm fine."

"Okay," he says, nodding his head, his brown hair a little longer than the last time I saw him, but the streaks of summer are still there. "We'll talk later."

"Yeah," I nod. "I'll save you a dance."

His smile grows wide. "Sounds perfect."

I watch as he walks over to join Tucker and Micah at the corn hole game that's in session. Seeing the three of them together makes it feel like old times and nostalgia settles in hard. I almost tear up until I feel a warm hand wrap around my waist and Annie's familiar scent waft over me.

"It's good to see all of y'all together," she says, squeezing a little.

I turn and give her my most honest smile. "Yeah."

"You okay?"

This must be the question of the night.

"Of course. Why?"

She shrugs, her soft brown curls falling to one side as she tilts her head to get a better look at me.

"You just look like you've got somethin' on your mind," she says. I watch as her eyes twinkle when she takes in the night. The lights hanging from the trees amplify her baby blues. It's so funny how Micah is so much like her, and Deacon is so much like Sam, but somehow they're both so much like the other—a perfect mix.

"Just takin' in all of this," I tell her, waving my hand across the yard, hoping she doesn't read what's going on because this is supposed to be a special night for her and Sam. She shouldn't be worried about me. Besides, there's no way I can tell her the truth, not about this. "Everything looks so beautiful. Happy Anniversary, by the way."

"Thank you, sweetie." She leans her head into mine.

After Annie goes off to find Sam, I mingle.

I talk to Ms. Becky, who offers me a job at her bakery, which I politely decline. I'm pretty good at baking, and I do want to make some money to put aside for my senior year, but I'm hoping to do that by selling some of my paintings. I've been busy and have quite the collection going.

One thing about Deacon being gone is that I've had a lot of free time to be in my head, which translates to more paint on canvases. I'd never tell him, but he's been the inspiration for most of the recent pieces I've done. Stacey tells me they look sad, but that's just because I've used a lot of blue . . . and that's because Deacon's eyes are a mixture of blue and green and some days, they're all I can see.

When it's time for dinner, I sit with my dad and watch Deacon from afar. He's so wrapped up in his conversation with Micah and Tucker that he never even turns to look at me. So much has changed in the short time he's been gone. I almost feel invisible or like an outsider looking in, and as much as it hurts, I can't look away.

I listen to him tell them all about the fraternity he's in and all the good places to eat around campus, including the restaurant he works at. Then, I listen to him go on and on about a *really cool* building he found that he wants to buy. He's happy. I can see that. And he's still the Deacon I've always known and loved.

Most guys Deacon's age are into girls and partying, but not him. He's trying to figure out what kind of loan he'll need to purchase this building.

I listen as he and Micah make pipe dreams about opening a restaurant together. They talk animatedly about what they could do with it and what kind of food they'd serve.

I smile because I have to. Because if Deacon is happy, then I'm happy. But the more he talks, the more I realize he's building an entire life in Baton Rouge. No, it's not *that* far away. But it's far enough that it doesn't include me.

Realization settles in as I blindly eat my food and sip my sweet tea: Deacon's in college and I'm in high school, and those two worlds don't mix.

He has frat brothers and a job and dreams.

I have homework and my paintings and hanging out with Stacey.

For sixteen years our worlds meshed perfectly. But now, they merely parallel. Sure, he'll be home for important occasions, like tonight. I'll probably see him on breaks from college, *if* he's not working or doing something with his fraternity. But the slow days of lying out by the pond or walking the dirt trail between our houses, those days are gone.

Finally, as dessert is served, Deacon's eyes fall on me. He holds up a fork full of cake with pink icing and waggles his eyebrows. I can't help the smile that pulls on my lips. After everything, in spite of everything, he's still *my* Deacon.

I LOOK OUT THE GLASS doors of the Landry's kitchen. I just helped Annie make sure the last of the food was put away. If truth be told, I've been procrastinating for the last hour. Deacon is still outside with the guys, but I was hoping that we'd be able to talk tonight. I know he'll be here tomorrow, but we have mass, and I'm afraid he'll leave before I get a chance to talk to him.

"Need me to drive you home?" Sam asks as he walks into the kitchen. "Annie went upstairs to get out of those God forsaken shoes." He laughs shaking his head. "I don't know how you women do it."

"Not me," I say, kicking up a leg to show him my sensible flats. "I'm not down with all of that pain is beauty mumbo jumbo."

"Good," he laughs. "Keep it that way. Besides, you're pretty enough. You get any prettier, and Clay and I are gonna have to start standin' down on the main road with our shotguns."

"Please!" I exclaim, rolling my eyes. "I don't even have a boyfriend." I don't add that I would like to have one and that I would like it to be his son. He doesn't need to know that. I can only imagine the fallout from that bomb.

"So you need a ride home?"

"No, I'm sure Tucker will be ready before too long. Besides," I tell him, quirking an eyebrow, "it's not like somethin's gonna get me."

He laughs, leaning against the counter.

"You never know. You can't be too careful."

"Thanks, but I'll be fine."

He takes a deep breath and cranes his neck to see outside. "Those boys are probably gonna be out there half the night. If you change your mind, come find me. I'll be watchin' the ball game in the den. I TiVo'd it." He raises his eyebrows like I should be impressed, and I am because Sam might be a genius lawyer, but he sucks at technology.

"Look at you, Mr. TiVo."

"Be sure to tell Deacon. He thinks I can't do anything now that he's not livin' here."

Does everyone have to remind me of that?

"I'll be sure to give you a glowin' review."

"And that's why you're my favorite."

I smile and laugh, shaking my head as he leaves the kitchen.

Walking over to the glass doors, I watch as the boys laugh and occasionally punch each other in various body parts. This could go in all night, and I'm tired.

Just when I open the door and think I'm going to forget about it and take the shortcut home, Deacon glances up this way and sees me watching. He says something, slaps Tucker on the back and jogs up to the house.

"Are you headin' home?" he asks as he slows to a walk when he gets to the patio.

"Yeah, I'm tired."

"Mind if I walk with you?"

"No," I say, shaking my head and trying to feign indifference, but inside my heart does a flip.

Our talk starts off casual.

"How's LSU?"

"How's FS High?"

"How's the job?"

"How's the paintin'?"

And then it starts to take a turn to where we need it to be. "Missin' home yet?" I ask.

"Yeah," he admits, his hands pushed down in his pockets. "It's kinda weird, ya know? When I'm there, I love bein' there. But when I'm home, I realize how much I miss everything here and how much I love bein' here."

"I bet the food isn't nearly as good as your mama's," I tease, loving the feel of the ease we've always known.

"Not even close," he says, laughing lightly.

When the lingering fire from the pit in the backyard is a distant glow behind us, he takes his hands out of his pockets and slips an arm around my waist and pulls me to him. Kissing the top of my head, he breathes deeply. "I've missed you most."

Tears prickle my eyes, and I have to force them open, so they don't slip out. It's what I wanted him to say, that he missed me, but now that he's said it, it kills me because deep down I know things won't be like I want them to be. Deacon isn't coming home anytime soon. But it doesn't keep me from telling him how I feel.

"I didn't realize how much I'd miss you," I confess.

"I'm sorry I didn't come home when I said I would."

"It's okay."

"No, it's not," he says, his voice low and regretful. "I promised, and I didn't keep it. I'm really sorry."

We walk in silence until the faint light from my porch is visible. I slow my steps, not ready to give up this alone time with Deacon and knowing there're things we still need to say.

"You told me you couldn't make me any promises," I reminded him.

"Cami, I—" he starts, but I cut him off, because if he's getting ready to say that we shouldn't have done what we did, it'll kill me. So, I put my hand gently over his mouth and force him to hear me out.

"And I told you I wanted to do it anyway. I still don't have any regrets."

I look up at him, letting my hand slip from his mouth, and silently plead with him to not say that he does. I want to go on believing that he wanted that as much as I did and that he doesn't regret it either.

"I know we're at two different places in our lives," I continue. "And I'm okay with just being your best friend. My only fear was losing you completely, but if you can promise that won't happen, I'll be okay."

"That will never happen. I'll always be your best friend. I might not be around as much, but if you need me, I'll be here for you." He gives me a slow, small smile as his eyes fall to the ground. "I wish I could promise you more, but it wouldn't be fair. You should be livin' it up and enjoyin' your last couple years of high school, not waitin' around for me."

I nod, swallowing down the pain and regret. Not regret for loving Deacon, just regret that we can't be together like I want us to be. I want it so bad. No one has ever had to tell me life isn't fair. I've known that my whole life. My mom died when I was six; I know life isn't fair. But right now, it sucks. And instead of crying and stomping my foot and demanding more, I bite the inside of my cheek to keep from crying and offer Deacon the most sincere smile I can muster.

"I feel the same," I croak out. "You're in college. It's supposed to be the best years of your life, right?" I smile up at him. "You shouldn't be worryin' about me."

"I'll always worry about you, Cami." His arms wrap protectively around my shoulders and my head nestles right under his chin. We fit perfectly together.

Three words are right on the tip of my tongue, but I know if I say them now, it'll only make this harder. So, I swallow them down along with my tears and wrap my arms around his waist, wishing I could anchor him here forever.

Wishing our lives didn't have to change.

Wishing we could grow up, but still be the same Cami and Deacon.

But that's not how life works.

People change.

They grow up.

They move on.

And I still wouldn't change a single thing.

Even though my heart is currently breaking into tiny pieces.

All of those pieces will always belong to Deacon Landry.

Chapter Eleven

Camille

Present

*A*S SAM PULLS INTO A spot near the emergency room entrance, my hand is on the handle, ready to jump out when he puts the truck in park.

I run to the back doors, still praying the whole way that when they bring Deacon out of the ambulance he'll be awake. It doesn't take long before the doors open, and I stand back to give them plenty of room.

One guy jumps out, and it's then that I finally get a glimpse of Deacon. His dark hair is a mess and partially matted down to his forehead. An oxygen mask is covering his beautiful face. And his eyes are still closed.

"Deacon?" I call out, thinking that maybe if he hears me, he'll open them.

"Let's go inside, Cam." Sam once again takes my shoulders and leads me away, when all I want to do is go to him. But like when we were still at the restaurant, there are three people surrounding him, making it difficult to be anywhere near him.

"Deacon," I say again, but this time, it's more of a demand. He *has* to open his eyes. He *has* to be okay.

They take him through the double doors, and people in scrubs and white coats start barking out and taking orders. The entire area is buzzing with activity, and we're told to go to the family waiting area and that a doctor will be out to speak with us shortly.

I look up at Sam, expecting him to refuse to leave, but he doesn't, and he takes me with him. We walk out into the stark white room with blue chairs, and we both stand there. I don't know what Sam's thinking, but I know what I'm thinking.

How did this happen?

How did I go from feeling like I finally caught the one castle I've wanted my entire life—my Deacon—to being so scared I'm going to lose him?

It's crazy how fast life can change. It's crazy how only a few hours ago, I watched him wrestle with Carter. He was so full of life, just like always. The life of the party. And now, he's lying on a stretcher in an emergency room, and I don't know if he's going to walk out of here. I don't know if I'm going to get to marry my best friend, the love of my life.

How in the world did this happen?

CHAPTER *Twelve*

Camille

Past

"WHAT'S ALL THIS MOPIN' ABOUT?" Annie asks, sliding a batch of cookies into the oven. She thinks food fixes everything, and it usually does, but not today.

"I don't know," I groan, leaning over the counter with my head in my arms.

Annie walks over and pulls my hands away from my face. "You know you can talk to me. Anytime. About anything."

"I know."

"You've been goin' through a lot of changes lately. And I know this time of year is hard, anyway." She sighs and mimics my pose on the other side of the counter, leaning in. "I think about her too, you know?"

"I know."

"I think about her all the time, but I especially think about her this time of year. It's hard to believe she's been gone ten years."

The sad look in her eyes makes me wonder if that's what mine look like. It also reminds me that I'm not the only one who misses her—my daddy misses her, Tucker misses her, Annie misses her—and something about not feeling alone in my grief makes it easier to bear.

"I do miss her, and I *am* sad, but I don't think that's what has me all mopey," I tell her, sifting through my feelings.

"Then what is it?"

I shrug and then let out an exasperated sigh.

"I'm just . . . I don't know." I huff, letting my shoulders slump. "I can't paint. I try. Every day after school, I pull out a fresh canvas, but I end up sitting there and staring at it until it's time to cook dinner. I can't see anything in my mind that's worth painting. Normally, I have, like, visions or something of a painting. I can just see it. I see the shapes and the colors and that transfers from my brain to the canvas, but lately . . . nothin'."

"I know what you need," she says.

I look at her with a quizzical stare. "What?"

Something tells me she's going to suggest cookies or pie, but I've tried all of that, and it hasn't worked.

"You need to go to the barn."

I look over my shoulder in the direction of the barn. "Am I in trouble?" I ask, looking back at her.

Sometimes, when we were little, if we were all arguing, Annie and Sam would send us to the barn to hash out our disagreements and get an attitude adjustment. Sam would put us to work sweeping or something.

"No," Annie says, laughing as she walks around the counter. Grabbing my shoulders, she forces me to look at her. "I think you need a change of scenery."

"You think I need to take my canvas to the barn?" I ask, still not following.

"No, I think you need to pick back up on your mural . . . use the barn as your canvas."

Memories of a younger me hit strong. I remember the year after my mama died, my daddy didn't know what to do to help me get out of my head and let my feelings out. Annie had given me some paint and brushes and dressed me in one of her old shirts and sent me to the barn. She told me to paint whatever I wanted, anything that was floating through my head, I could put it on the wall of the barn. And I did. And it was the best therapy money couldn't buy.

"You're right," I tell her. "I'm gonna go get my paints."

"That's my girl," Annie says, her face beaming.

With a quick kiss to her cheek, I head out the back doors and practically run to the barn.

When I push open the heavy door, I'm instantly hit with nostalgia. I'd forgotten how much fun the boys and I had in here as kids, minus the chores, of course. I open the other door as far as it'll go, letting the natural light shine through. The sun will only be up for a couple more hours, and I don't want to waste another minute.

As I take in the large wall that I used to stand at for hours, I remember. I can almost see the seven-year-old me in my oversized shirt and hair in a ponytail. My piece de resistance was the castle done up in pinks and purples, but even it is smaller than I remember. There are a few random hearts, rainbows, and a horrible-looking unicorn painted around the castle, but nothing that makes a complete picture. It just shows what a dreamer I was, even at a young age, and I have to smile because I haven't changed that much. I still love to dream. My dreams are just more realistic now. Well, realistic in the sense that they're no longer about castles and fairytales.

My mind wanders to Deacon, and I let out a deep sigh. I miss him every day. Even though he's been home a few times since his parents' anniversary party in October, it's just not the same. Even at Thanksgiving and Christmas, he was around, but he spent most of his time with Micah and Tucker hanging out at the creek and helping Annie around the house.

It might sound crazy, but I know the reason I haven't been painting lately is because Deacon isn't here. I guess I've always thought of him as my muse in the same way he's always thought of me as his good luck charm. Sometimes a conversation with him would be the spark for a painting, and I'd have to run home to get it onto canvas before it escaped me. He's always encouraged me to dream big and out loud and, because of that, I was never without fresh ideas. With him gone, there's a huge void.

Gathering my paints and brushes, I pull up an old stool and stare at the wall for a while, trying to decide on something and finally inspiration strikes.

I spend the next hour and a half painting, and I'm not at all surprised that Annie was right. This is exactly what I needed. Not once did I think of my mom or Deacon or anything else as I worked. My mind was clear and I felt like an athlete who gets in the *'zone'* during a game and can't be distracted.

Standing back, I take in the swirls and abstract strokes. It's mostly greens and blues, shades that represent this time of my life. The blues remind me of the sky and the clouds I love to get lost in while I'm daydreaming. The greens represent newness and a fresh start. As a whole, it will make a very pretty background, leaving my options open for what I decide to paint next.

After cleaning up my supplies, I close both barn doors and walk home, relaxed and exhausted, but more content than I've felt in months.

A week later, I'm standing in the same spot, looking over my work I've done so far on the mural. I finally decided to show Stacey, because she wouldn't leave me alone, always asking what I'm doing and why I can't hang out. And now, I'm waiting for her reaction.

"So what is it?" Stacey asks, sitting on a blanket on the floor of the barn, staring up at my work.

I can't help but laugh. For some reason, it just strikes me funny. I feel like a little kid who's made a drawing at school, and the parent is too afraid to make an assumption. *"Tell me about your picture, Timmy."*

"I'm serious," Stacey whines.

"Well," I start, clearing my throat. "The blues and white are supposed to be clouds. And the greens are supposed to represent the fields and grass." I motion with my hand, and Stacey follows with her eyes, nodding.

"Okay, I see that," she says, tilting her head.

"I wanted to leave the original castle and all of the other smaller paintings I did when I was younger. So, I decided to make the fresh paint more abstract. I'm thinking about painting some large trees that resemble the ones that line the lane in front of the plantation."

"Oooooh, that would be pretty," she gushes. "You're so talented."

"Stop."

"I'm serious. I do good to draw hearts," she says, laughing. "One of these days, someone is going to pay a lot of money for a Camille Benoit original." I laugh, shaking my head at her. Only your best friend has that kind of belief in you.

"Thanks, Stace."

"I only speak the truth." We sit on the dusty wooden floor for a few more minutes, just taking in the painted wall and listening to the outside world filtering into the barn.

"I think I'm gonna have sex with Bryan," Stacey blurts out.

My head does a slow turn in her direction, and I try to school my facial expression so she doesn't see my disapproval. Bryan Vincent only likes her for her boobs. He's not v-card material. But I know Stacey, and if I make my disapproval known, it'll make her want to do it with him that much more. It's the same reason why I stopped telling her how Tucker wasn't worth waiting around for, besides the fact that Tucker was never going to ask her out.

She's my best friend and in his book, best friends are off limits. That especially applies to Deacon and me. Well, in Tucker's eyes, there never could be a *Deacon and me.*

"Bryan, huh?" I ask, trying to sound indifferent.

"Yeah, I mean, we've been goin' out for over a month, and I'm tired of waitin'."

I can't help the chuckle that escapes and the eye roll that follows.

"Don't give it up to Bryan just because you're tired of waitin'. That's the worst reason ever. Besides, what happened to roses and moonlit nights? You can't abandon your dreams of the perfect night yet."

Stacey sighs and leans back on her elbows, stretching her legs out in front of her. "Do you think you'll graduate a virgin?" she asks. I swallow, wishing I would've just told her about Deacon and me when it happened.

"Uh . . ." I can't lie. She's my best friend. Best friends don't lie.

Instead of lying or admitting guilt, I stand and begin to pace in front of the wall, pretending like I'm examining my work, avoiding her stare and her question.

"Camille Benoit."

I stop pacing, but I don't turn to look at her. She'd see right through me.

"What are you not tellin' me?" she asks, standing up behind me and I can almost hear her hands land on her hips.

Finally, I decide to face the music and rip the band-aid off. I turn in her direction, but my eyes stay glued to the wooden plank beneath my feet. "I had sex with Deacon."

The laugh that erupts is half incredulous and half hysterical. "Right. And I had sex with Matthew McConaughey."

When I keep my head down and don't laugh or say anything in response, she takes a step closer.

"You had sex with Deacon." It's not a question. It's a statement.

I nod, finally raising my head to look at her. "Yep."

"When?"

"The night of the bonfire before he left for college."

"Where?"

"The back of his truck." I realize now that the back of an old pick-up truck probably isn't the most romantic place to lose your virginity, but it was perfect. For me, anyway.

"Why didn't you tell me?" she asks, and I can see the slight hurt in her eyes.

"I don't know," I tell her, shaking my head. "I guess I felt like I was betrayin' Deacon somehow . . . like I had to protect what we had, but . . ." I trail off because we don't have anything. He's Deacon, and I'm Cami, but we're not Deacon and Cami.

"So, are y'all like secretly datin' or somethin'?" she asks, her voice going higher as she tries to mentally put it all together.

"No." I shake my head. "I mean, I wish, but no."

"Why not? You two are perfect for each other. Everyone knows that, including the two of you." Stacey's pointed stare makes me squirm. I don't want to talk about this. It still hurts.

"Because it's just not in the cards for us."

She groans her dissatisfaction and rolls her eyes until realization dawns on her. "That's why you wanted to go to Baton Rouge a couple of months ago."

"Yeah," I admit. "I just needed to talk to him. I felt like he was avoidin' me and I couldn't let that be how things ended."

"So, did you ever get a chance to talk to him?"

"At Sam and Annie's anniversary party. Well, later that night. He walked me home, and we talked."

"And?"

"And, we're just . . . friends."

Closing the distance between us, she wraps her arms around my shoulders and hugs me tight. "Are you okay?"

This is why Stacey and I are best friends, because she gets me and even when I haven't told her about the biggest event in my life, to date, she forgives me and wants to know if I'm okay . . . because she knows how much I want to be more than friends with Deacon Landry.

"I'm fine," I sigh into her shoulder, not letting go.

"I'm sorry it didn't work out."

"It's okay."

"Do you regret it?" she asks, pulling back to look me in the face.

"No. I can't imagine it happening any other way; everything was perfect, except for how it ended, but it's not the end of the world. Deacon and I are still friends, and that's all that matters."

"Well, shit. Now, I've gotta get laid."

I laugh. Hard. I laugh so hard there are tears in my eyes. "Please don't have sex with Bryan. He only likes you for your boobs, and I'm not just saying that because I don't like him. So, don't do that reverse psychology shit and go have sex with him just because I say not to."

"Fine," she huffs, rolling her eyes. "Who's Tucker into these days?"

I laugh again. "You don't wanna know."

"I refuse to be the only girl who graduates a virgin."

"Just look at it this way, you can graduate being the girl who has her v-card *and* her heart still intact."

A sad smile pulls at her lips before she gives me another hug.

"You're gonna be just fine, Camille Benoit."

Even though I'm sad things didn't work out for Deacon and me, I realize Stacey's words are right.

I *am* gonna be okay.

CHAPTER

Thirteen

Camille

Present

"SAM!" ANNIE'S VOICE RINGS OUT across the mostly-empty room, and Sam and I both turn in its direction to see her pushing her way through the door of the ER. "Where's Deacon?"

"He's in good hands," Sam says as his arms wrap around Annie and he pulls her to him. Unlike me, she doesn't hold back. She clings to Sam and cries.

"How did this happen?" she sobs. "What happened?"

"All I know is that there was a fire. It broke out toward the front of the restaurant. Could've been electrical or something. They don't know." Sam's voice is also thick with emotion now, and I feel the tears trickle down my cheeks.

"Yeah, but why was Deacon still in there? Why didn't he get out?"

Sam shakes his head and rubs a hand over his eyes. "I don't know. They said the side door was jammed. They broke it open and found him in the kitchen. They think he probably passed out from the smoke."

"Oh, God," Annie says, her hand going to her mouth, and I feel myself do the same. "Can I see him?"

"Not yet," Sam says as he continues to rub her back. "The nurse said a doctor would be out to talk to us soon."

"Did you call Micah?" Her voice sounds so small and pained. I can't imagine what she must be going through. I love Deacon with every fiber of my being, but she's his mother. And as mothers, it's our job to protect our children, no matter how old they are.

"I called him. He should be here soon." Sam's eyes gaze out over the top of her head as she buries her face into his chest. "Deacon's gonna be fine."

"God, I hope so."

Me, too.

It's my prayer, the only thing that's on repeat in my mind right now. *Please, God, let him be okay.*

I'm to the point I'd make deals, sell off part of my soul, just as long as he makes it. There was a time in my life when I thought the most painful thing that could happen, concerning Deacon, was losing him to someone else. But I was wrong.

The thought of Deacon not being in this world, with me or anyone else. That's the most painful. And right now, it's ripping my heart right out of my chest.

CHAPTER Fourteen

Camille

Past

"TWO MORE DAYS, CAMI. TWO!" Stacey squeals, rolling onto her back and kicking her legs in the air.

"Damn, Stacey, I think you're more excited about my birthday than I am."

We're in my room pretending to study, but I don't know why we're bothering. My daddy is outside working on the tractor and Tucker hasn't been home in months since he went out on the road with his band. So, we pretty much have the house to ourselves.

Stacey pushes herself off my floor and plops down by me on my bed, making my pencil slip against the notepad in my lap and giving my doodle of a guitar an extra string. She doesn't notice, though; she's too fired up.

"Of course, I'm excited. You'll finally be eighteen and, like, an adult!" She ignores my laughter and continues. "I'm serious. You can join the military, vote, and pretty much anything else you want to do and no one can tell you no. The best part is that you'll finally be able to go to the bar with me. I'm so tired of going out with my cousin. I swear that girl has no standards at all. You should see the coullions she hooks up with."

"You're right, Stace. I can't wait to go dancin' with you at Fat Woody's. It'll be a dream come true," I say in between giggles.

"It'll be fun, and you know it. Besides, it'll be good for you to get out and socialize before you abandon me."

I grab a pillow from the bed and smack her in the head with it. "I'm not abandoning you; I'm just movin' to New Orleans a few months early. You're the one going off to college two hours away!"

She takes the weaponized pillow and lays her head on it. "I know, but I'll visit you as much as I can, and we can party on Bourbon Street." She pauses to waggle her eyebrows at me. "You know no one will care that we're not old enough to drink yet."

"Sounds like a plan," I laugh. Stacey has the luxury of a college fund. I, on the other hand, have the luxury of applying for student loans. So, instead of waiting around for college to start and working some local job to save money, I decided to move to New Orleans this summer and try to sell my paintings. I've seen other people do it. I've been to New Orleans several times with my family. The artists on Jackson Square have always been mesmerizing to me. I love how every person is so unique, and I'm hoping to find my niche.

It's going to be hard not seeing Stacey every day, but I won't dwell on it right now. I just want to enjoy this time with her before I leave.

"What did your dad say when you told him you wanted to move this summer, instead of waiting for the fall semester to start?"

"Honestly, he was pretty cool about it. I don't know if he thinks I'll change my mind when the time comes or what, but he hasn't said much. I'm kinda worried about leavin' him, though," I admit, hating the way my stomach feels when I think about leaving Daddy by himself.

"Oh, your daddy will be just fine. There are still plenty of women in these parts that are waitin' for the right moment to pounce him. I bet they'd even help you pack your bags to get you out of the house quicker."

"Stop," I groan, covering my face with my notepad. "You're probably right, but I do not want to think about that right now."

"So, how's Tucker doin'?" Stacey asks.

I shrug. "He seems to be doing well. His liver, on the other hand, maybe not so much." His band left shortly after the holidays and traveled along the west coast before driving across the country playing anywhere and everywhere they could. He says he'll be here for my graduation so he can take a break before the band heads to the east coast for the summer and I hope he does. I actually miss the shithead. It's too quiet without him here.

"I've been sketchin' up some ideas for flyers for the band to use. What do you think?" I show her the drawings in my notepad.

"These are incredible, Cami. You're gonna hit the big time in New Orleans. I can feel it."

AS I STAND BACK AND observe my work, I'm filled with a serious sense of accomplishment. In the past year and a half, I've managed to slap paint on almost this entire barn wall. Sam even built me my very own scaffolding, with a harness and everything. There are large brown tree trunks that branch up toward the ceiling and burst with green. Some of the foliage is more on the oak side, but some of it resembles the gorgeous weeping willows Annie has planted in the back of the plantation. And no tree is complete without moss dripping from its branches. That's what I've been working on most recently.

I haven't had time to work on the mural as much as I would've liked. Being a senior has kept me busy. Now, that we're coming to the end of the year, and graduation is creeping up on us, it's crazy.

I wipe the back of my hand over my forehead and realize I had some brown paint on it that's now smeared across my face. Awesome.

Springtime in Louisiana can get toasty. It's already eighty-something degrees today and even though the two big barn doors are wide open, I haven't felt much of a breeze since I've been in here. I guess it's time to trade in my trusty overalls for a pair of shorts. Since I clearly can't disrobe in the barn, I unhook my straps and pull my t-shirt over my head, leaving me in my sports bra, and fasten the straps on my overalls back.

Better. At least my skin can breathe.

Sitting on the bottom step of the stairs, I pick up the sweet tea I brought out with me and chug half of it. As I lean back and press the cool glass to my forehead, I scan over the wall and decide what I want to paint next.

After a few minutes, the combination of fewer clothes and refreshing drink has me feeling revived. Just as I'm getting ready to climb back up my ladder to finish some detail on the moss I've been adding to the trees, the shuffle of feet catches my attention. Turning, I practically dump my palette of paint on the floor.

Standing in the doorway with a huge smile is none other than Deacon Landry, and boy is he a sight for sore eyes. He's lost some of the bulk he'd gained during his senior year playing football. His muscles are now a lot leaner, longer. His hair is longer too. He's got the typical frat boy shag going on, and it's totally working for him. The familiar sun-kissed streaks are more prominent, framing his face and making his blue-green eyes stand out even more than normal. I haven't seen him in over a month. Maybe it's been two. Annie and Sam have been in Baton Rouge quite a bit lately for benefit dinners and charity events, so he hasn't been home much.

"Hey," I finally say, setting my paints and brush down on the floor and rubbing my hands against my legs.

"Hey, almost-eighteen-year-old," he says, a bright smile splitting his gorgeous face.

I can't help the blush that heats up my cheeks. I don't know if it's from him reminding me that I'm almost a legal adult or his presence or the smile. Maybe a combination of the three. I think I used to be immune to a lot of his charms because I was around him all the time. With him being gone so much, my resistance is at an all-time low.

I even feel a slight squeak in my voice when I laugh, making me sound like I'm nervous. That's how the girls at school used to act around Deacon, not me. Clearing my throat, I try again, hoping I sound normal. "What brings you here?" I ask.

"What? I can't come home when I want?" He feins hurt, arms out to the side like he's full of innocence. That's when I notice the box. It's small and wrapped with a white bow on top.

I laugh again and try to hide my smile, but he sees it.

"What?" he asks, looking at the box. "You think this is for you?"

"No," I say, shaking my head. "I'm sure it's for some other almost-eighteen-year-old."

He steps further into the barn and turns toward the wall. I watch him as his eyes rake over the painting. It's large. The biggest piece I've ever done. And an old part of me, the one that's always wanted Deacon's approval, holds her breath and waits. When a slow smile graces his face, I feel my shoulders relax and a breath ease in and out of my lungs.

"Mama told me you were working in the barn. I thought maybe you got in trouble," he says, not taking his eyes off the wall.

I can't help the laugh that bubbles out of me. I've missed him. I've missed having someone who gets me; someone who knows where I come from and understands me on a deep level. Sure, Stacey gets me, and Micah is still around, but I miss the way things were when all of us were together. Except the part where they always used to tell me what to do and try to control my life, that part I can live without.

"Who's around to get in trouble with?" I ask, still giggling.

"Micah," he says, shrugging. "He knows how to piss people off."

I roll my eyes. "Micah and I haven't had a disagreement since sophomore year when I let Stacey borrow his Goonies movie without askin'."

"Ah, yes. Goonies Gate. Didn't you lie and say you couldn't find it?"

"Maybe. I just didn't realize he'd go all ballistic over a VHS tape."

"Micah is very protective over his VHS collection."

"Apparently."

We both laugh, looking anywhere but at each other.

"The painting is great," he finally says, gesturing to the wall. "I love the trees and the way you incorporated your old stuff into the new. It's a shame it's stuck out here in this barn."

"Thanks." I laugh lightly, always feeling uncomfortable when people offer a compliment, especially about my painting. "I'm kinda glad it's stuck out here in the barn. It's too personal to be on a canvas."

He nods his head, still looking at the wall. "I can see that," he says, walking over to touch the wall where the castle is painted.

"I just couldn't cover up the past, ya know?"

"You shouldn't. The past is what makes us who we are, right?"

"Yeah," I reply, feeling my heart puff up. It's crazy how just sharing a space and conversation with Deacon seems to take me back and make me forget time and distance.

"I brought you this," he says abruptly, handing me the wrapped box. "Happy Birthday."

I take the box and hold it close to me, trying to judge its contents by the weight.

"This isn't Christmas. You don't have to shake it and make guesses. Open it."

It's light, so I'm guessing . . . jewelry?

Gingerly, I slip my finger under the flap, tearing the tape on the wrapping paper. When I'm down to just the box, I crack the lid and see a small castle. It's pewter and no bigger than a Matchbox car.

It's perfect.

"I love it," I tell him, turning it over in my hand and rubbing my thumb against the detailed edges.

"It's just somethin' I found at this old antique store in Baton Rouge. I was in there killin' time the other day and saw it and immediately thought of you. I know it's not much, but . . ."

"Thank you," I tell him, wrapping my arms around his neck and loving the way he feels against me. In moments like this, it's like no time has passed. If I close my eyes and just breathe deeply, we're back out by the pond, lying on our backs and watching clouds pass overhead.

"You're welcome," his arms tighten around me before loosening their hold.

We both clear our throats and I glance around the barn, looking for a distraction. As I go about picking up the few discarded pieces of wrapping paper, I try not to think about how good it felt to touch him.

"I also have some good news," he says as he walks back toward the barn door, putting some distance between us.

"Oh? So, this visit isn't just for my birthday?"

He smiles. "It is, but I also wanted to tell you this in person."

"Well, you've got me all intrigued now. Tell me."

"I got a loan for that buildin' I've wanted to buy. My application was approved yesterday, and I was able to get the owner to lower his sellin' price."

"Oh, my God, Deacon! That's so great," I squeal and wrap my arms around his neck, hugging him tightly.

His arms wrap around my waist, and my feet leave the floor.

I kiss his cheek before he sits me back down.

"I'm really happy for you," I tell him.

"Thanks," he says, scratching the back of his neck. "You're the first to know. Well, besides Micah. I came to tell Mom and Dad, but I just had to tell you first."

That little tidbit of information causes my breath to catch. The fact that he still thinks of me as someone he wants to share pieces of his life with makes my heart beat faster.

"I also want you to come to a little party we're throwing in a couple of weeks. I should be able to close on the building by the end of the month, and I want to have a celebration, just family and some close friends. The building is a mess, but it'll be cool."

"I wouldn't miss it."

"Really?"

"Of course."

"Okay." He smiles. "Well, I better go talk to Mama before I have to leave. I've gotta get back for a late shift."

"Thanks for this," I say, holding my gift. "And congrats again."

He nods and waves as he exits the barn. And I'm left standing there, holding a small pewter castle to my chest.

MICAH AND I RIDE TO Baton Rouge in comfortable silence; the only noise is an old country station playing low on the radio of his Jeep. His new ride was purchased with a portion of his inheritance, the majority of which he's saving for renovations on the building we're going to tonight. I'm so proud of him and Deacon.

They have a dream, and they're going for it.

Some people might think they're not old enough to take on a venture like this, but those people don't know Deacon and Micah like I do. They're driven, and when they have a goal, they pretty much succumb to tunnel-vision, only seeing what's in front of them. And they'll do anything to get it.

"You excited?" I ask as we exit off the highway.

"Yeah," Micah says, looking over his shoulder. "I feel all jittery inside, like right before I go out on the field for a big game."

"I can see that," I say, chuckling. "This is a pretty big deal."

He nods, focused on the road and the turns he's making to get us where we're going.

"So, who's all gonna be there?"

"Uh, just us and Deacon. Dad and Mom are supposed to stop by for a few. Other than that, just some of Deacon's friends from school."

"I wish Tucker could be here for this."

"Me too."

"I miss him," I confess, looking out the window as we get closer to campus, which must mean we're closer to the building.

"Me too," Micah says. "I'm glad he's out doin' his thing, but I'm ready for him to come home. At least for a while."

We pull up in front of what looks like an abandoned building. The windows are blacked out and unlike the adjoining buildings, there's no signage, no lighting.

I recognize Deacon's truck, but the rest of the vehicles parked close by aren't familiar, and suddenly I'm nervous.

I've never interacted with Deacon at college or his friends. I've wanted to, but my daddy hasn't let me. He always says a college campus isn't the place for a young lady. But Micah and Tucker come and hang out frequently. Double standards piss me off.

What if they think I'm some immature high schooler?

My hands fidget as we walk up the sidewalk.

"Nervous?" Micah asks, eyeing me before opening the door.

"No."

He gives me a look, one eyebrow raised. "Don't be nervous. I've met most of his friends, and they're all cool."

"Okay," I say, swallowing down my insecurities.

Micah holds the door for me, and I walk in.

The place is dimly lit with a couple of tables set up in the center of the wide open floor. Some random building supplies are stacked against the walls, and there's more dust than you can shake a stick at, but it's awesome.

The place gives industrial a whole new meaning, but I can see the potential—tall ceilings, a portion of it open to the second floor, dropped lighting, metal railing. It's cool. And if I were to be completely honest, I'm kind of in awe of the fact that Deacon and Micah now own it.

"There he is," Deacon's voice rings out, clapping his brother on his shoulder and pulling him into a hug. "Everybody, this is my brother Micah. Micah, everybody."

I watch as Micah gives a casual two-finger wave, wishing I could be half as cool and collected as he is.

"And this is Cami." Deacon motions to me, smiling and everyone says hello. They all seem friendly, so I make an effort and begin making my way around the room, introducing myself.

The small crowd begins to mingle, and Deacon serves up drinks, alcoholic, I'm sure. He offers me one, but I decline. If Micah drinks, I want to be able to drive home. My daddy will shoot us both if I'm not home before my curfew.

"Thanks for comin'," Deacon says as he grabs me a plain Coke from an ice chest.

"I wouldn't have missed it." I accept the drink and try not to react when our fingers graze during the exchange.

"So, what do you think?" he asks, gesturing to the building.

"I think it's great," I tell him. "I can see why you wanted to buy it." I smile up at him and hope that it doesn't look as awkward as it feels. I've always felt close to Deacon, but I feel our paths drifting, and the divide physically pains me.

"Thanks." He stops and holds my gaze. "I mean it. I'm glad you came."

Deacon goes on, visiting with people and I stand back and watch. Micah seems to fit right in. He and Deacon have always been good at stuff like this—mingling, being the life of the party—where I've always been more of an observer.

During my observations, my attention goes to a girl with short dark hair who seems to be very familiar with Deacon. I watch as she laughs and touches his arm. When he turns to her, she leans into him, and the simple action makes my blood run cold.

At first, I think they must just be close friends, but when Deacon's hand comes to rest on her hip, I realize they're probably more.

To anyone else, the actions probably seem simple, innocent, but to me, they're anything but. Her hands are touching the person I want to touch. She has what I want. And he's looking at her like he only used to look at me. All of it makes my heart ache as it splits in two. To keep myself from crying, I try to think of something else, anything but the two of them. But I can't.

Who is she?

What's her name?

I remember being introduced, but I can't think of it through my jealous haze.

Jenny?

Janice?

Janie?

Yeah, Janie.

I rack my brain, trying to think if I remember her name ever being brought up in conversation, but come up empty handed.

His lips graze the top of her head, and that's a move I know. Watching it happen to someone else is like a punch in the gut I wasn't expecting. I feel my breath leave my body, and I force a neutral expression on my face. I can't make a scene here. This is Deacon and Micah's night. And no matter what, I can't cry. Maybe tonight, when I'm alone in my bed, but not here. Not in front of all these people. Definitely, not in front of her or him.

He's happy.

He's living a life I'm no longer a part of.

He smiles as he scans the room and when our eyes meet, I can't miss the slight change in his. Maybe it's regret? Maybe it's sadness? Even though I can't imagine him being sad on a night like this. So, I give him the best smile I can muster, because he deserves it.

He deserves happiness.

And so do I.

Fifteen

Camille

Present

MICAH AND HIS NEW GIRLFRIEND, Dani, showed up a few minutes after Annie. My daddy and Kay soon followed. The only person from our immediate family who isn't here yet is Tucker. He drove by Ms. Becky's to check on Carter before driving this way.

I'll have to remember to give him an extra hug when he gets here.

As much of a pain in my ass as he was while we were growing up, he's a wonderful uncle to Carter, and he's pretty much the best brother I could ask for. Sure, he's a little rough around the edges, but he's soft on the inside, and he's got a heart bigger than Dallas.

"Stop," Annie says, gently pulling my hand away from my mouth. "You're gonna bite them down to the quick."

"I can't help it." When my teeth no longer have my nails to chew on, they go to my inner cheek. I'm sure I'll draw blood on some part of my body before the doctor finally gets out here to talk to us. "I don't know what's taking so long. They should've come out here by now. I mean, it's been—"

"They'll be out soon." Annie cuts me off mid-sentence. Her no-nonsense way is back in full force. She's in control, like always. Her hand comes down on my knee, and she squeezes it in reassurance.

I take a minute to look around at the waiting room.

My daddy and Sam are over in one corner talking, and they look very serious. Both of them have their arms crossed over their chests and their brows are furrowed. I can't make out what they're saying, but I hear the low murmurs. Kay is sitting on the other side of me, flipping through a magazine, but I can tell she's not looking at it. It's just giving her something to do to occupy the minutes. Micah and Dani are sitting across from us, and Micah's face is hard. He hasn't taken his eyes off the door that leads to the ER since he sat down.

Dani, the newest addition to our group, is sitting at Micah's side, rubbing soothing circles on his back. Every once in a while her eyes turn to me and the smile she gives is sad. She loves Deacon. They made a connection when she came to do an article on the plantation a few months ago. Deacon showed her around and gave her insider information on Pockets. They've been buds ever since. So, I know this is affecting her as much as the rest of us.

The longer we wait, the more the bottom falls out of my stomach and my heart. I'm not a medical professional, but I know that if Deacon is in some kind of coma or something, the longer he's out, the worse it is. And that thought makes me feel like I'm going to be sick.

"I need to see him," I whisper to no one in particular.

Annie squeezes my knee and then her hand finds mine.

I want to ask how long is too long . . . what does it mean if he doesn't wake up . . . but I can't let my fears take flight. I can't speak that out into the universe.

I've been nervous a time or two in my life, but nothing like this. My entire insides want to give way to the emotion that's been bubbling up since the moment I heard those sirens. My muscles hurt from struggling to keep myself from shaking.

Looking at my watch, I do the math. It was a little after ten this morning when I heard the sirens, and now it's almost noon. So, two hours have passed since this all started. Two hours isn't that long, right?

The drive here was half of that. Surely, he's awake by now. Surely, they're just cleaning him up before they come out and tell us that everything's fine.

With a bolt, I stand up out of the hard plastic seat, and I begin to walk down the hall toward the double doors. I can't sit any longer. I can't just sit while Deacon is less than a few hundred feet away from me . . . and he might be fighting for his life. I want to fight for him. I want to do something besides take up space in the waiting room. But if they won't let me back there, I'll be right here when they finally come out.

When I feel an arm entangle with mine, I assume it's Annie, but it's not. "You okay, honey?" Kay's voice is soft, and she doesn't try to make me sit down or tell me to stop worrying. She just falls into step beside me.

"I am, if he is," I tell her, honesty soaking my words. I couldn't say that to Annie, but I can to Kay. She's like a mom to me. She came into my daddy's life at the perfect time, and they're perfect for each other. In all the years since my mama passed, I could never imagine my daddy with someone else, but that's because I never saw him with Kay. It's like my mama handpicked her for him . . . for us. The thought brings even more tears to my eyes, and I can't hold them back any longer.

"Shhhh," Kay says, drawing me close to her and smoothing my hair.

She doesn't tell me everything's going to be okay because no one knows that. She just holds me and gives me a shoulder to cry on. It's what I need, and so I cling to her and let her hold me.

Sixteen

Camille

Past

MY DADDY CALLED ME TWO days ago, asking if I could come home for the weekend. Of course, I said I would. Besides the fact that he sounded like he had something important to tell me, it's been a few months since I've been home.

But now, as I'm driving down the two-lane highway, I feel anxious. He didn't say what the nature of his call was. I'm sure if it was anything bad, he would've given me some warning. On my weekly phone calls with Annie, she's made it sound like he's doing great. So, I don't think it's about his health or anything.

At least, I pray it's not.

When my tires finally meet gravel, my chest feels lighter, and I breathe a little easier.

Home.

It never gets old, and it always feels good.

I take a second to roll my windows down and let as much of the fresh, unpolluted Louisiana air inside my truck as possible. If I could bottle it up and take it back to New Orleans with me, I would. Dust and all.

Passing by the Landry's, I smile. Annie's azaleas are green and ready to bloom, and her lilacs are putting on a gorgeous show of pale purple.

Begrudgingly, I drive slowly past the large white house and continue down the road.

The first thing I notice when I turn off the road and pull up to the front of my house is an unfamiliar car. I know it's not Tucker because his hippy van he uses to travel around the country is parked on the other side. And I doubt my daddy called me home to show me a new car. He's never bought a new car. Doesn't believe in them.

Turning off my truck, I step out, cautiously looking over the sleek black sedan.

"Daddy," I call out as I walk through the door, letting the screen bounce behind me and tossing my backpack into the hallway.

And that's when I hear it—a woman's laughter.

And then I smell it—baked apple pie.

Rounding the corner into the kitchen, there at the table sits my daddy and Tucker and Mrs. Bellenger, my high school Home Ec teacher.

Or is it Ms.?

Her husband died in a freak boating accident about ten years ago and left her with loads of cash. We always wondered why she kept teaching.

"Cam," my dad says with a huge smile on his face as he walks across the kitchen and wraps me up in his arms. "Glad you came home."

I hug him back, squeezing hard. "Me too," I say, tilting my head and raising my brows, like *is there somethin' you want to tell me?*

"Camille LuAnne Benoit, get over here and give your brother a hug," Tucker demands. When we were kids, he loved it when Annie middle and last named me, because it usually meant I was in trouble, but that didn't happen often. I can't say the same for him, Micah, and Deacon, though. Their middle names were used more than *the* and *but*.

I hug Tucker and look at him long and hard. "You're gone too much," I tell him, pulling at the front of his plaid shirt with pearl snaps.

"You need to move home," he retorts.

I scowl at him and shake my head. "At least I come home more than twice a year."

"I don't like you livin' in New Orleans all by yourself," he says, sitting back down at the table and cutting himself another slice of that good smelling pie. "I wish you'd live in the dorms like a regular college student."

I look over to see Mrs. Bellenger just watching us.

"Well, I'm nineteen years old. So, you don't get to boss me around anymore," I say through my teeth as I give Mrs. Bellenger a big smile. "I need to be closer to the square so I can sell my paintings."

Daddy clears his throat from behind me, and I turn to look at him over my shoulder. I can tell he has something to say by the way he lets out a deep breath and his eyebrows go up to his forehead like he's giving himself an internal pep talk.

"Hi, Mrs. Bellenger," I finally say when no one else says anything. "How are you?"

She stands and gives me a hug. "I'm just great," she says, patting my back. I give Tucker a confused expression over her shoulder, but he just stuffs his pie hole with more pie. "And call me Kay."

Kay? Maybe that is her name. Isn't that weird? You never think of teachers having real first names.

"Okay . . . Kay," I say, smiling as she sits down and pats the seat next to her.

When I sit, she takes a clean plate off the stack in the middle of the table and serves me up a large piece of pie. "I'm sure you're hungry after your drive," she says. "Would you like milk . . . or coffee?"

She stands from the table and goes over to the cabinet where we keep the cups and waits for me to answer.

Why is she offering me something to drink in my house?

I hear Tucker snicker, but it's my daddy I turn to for an answer, even though I didn't speak it out loud. He has to know what I'm thinking.

But instead of saying a word, he walks over to Mrs. Bellenger and slides his arm around her waist, pulling her into his side.

And suddenly, everything makes sense.

Why he's always so busy when I call him.

Why there were unfamiliar leftover dishes in the refrigerator the last time I was home.

Why he's always out on Friday nights.

Why he was so happy and at ease when he visited for Thanksgiving.

"You're datin' Mrs. Bellenger?" I ask, a slight laugh in my voice. "Oh, my God. How did I not see this?"

She had a thing for my dad. I remember. Back when I was in tenth grade, she stayed late for an entire week while I perfected this lemon meringue pie for my daddy's birthday. And she would always ask about him. And I saw the way she looked at him when he came to our parents' night.

"Well, actually," my dad finally says, gaining back his ability to speak. "We're engaged."

I turn to look at Tucker, imagining a look on his face similar to the one I'm sure is on mine—shock, awe, dismay—but no. He's just sitting there with a smirk on his face.

"Did you know?" I ask, not accusatory, just curious.

"Yep," he says, laughing and shaking his head. "Well, I mean, I knew before you, but not before today."

"Uh, congratulations," I say, turning back to my dad and Kay. They're both standing there with worrisome expressions, like they're just waiting for something bad to happen. When I smile, they ease up a little. But it's not until I walk over to them, giving them both a hug, that they finally breathe easy.

"I'm happy for you," I tell them, but I mean it most for my daddy. I am. I want him to be happy, and I don't want him to be lonely. So, seeing him with Mrs. Bellenger—KAY—It's a good thing. It's weird and completely unexpected, but good.

After dinner, the four of us sit around the table and visit. It's nice to hang out with Tucker. I haven't had a chance to do that since Christmas. And Mrs. Bellenger is really funny. I can see why my daddy likes her . . . or loves her, I guess.

Engaged, I remind myself.

The corner of her eyes crinkle when she smiles, and she looks at him like he hung the moon.

It's weird seeing him with someone like this. I was so young when my mama died. I remember them being affectionate toward one another, her sometimes sitting on his lap while they watched television, but I don't remember specifics.

But my daddy is sweet and thoughtful. He occasionally brushes her shoulder or reaches his hand across the table and locks pinkies with her. He listens so intently to her stories and laughs at all of her jokes.

Dinner is amazing. She made jambalaya, and it is close to beating Annie's, but I'd never tell her that . . . either of them. Even though I live in New Orleans, and it's a food lover's paradise, nothing beats home-cooked meals.

I WAKE UP THE NEXT morning and have to remind myself where I am. It's weird how things have changed, but waking up in my old bed feels good. I stretch like a cat on a cool summer's day and soak up the tiny rays of sunlight that make their way through the large oak outside my window. I left the window cracked last night, and nothing but earthy goodness is seeping through this morning.

Taking a deep breath, I also pick up a hint of coffee, and I can't stay in bed any longer. Besides, I'm planning on driving back today, and I want to see Annie and Sam before I leave.

Quietly, I make my way down the hall and expect to see my daddy or Kay milling around in the kitchen, but I'm surprised when it's my big brother standing over the coffee pot, waiting for it to finish.

"Are we the first ones up?" I ask, looking around the house. I don't know why, but last night I was so caught up in the news and the conversation that I missed the tiny new touches in the house. It's obvious that Kay has made her mark. Part of me is a teeny tiny bit sad, but the bigger part is happy.

"No," Tucker says, pouring two cups of coffee when the pot stops percolating. "Dad and Kay went for a drive down to the back forty. He said there was some fence down yesterday, and he wanted to get it patched up this mornin'."

"And Kay went with him?" I ask, putting my lips to the welcomed mug and inhaling before I sip.

"Yeah, I think she goes out there with him almost every day," he says as we walk out onto the porch.

"I'm happy," I say, out of the blue. "I'm happy for him . . . for them. They seem like they're really in love."

"Yeah," Tucker agrees, sitting down beside me on our front porch swing. "How about you?" he asks. "Are you happy?"

"Yeah," I say, cocking my head at him in confusion. "Why?"

"I don't know. I just want you to be happy, and I don't see you often enough. So, I worry."

"Don't worry," I say, quietly, patting his leg. I want to say more, but the words are stuck in my throat. If you'd asked me a few years ago if I'd ever miss his meddling ways, I would've given you a strong and hearty hell no, but now, there are so many days I miss my brother . . . and Deacon and Micah. I miss feeling like I always have someone in my corner, even if they did get on my nerves. Having someone fight for you and for what's best for you is not the worst thing in the world. I see that now.

"Have you seen Deacon and Micah lately?" I ask, feeling the familiar pain in my chest at the mention of Deacon's name. I miss him so much it physically hurts.

"Yeah, I spent a few days with them a month or so ago when we were passing through."

"How are they?" I ask, staring out across the front yard.

"Good. Busy. Deacon asked how you were," he says and lets it hang in the air. I don't know what my brother knows and doesn't know, but I often wonder if he's ever caught on to my feelings for Deacon. If he has, he's never said anything.

"Oh?" I ask, trying to sound nonchalant.

"Yeah, he said it had been a while since he'd seen you and was wondering how you were doing." He takes a large sip of his coffee and doesn't look my way when he says, "I'm surprised ya'll don't talk much."

"Why?" I don't know why I ask why. Maybe because I think Tucker's going to have some information that'll make my heart feel better. Maybe because I think he knows something I don't.

"Because the two of you were always so close. There for a while I thought you might, I don't know, go out or something." And this time, I feel like Tucker is baiting me.

"No," I say quickly and adamantly. "Just friends."

"Crazy how things change, huh?"

"Yeah."

Tucker's arm wraps around my shoulder, and he brings me in for a hug. "I miss you."

"I never thought I'd hear those three words come out of your mouth," I say, needing to lighten the mood before things get too serious.

"Stop," he chides. "You know I love you."

"I do. And I love you too."

"Don't forget it."

"Never."

Seventeen

Camille

Present

MY BROTHER WALKING THROUGH THE doors of the hospital brings me a small sense of relief. I don't know why, but his presence calms me. He's always been there for me. He was the first person I hugged when I found out our mama died. He was the one waiting on me after my first day of school. He beat up J. J. Smith in second grade for making fun of me when I accidentally peed my pants. When I was younger, his meddling ways were something I was always trying to get away from, but now, I appreciate him and his protectiveness. I know that if he's around, no one's going to hurt me.

And even though he can't protect me or my heart today, I still want him near me.

He doesn't say anything, probably fighting emotions like the rest of us. So, instead, he wraps his arms around me and pulls me to him. I feel his hard breaths on the top of my head, and then he presses a kiss to my hair.

"How was Carter?" I ask, needing to focus on something besides the fact that the doctor still hasn't been out to talk to us.

"Fine." Tucker's voice is gruff. "He wanted to come with me." I hear the break in his voice with that statement, and I squeeze tighter.

"Thank you for goin' by to check on him."

He takes another deep breath before saying, "Of course."

"It's better that he doesn't know what's going on right now," I tell him, trying to help him feel better about leaving Carter at Ms. Becky's, because I know how hard it is for him to say no to his nephew. "This wouldn't be good for him."

"No, I know. I told him one of us would be back to get him in a couple of hours. He asked for Deke."

Those words break me. I feel the crack deep inside my chest.

Deacon is all that Carter has ever known as a father figure. We'd planned for Deacon to adopt Carter after the wedding, but we were waiting to tell him, wanting it to be a wedding surprise for him.

How will I tell him?

How will he bounce back from this?

I know kids are resilient, but I don't want Carter to have to be. I don't want him experiencing that level of heartache at such a young age like I did.

I don't want history to repeat itself.

I want Deacon.

I want him to be Carter's father.

I want the life we've planned . . . the one we've waited so long for.

Once again, I'm left with the feeling that my life is spiraling, and I'm grasping onto Tucker, needing something to anchor me . . . something to keep me from falling.

Eighteen

Camille

Past

I LOVE JACKSON SQUARE FIRST thing in the morning.

The beauty of the cathedral, old buildings, and the landscaping of the park is breathtaking. It's exciting to be here surrounded by all of the talented artists. Every inch of this place inspires me. There's also the freshness of a new day that is comforting. The crowds of tourists haven't picked up yet, and the streets are clean for the time being. All of the vendors are setting up for the day while shopkeepers are opening their doors.

It's like a fresh lease on life with possibility permeating the air.

Maybe a portion of this good mood and positivity can be attributed to selling ten pieces yesterday. Ten. In one day. It's the best business I've done in a day since last summer, and it gives me hope and validation. The lady who purchased two of the canvases said she had a friend she wanted me to meet. She said he's very charming and happens to run a small gallery down on Harrison Avenue.

Maybe he'll show up today?

Maybe he'll like what he sees?

Having my art displayed in a gallery would be life changing, a dream come true. Even though I'm normally a dreamer with my head in the clouds, I'm also a realist. I hate getting my hopes up and being disappointed, so I'm trying not to think about it. Too much.

If he shows, he shows.

If he doesn't, I'll still be here, painting and selling my work.

One of my favorite parts about this place is being able to watch people all day. From the passers-by, I gain inspiration. The coolest part is painting, right there on the spot.

This is me.

This is who I am.

I feel free.

I feel like a wild horse running through an open field.

Okay, that might be the caffeine talking.

"Good morning," a deep voice says, catching me off guard.

I spin around to see a man standing a few feet away. He's knelt down by one of my larger canvases. The painting he's inspecting is the Mississippi River. It's a piece I painted just last week.

"Good morning," I reply, sitting my coffee down by my chair and getting up to stand behind the man, admiring my own work. I really love this painting.

"You must be Camille," he says, turning to look at me.

"I am," I say, my heart beating a little faster when he says my name. I'm not sure if it's a fight or flight mechanism from all of those stranger danger talks with my dad or if it's something else entirely. The way his eyes glisten in the early morning sun makes me take a longer look at him, holding his gaze.

"And you are?" I ask when all he does is stare up at me.

"Smitten," he says, giving me a wide smile, showing off his perfectly straight, bright white teeth.

"That's my favorite painting," I blurt out, unsure if he's talking about me or the canvas.

"It's lovely," he says, turning back. "I'd like to buy it."

"O-okay," I say, my breath catching in my throat and causing me to stutter.

"How much?"

"Fifty?" I don't know why my response comes out as a question. It's fifty. I sell the small paintings for twenty-five, the medium-sized paintings for fifty, and the large ones for a hundred. "Fifty," I say a little louder, without the question mark on the end.

"I'd say I'm getting a steal." He stands, taking the painting with him as he begins to walk down the wrought iron fence, looking at my other paintings on display.

"I still didn't get your name," I hedge, feeling weird that he knows mine, but I don't know his. I'm assuming he's the guy I was told about yesterday, but that doesn't mean anything.

"Tristan." He sits the painting down and offers me his hand. I hesitantly place mine in his and watch in awe as he places his lips on my skin. I've only seen someone do this in movies and read about it in books, but experiencing it first-hand has my stomach doing somersaults. "Tristan Harding."

I stare at his dark eyes for a split-second too long. Clearing my throat and shaking my head slightly, "Camille Benoit."

"Such a beautiful name for a beautiful woman."

Woman?

Me?

"Uh, thank you," I say, once again a statement becoming a question when I don't mean for it to be.

"You're very talented, Camille Benoit. Where did you learn to paint like this?" he asks, turning his head back to my work, but his hand still holding mine.

"I, uh, I taught myself."

"No art classes?"

"Well, yes, I've been a student at UNO the last couple of years."

"Very nice. I've witnessed some great talent come from that school," he says, finally letting my hand go and it falls back to my side. "They're fortunate to have you."

"I'm sure it's the other way around," I say, honestly. "I love my classes, and I've learned so much but, really, I just want to paint. Comin' here and sellin' my work seemed like a good way to get some real life experience outside of the classroom."

"I agree. And I'm glad I found you here." He pulls out a business card from the pocket of his double-breasted suit coat. "I'd love to take you to dinner sometime. We can discuss your art. I also have a gallery—"

"Down on Harrison," I interrupt.

"Yes. Technically, my parents own it, but they left it for me to run."

"The lady who was here yesterday told me."

"Cynthia. She's one of my assistants. Always on the look-out for a fresh perspective. And you have that."

"Thank you." Hearing his words of praise are good for my soul.

After he makes his purchases, two medium canvases, bringing my weekly total to fourteen, which is my new record and more than enough to pay my rent for the month.

"Thank you, Mr. Harding."

"Tristan," he corrects.

"Tristan," I repeat, a slight blush creeping up on my cheeks.

"I'll see you around, sweet Camille."

"SO, HOW HAVE CLASSES BEEN going?" Tristan asks, dabbing at the corner of his mouth with a linen napkin.

I take a drink of my sparkling water and swallow quietly.

"Good," I tell him, looking around the dimly lit room and having a hard time believing I'm here. It's making me tongue-tied and nervous. Tristan is so different from anyone I've met since I've been here and I've met a lot of different people. New Orleans is full of unique individuals, but something about Tristan draws me to him.

"Do you feel like your classes are paying off?" he asks, his eyes squinting like they do when he's analyzing a painting.

"I do," I say, matter-of-factly. "Before college, I'd never had the chance to study art. I feel like I have an even deeper appreciation for it and my classes have helped me hone my craft."

"They say all artists need to know their purpose. Do you feel like you've found yours?"

"Yes," I say, with conviction.

"And what is that?" he asks, almost challenging me.

"Well," I say, leaning back on my hands. "I think originally, my purpose was escape. I was escaping from my life, from the events that were out of my control. Painting gave me a voice and a way to express my grief. Through that, I found a love for expressing myself on canvas. It's also a way of preserving the past and memories. I think purpose changes as we change. Sometimes, my purpose is so simple, like just wanting to capture a moment of beauty."

"That's beautiful," he says thoughtfully.

I shrug under his compliment and sit up a little straighter on the blanket.

Tristan has set up a picnic, of sorts, in the middle of his art gallery. It's probably one of the most romantic things anyone has ever done for me. There was a single rose and a bottle of wine and sparkling water and cheeses and fruit . . . so many things that are completely different and new . . . like, Tristan. He's so unexpected and intriguing.

"Camille, you know what you want. You know why you paint. You have a clear perspective and vision. That's what makes an artist special." He pauses to stare at me across the blanket, tipping his wine glass to his lips before he continues. "You have something that can't be taught. It's a natural gift."

Taking a deep breath, my stomach flips, just like it does when he brushes my skin with his fingers or twirls a strand of my hair. His words get to me.

I've always had people in my life who believe in me, but there's something different about Tristan telling me how good he thinks I am. He knows art. So, for him to see something special in me, it makes me believe that maybe there is. Maybe I'm not just some girl with a paintbrush. Maybe, I can be someone.

"Thank you," I tell him, trying not to let my emotions get the best of me.

"No thanks needed. I only speak the truth."

His intense stare makes me feel uncomfortable, but not in a horrible way. It's like an electric current under my skin—like he's touching me with his eyes. I feel exposed and desired. Last week, after a late night coffee date, we almost kissed, but I got spooked and pulled back. Since then, he's only made small gestures toward me, like he's waiting for a sign or for me to say it's okay. But I don't know if it is. I don't know exactly what I feel for Tristan.

He's beyond handsome, with his dark hair and eyes that match. And he's so smart. And successful. But I'm still trying to figure out if I'm attracted to him because of who he is or the person he is. I'm not the kind of girl that falls into someone's arms because of what they can do for me.

"I have to go," I tell him, needing a little space so I can think. "I have to be up early to get my spot on the square in the morning."

"A brilliant artist like you shouldn't be peddling art on the street corner," he says with a touch of disgust in his voice that confuses me. That's where he met me was on the square . . . and he bought my art on the street corner.

"Come work for me."

"What?"

"Here," he says, looking around the dimly lit room. The paintings shroud in shadows, but still so beautiful. "I could use someone to field phone calls and be available for private showings. An art gallery doesn't run itself. It would give you a chance to make money while you're finishing school and I think you'd learn a lot about the business side of art."

"But you have Cynthia."

"Yes, but she's busy with other things. I need someone who's devoted to the gallery."

"But I have my paintings to sell . . . I have my spot."

"You can sell your paintings here. I've been meaning to talk to you about having a show," he says, his eyebrows lifting. "A Camille Benoit debut."

"Really?" I ask, and now my heart is beating fast for an entirely different reason. "A show?"

"Yes, I've been thinking about it since the first day I saw your work. If you can complete a few more pieces by the end of January, we could schedule something for February."

"With just my work?" I ask, still not sure if I understand him right. How can he mean a show with just my work?

"Just you."

"I don't even know what to say to that."

"You can say yes."

"I . . . I, well, I love selling my art on the square, but . . ."

"But you're better than that." His statement almost sounds like a reprimand. "Listen, you're going home for the holiday, right?"

"Yes, I leave in two days."

"Right, well, why don't you think about it and then let me know your answer when you return. I'll make reservations for us at Restaurant August." He stands and offers me his hand. When I'm on my feet, his hand leaves mine, and he wraps his arm around my waist.

"It'd make me happy if you'd say yes," he says, his voice and warm breath at my neck.

"I'll think about it," I say, smiling. I don't think Tristan is used to people not crumbling at his will.

A light growl escapes his mouth as his lips find the sensitive skin under my ear and my breath hitches.

"You," he says between nips. "You're going to make me work for what I want. Aren't you?"

I can only laugh lightly in response, my eyes closing on their own free will.

He pulls me back slightly, and his usual brown eyes are almost pitch black in the dim light.

"I always get what I want."

His lips are sure and confident, doing just that.

CHAPTER Nineteen

Camille

Present

*W*HEN THE DOORS OPEN AND a man in a white coat walks through, we all stand, our focus turning solely to him.

"Landry family?" he asks.

"That's us," Annie says, standing abruptly and walking over to join Sam. Micah walks over and stands behind her, placing his arm on her shoulder.

It's then that I realize I'm not a Landry. Not yet. Not technically, anyway. I may feel like I'm part of the family and I might be treated as part of the family, but I'm not. I have no earthly ties to Deacon, no authority. If I've ever needed a reason to marry him, it's right now. I want that. I want to be able to say that he's mine and for it to be true, in every sense of the word.

We've taken things slowly our entire lives, always feeling like we've had time, but the truth is we don't. Because as I stand here, waiting to hear what the doctor has to say, I know that forever would not be long enough. I need the past, the present, and the future and anything beyond that I can get.

He's mine.

I wish it were Deacon who just walked through that door.

I wish he were standing there showing off his dimples and smile.

I need him.

I need him so much it hurts.

As I wait for the doctor to speak, seconds feel like minutes and minutes feel like hours. On their own accord, my feet walk slowly to stand behind Micah, needing to be as close as possible to hear what the doctor has to say.

"How is he?" Annie asks. Her voice sounds like my heart feels—on edge, splintered, trying to hold itself together.

The doctor takes a deep breath and exhales, and I fight the urge to grab him and shake him. I don't know what's come over me, but if he doesn't say something in the next second, I might scream. The waiting is too much. The truth of the situation, although it might not be what we want to hear, will be better than the unknown.

The unknown is what kills. It's what allows fears to become reality and worst-case scenarios to infiltrate your mind.

The unknown is what has my heart clawing its way out of my chest.

"He's critical but stable. The next hour will be crucial."

"What does that mean?" Sam asks the question that's on the tip of my tongue.

"It means he's still unconscious, but his brain activity is good and his oxidation levels are improving, so we expect him to wake up soon. He's on a ventilator, but we'll take him off as soon as he shows us he can breathe on his own. Right now, his leg is being looked at. The x-ray showed no fracture. So, the laceration is being cleaned and stitched. He has a few 2nd-degree burns, but nothing too substantial."

"So he's gonna be okay?" I ask, feeling the first full breath enter my lungs since I drove up to the restaurant.

"Yes," the doctor says with confidence. "He's lucky. It could've been a lot worse."

"Oh, thank God," Annie sobs.

"Thank you," Sam adds. His voice is still tight with emotion, but relief is evident in his tone.

A cumulative sigh is heard from everyone else in the room, but I still feel on edge. I don't think I'll truly be able to relax until I see him with my own eyes and know he's okay. I need that smile and the dimples that light up a room. I need the look he saves just for me. The one that has always been mine. The one that tells me everything is right in the world.

"It's still going to be a while before we have him cleaned up and ready for visitors. A nurse will be out to let you know when he's in a room."

But he *is* going to wake up.

He *is* going to be okay.

And that is enough to keep my heart beating.

"I'm gonna call and check on Carter," I say to whoever's listening as everyone watches the doctor go back behind the doors.

Needing some fresh air and to hear my little boy's voice, I step outside the emergency room doors and dial Ms. Becky's number.

"Cami?" she answers with worry in her voice.

"Yes," I reply.

"How's Deacon?"

"He's . . . he's gonna be fine," I tell her, still needing to hear that for myself.

"Oh, thank goodness," she says quietly.

"How's Carter?"

"He's good, sitting out at one of the tables talking to Mr. Wilson."

I laugh lightly, loving the picture of Carter sitting at Ms. Becky's bakery, talking it up with Mr. Wilson. No telling what that conversation is about. "Can I talk to him?"

"Sure, sweetie."

I can hear a rustle as she covers the phone lightly and calls to Carter, telling him I'm on the phone.

"Mommy?" Carter's little voice comes through, and it warms me more than the afternoon sun.

"Hey, baby," I say, closing my eyes as I try to rein in my emotions. "Are you bein' good for Ms. Becky?"

"Yep."

His adorable four-year-old voice is almost too much for me to handle sometimes. I love this age. He's so smart and knows everything. I swear, he's four going on forty sometimes, but he's also still so small and impressionable. He soaks in everything he hears and sees, which often makes him act and sound just like the men in his life.

"Someone will be there to get you soon, okay?"

"Okay." He pauses, but I can hear the hesitation there, and I wonder what he's overheard through all of the chaos today. "Is Deke hurt?"

"Yeah, baby," I tell him because I've never been one to lie, especially to Carter. "But we just talked to the doctor, and he's gonna be just fine."

"Does he have a bad boo boo?"

"Yeah, on his leg."

"Is he gettin' stitches?"

He knows all about stitches because my daddy hurt his hand working on the tractor a few months ago and had to have a few. Now, anytime he gets a cut, he's worried about needing stitches.

"Probably."

"That's gonna hurt," he says, and I can hear the worry.

He loves Deacon so much, and his little heart is so tender.

"You should go hold his hand," he whispers.

"I'll see if they'll let me," I tell him, even though I know they're probably already stitching him up as we speak.

"I need to see him," Carter demands.

"Soon," I promise.

"Okay."

"I love you, baby,"

"Love you."

"Put Ms. Becky back on the phone."

He sighs and then the phone is rustled again before Ms. Becky picks back up. I tell her that someone will be by to get Carter in the next couple of hours, and she tells me not to worry.

I can't help worrying, especially about Carter. He's mine. Even though he's surrounded by people who love him, he's my responsibility. Sometimes, I feel like I'm overcompensating for the fact that his father isn't in his life, but I can't help it. The responsibility of loving him and caring for him is my most important job. Right now, my biggest concern is getting Deacon home to him.

In less than a week, Deacon and I will be married, and he will be Carter's father—the only one he's ever known or needs to know. Deep inside, I know even if Deacon and I hadn't made things work, he would've still been a constant in Carter's life. The fact that our paths finally crossed again, and this time at a point where we're both ready, makes me believe in fate and destiny and that everything happens for a reason.

Twenty

Camille

Past

THE DAY AFTER I GOT back from spending Christmas in French Settlement, I accepted Tristan's offer to work the front desk in his gallery. I also accepted his offer to stay the night at his apartment, and our relationship instantly went from lukewarm to boiling. Tristan and I have great sex. We're good in bed. Outside of bed, we're okay. I've always heard that there's a fine line between love and hate and that people in love fight passionately. I'm not sure if I'm in love with Tristan, but the passionate part is there. It's been a learning experience, to say the least.

"Rise and shine, Mon Cheri." Tristan wakes me with kisses to my shoulder and neck before sweeping my hair to the side and moving down my naked back. The stubble on his chin tickles my side, and I can't keep still any longer. I giggle and turn over, wrapping my arms around his neck.

"Ah, there's my beautiful angel," he whispers before kissing the tip of my nose.

I love when he wakes me like this. I don't spend every night at

Tristan's apartment but, when I do stay over, he's always so sweet in the mornings. He also loves morning sex, so it's a win-win situation because I love sex with Tristan. I love the way he makes me feel. I've never felt so wanted and worshiped. It's addictive.

After we've both showered and had breakfast, Tristan reads the paper while sitting on the balcony outside of his bedroom and I get ready for work.

"Are we riding together this morning?" I ask while pulling my hair up in a bun. I don't have classes today, which means, I'll be at the gallery.

"Camille, you know how I feel about us arriving to work together."

I do, and I don't like it. Occasionally, I'll bring the subject up to see if he's changed his mind. He doesn't like it when I do that either. A couple of weeks ago, he accused me of playing house. It made me so mad I didn't stay over for a week. I honestly had no plans of staying over ever again, because he made me feel childish. Then he showed up at my apartment, with an expensive bottle of wine, telling me how sorry he was and that he was stressed over an art deal that he'd been working day and night on.

I know the gallery is stressful, so I forgave him. But, I don't like feeling like a dirty secret, so I still push occasionally. It wouldn't hurt for him to acknowledge our relationship in public.

"I just don't see what the big deal is," I tell him.

Tristan sighs and puts his newspaper down. "It's tacky, and I'm growing very tired of you pushing me on this. I will not parade my personal life in front of my employees."

I finish getting ready, putting on a bracelet Tristan bought me and grab my purse. "You're right; it's much more tasteful to let them gossip about me fuckin' the boss rather than you and I puttin' up a united front."

He throws the paper onto the floor and is in front of me within seconds. His hands grab my waist tightly, pulling me against his chest. His mouth is so close to my ear that it makes me squirm, but he doesn't let go.

"You are fucking the boss. Don't forget it." He sucks on the skin just behind my ear long and hard, leaving a mark. Bastard. This isn't some macho way to claim me as his; it's his way of reminding me that he calls the shots here. "Now, get to work before I dock your pay for being late," he commands.

"You're an asshole," I mutter, as I walk out of the room.

"Don't forget to take your hair down, Camille. I'd hate for that hickey I just gave you to cause any problems today," he calls after me.

I ignore him and leave my hair up. Fuck him for trying to control and manipulate me like that. He may, technically, be my employer and my boyfriend, but that doesn't mean I have to do what he says.

I'm practically seething when I get downstairs, so instead of taking a streetcar or the bus, I decide to walk to work to give myself time to calm down. I welcome the morning sun and the interesting people I pass. They all help take my mind off Tristan and put me in a better mood.

I hate it when we fight, but he can be so temperamental and pushy. I've never been one to let someone walk all over me. We're both so stubborn, but we're also passionate, especially when we make up. I guess that's why our relationship works.

After work, I take the bus to my apartment. Tristan wasn't at the gallery very much today, and when he was, I did my best to avoid him. I'm just not in the mood to put up with him and a night alone should be good for both of us.

Bright and early the next morning, I'm startled by a knock on my door. I check the peephole and sigh when I see that it's Tristan. Opening the door, I greet him with an unamused expression and my hands on my hips.

"Mon Cherie . . . Mon Cherie," he grovels, wrapping his arms around me and hugging me tight. "Please forgive me."

"Forgive you for what?"

"For being the controlling asshole that I am. I let my ego get the better of me again, and for that, I am truly sorry, Camille." I watch for telltale signs of a lie because this seems to be a pattern with him. But he never breaks eye contact with me, and I want so badly to believe him.

"I'm tired of these stupid fights, Tristan. If we're going to be together, it has to be all or nothing. I won't be your plaything. When you won't be seen comin' to work with me, it makes me feel dirty . . . like we're doin' somethin' wrong," I confess, leaning into him. Sometimes, when we argue like this, I wonder if he thinks I'm immature, but I can't help what I feel.

"Of course, my darling," he whispers in between the kisses he's placing on my neck. "You're right, and I'm a fool to treat you like you're anything less than the goddess you are."

That's laying it on a bit thick, but who am I to stop him?

He pulls back and reaches into his breast pocket. When his hand reappears, a necklace is dangling from his finger, sparkling in the early morning sun. It's gold and covered with tiny diamonds that meet in the middle where a larger stone hangs. It's not my style, but it is beautiful.

"For you." He unlatches the necklace and drapes it around my neck. Standing back, he admires it . . . and maybe me, as well. I'm not sure.

"Thank you," I tell him with sincerity, my fingers tracing the delicate chain. "But it's not necessary. You don't have to buy me somethin' every time we fight."

"I bought it for you because I care deeply for you and I want you to have something beautiful to wear to your first gallery exhibit."

"What do you mean?" I ask, trying not to get my hopes up because he's mentioned showing some of my paintings before, numerous times, but it's never happened.

"I'm going to have a showcase at the gallery for your art. I've told you that."

"I know, but I . . ." My words drift away before I start another argument. "Thank you, Tristan."

Jumping into his arms, I let the anger from our fight fade away. I don't want him to try to buy my affections, but if he's seriously planning on showing my art, that must mean he respects me as an artist . . . and a girlfriend. Truthfully, that's all I want.

"Now, Mon Cherie," he says, untangling my legs from his waist and placing me back on my feet. "I want you to go to your bedroom, take off your clothes, and wait for me."

His deep voice makes my entire body tingle, and the way he's looking at me makes my heart race. I begin unbuttoning my blouse as I walk down the hall but stop when I hear him call my name.

"Camille, leave the necklace on."

IT'S FUNNY, WHEN I'M HERE in New Orleans, I can feel the twinge of being homesick, but it doesn't bother me much. But when I'm in French Settlement, I often wonder what the heck I'm doing in New Orleans. I have to remind myself of Tristan and the gallery and everything I've accomplished since I left home . . . and none of that would've been possible had I never left.

Sometimes, we have to do things because it's what's right for us, for the time we're at in our lives.

Today, I'm feeling particularly homesick, so before I make my much-needed phone call to Annie, I grab a latte and sit on a bench at the local park. It's the closest I can get to actually having coffee with her at the plantation.

"I was just tellin' Sam that you'd better not miss our phone date," she says instead of answering the phone with the traditional 'hello'.

"I'm glad I called then. I don't need to be in the dog house," I say, jokingly.

"Like you've ever been in the dog house a day in your life," she says with a laugh. I love her laugh; it's almost as good as her hugs—able to mend a broken heart and right all the wrongs in the world when needed. "Alright, spill it," she demands. "I can already tell somethin's on your mind, and I want to know everything."

"I don't know." I sigh, trying to decide where to begin.

"Is it school?"

"No, school's great. I mean, I'm super busy tryin' to finish everything so I can graduate next semester, but I still love it." I sigh again and pause. "I guess I'm just worried I'm losin' my inspiration. I don't know what to paint anymore. And when I do, it feels forced." I groan at the admission and slump down on the bench.

"Sounds like you need to take a break and relax a bit."

"That'd be amazing, but I just don't have time. Tristan has me workin' all day and night lately, helpin' him get the gallery ready for a big-time local artist's show. It's not the work I mind. I find this side of the art world very interesting, but I hate that it's zappin' all my creative energy."

"So, when are you gonna have *your* opening night?"

"I still don't know. Tristan said he's tryin' to find a time for me on the calendar, but . . ." There's no need to finish my sentence because it's always the same. He's been promising me my own show since we first met, but still nothing. I rarely ask him about it because I don't want him to think that's the only reason I'm with him. It's not. He's smart and handsome and great in bed. We have fun together when we're not arguing, and he can be very sweet when he wants to be. It just bugs me that he doesn't seem to respect, or even like, my art . . . not like he used to, anyway. I mean, it's what brought us together in the first place.

"Well, then what else is botherin' you? And if you say nothin', I might whip you."

I can't help but laugh. I wouldn't put it past her to drive down here and set me straight if I needed it.

I let out another deep sigh. "I think I'm just havin' one of those moments where I question every decision I've ever made." I try to laugh so that my words don't sound so heavy, but it falls flat.

She's quiet for a couple of minutes before she says, "I thought you were happy in New Orleans?"

"I am. On most days."

"And the days you're not?"

"I miss home."

"Then come home," she says like it's such an easy thing to do.

"I can't just leave, and besides, I love it here. I do."

"Then what's goin' on that makes you unhappy? Does this have anything to do with Tristan?" She says his name like she's trying it out, not wanting to commit to it, and I feel awful for not sharing more of this part of my life with her. "Tell me about him. All I know is that he owns a gallery."

"Well, his parents own it. He runs it for them."

"And?"

"And, he's great . . . on most days."

"And the days he's not?" she asks. Her voice takes a sudden turn and doesn't sound like her usual chipper tone.

"I don't know," I hesitate. I hate this because I do care for Tristan and I don't want to talk badly about him, especially to Annie, because I want her to like him, but everything that's wanting to come out of my mouth right now would solidify her opinion of him.

"You can tell me, Cami . . . and you know, it always stays right here," she says, reassuring me.

"We argue a lot," I admit. "Not all the time, but occasionally, and the times we're not arguing, I feel like I'm biting my tongue to keep from starting somethin'. Lately, I feel like I can't do anything right by him. He never takes an interest in my art anymore, and if I do show him something, he has something critical to say. But then there are days when I feel like he gets me and appreciates me, as an artist and as a girlfriend. I'm just not sure what to do."

"Well," she begins. I can tell she's trying to be diplomatic. "Relationships are never easy. And with love comes passion, and sometimes, that means arguments, especially when you're trying to figure each other out."

Yeah, I get that.

"But, Cami, honey," she continues. "No matter what, you've got to stay true to you. Don't let him dull your shine. If it's not working out, it's not working out. You can't fit a square peg in a round hole."

I laugh, shaking my head. You just gotta love Annie's analogies. But it makes sense. And I guess it's up to me to decide if Tristan is a square peg or not . . . or am I the peg? I don't know, but I'll figure it out. I have to, because if I don't, I might just lose myself, and I refuse to let that happen.

I'm Camille Benoit.

I might bend, but I won't break.

"I'M SO EXCITED TO SEE Tucker perform tonight," I tell Tristan as I step out of my work clothes and walk into his closet.

"I can tell," he replies. "I can't even remember the last time I've seen you so happy."

Even though he can't see me, I still roll my eyes and try to ignore the resentment in his tone. I refuse to feel guilty for being happy about seeing my brother tonight. And, as far as the last time I was this happy, I know exactly when it was. It was a few months ago, on the opening night of my show. That night was a dream come true and has brought some new opportunities for me, but I know not to bring it up to Tristan right now. It would just put him in an even worse mood.

After dressing, I twirl in front of Tristan's full-length mirror and admire my reflection. I finally look like a woman . . . I feel like one, too. I'm making it in a big city by myself, doing what I love, and I'm enjoying the little bit of success I've had. The jeans I'm wearing tonight were a gift to myself after my opening at the gallery. It's the first pair of designer anything I've ever had and, although it was hard paying so much for denim, I have to admit they make my ass look good.

Tristan is getting dressed by his bed, and I admire him. His body is long and lean, even though he's only a few inches taller than I am, and I love watching his back muscles twist and turn as he moves. He's very graceful, meticulous with every step. We're so different. Sometimes I wonder if we'll stay together for very long, or if we even should. I know I'm not in love with him, but I do love him. I try not to compare him to Deacon, but there are times when I just can't help it. I doubt any man can make me feel like Deacon did, and it's unfair to hold others up against him.

I walk over to Tristan and wrap my arms around him from behind. He halts his movements but doesn't say anything.

"I don't want to fight; I just want to see my brother and have some fun. I know where we're going isn't your style, but can you let loose and try to enjoy yourself tonight? For me? It's important to me."

He takes one of my hands and pulls it to his mouth and kisses it. "Of course, I can, Camille. I've never seen this side of you; I'm anxious to meet your brother and see what all the fuss is about." He laughs and turns around so he can kiss me properly, and I melt into his arms.

"Everyone loves Tucker, so I'm sure you will, too," I assure him.

To be honest, I'm incredibly nervous for Tristan and Tucker to meet. Tonight has the possibility to go really well or become a complete disaster, but I try not to worry too much.

Half an hour later, we're in Tristan's car headed to a side of the city we rarely venture to. I can tell Tristan isn't happy, and it worries me that this night might not go how I'd hoped. When he's like this, anything and everything can set him off.

I try not to let his mood get to me, and when we pull up outside of the bar, I feel the excitement bubble up inside me.

Inside, the bar is crowded, and the music is already loud. We find a table just as Tucker strums the opening chords.

It's so great to see him on stage again. He's such a natural at performing. I know he's my brother, and I'm probably biased, but he's awesome, and I think he's got even better since the last time I saw him play live. It won't surprise me if he makes it big one day. The amazing thing about him, though, is that he doesn't care if he becomes a huge rock star; he just wants to play music. I admire that about him. He's happy just to do what he loves.

Tristan won't get on the dance floor with me, so I stand up by our table and dance there instead. I also say a silent prayer that the stick up his ass falls out one of these days. My voice is almost hoarse from yelling and singing so much, but I don't care. Seeing Tucker up on the stage fills me with so much pride and nostalgia, and I'm having a great time. I only wish Stacey was here with me. She'd dance with me for sure.

I'm startled when I feel Tristan stand behind me; his body pressed against my back. Thinking that stick finally fell out, I lean back against him and grind my ass on his crotch. His hands grab my hips and stop their movements immediately.

"Have some class and act like a lady, Camille," he scolds. "I'm only standing here because of the attention you're attracting from the other men. They can't keep their eyes off you, so I have to show them you belong to me."

Yep, that stick is firmly in place. Good to know.

The set ends, and I see Tucker set his guitar on the stage before stepping off and heading our way. Now is not the time for a fight, but I can't keep my mouth shut.

"Would you like for me to stretch my leg out so you can piss on it and mark me properly?"

"You're such a child, Camille. I can't believe I agreed to come here tonight. I knew it was a mistake."

"You're free to leave any time you want, Tristan. Contrary to your opinion of me, I'm a big girl and can get home on my own."

Before he can respond, Tucker makes his way to us and grabs me, picking me up and spinning us around until I'm threatening to throw up on him.

"Hey, little sis! Havin' fun?" Tucker is sweaty and gross, but he's truly a sight for my homesick eyes.

"Of course, I am. You and the band sound great tonight. The crowd loves y'all, too," I say.

A throat clears beside me, and I'm reminded that I'm not alone, even though a part of me wishes I were. It would be nice just to hang out with Tucker like old times, without the judgmental glare of Tristan. "Tucker, I'd like you to meet my boyfriend, Tristan Harding." I place my hand on Tristan's arm. "Tristan, this is my brother, Tucker."

"Nice to meet ya, Tristan," Tucker says, shaking his hand. "I need a beer. Y'all want one?"

"A red wine?" Tristan counters, causing Tucker to bark out a harsh laugh.

"Dude, look around," Tucker says, gesturing to the rough interior and dim lights. Lit up beer signs litter the walls. "Even if they did have wine, I'd advise you not to drink it."

"Right," Tristan says, his voice taking on a strong better-than-you vibe that I've heard from him a time or two, but I don't like it. I hate it.

I narrow my eyes at him, trying to tell him without words to stop acting like a pretentious prick.

"I'll just have a sparkling water, then," he says as he slides back into a chair at the table.

Tucker looks at me, eyebrows raised. "Are you kidding me?" he mouths from behind Tristan.

I give him a tight-lipped smile. "Two waters," I tell Tucker, pleading with every ounce of my being for him to not . . . just not. I can't handle a big showdown right here in the middle of the bar. This is supposed to be a fun night, and it has been, sorta, but Tucker beating up my boyfriend would be a definite turn for the worse.

"Alright, two waters, comin' right up," he says, leaning in to kiss my cheek and then turning toward the bar. I watch him as he walks right up, the waitresses giving him their undivided attention.

"Interesting," Tristan mumbles from behind me.

I turn to him, daring him to say one more thing about Tucker. For once, he doesn't say something pretentious or smart ass. He keeps his mouth shut. And I thank the Lord for small miracles.

When Tucker returns, the three of us sit at the table, and I try to find some common ground between the two of them, bringing up the fact that Tristan plays a couple of instruments.

"Oh, really," Tucker says, leaning forward and putting forth a good effort. "What do you play?"

"I play the piano and the violin," Tristan says, not willing to budge an inch. "I went to a private school and was professionally trained by one of the best teachers in North America. How about you?"

"Taught myself," Tucker says proudly, tipping up his bottle of beer. "After our mama died, Cami picked up painting, and I picked up a guitar."

"That's interesting," Tristan says taking a sip of his water, but the scowl on his face tells me it's not up to snuff. When he sets the glass down, he pushes it to the middle of the table.

Is *interesting* his new favorite word, or has he lost the ability to converse and be a decent human being?

My insides are a jumbled mess, and I'm seriously considering telling him to take a hike, but just like always, he knows when he's been an ass, and he starts to backtrack.

"I've always admired self-taught people." He adjusts in his seat and clears his throat. "I think it says a lot about a person and also their talent."

Tucker looks over at him, but I can tell by the squint of his eyes that he thinks Tristan is feeding him a load of shit, saying what he thinks Tucker wants to hear.

"Like, Camille," Tristan says smoothly. "She's a wonderful painter, full of natural talent. A little rough around the edges, but with the right guidance, she'll be somebody one day." He smiles over at me, obviously pleased with himself. I'm sure he thinks he's scored points with Tucker, but I can tell by the heated look on Tucker's face that Tristan is failing miserably.

"I've gotta get ready for our second set," Tucker says abruptly, downing the last of his beer and slamming the bottle back on the table.

"Another set?" Tristan asks.

Tucker just stares Tristan down, daring him to say another word.

"I'm going to go get the car," Tristan says coolly. "Tucker, it was nice meeting you."

The stare down continues as Tristan and Tucker both stand, and for a brief second I'm afraid the glares won't be enough and fists will start flying.

"Likewise," Tucker grits out.

"Give me a minute," I tell Tristan without looking at him. I hear him scoot his chair back to the table with more force than necessary, and what I want to tell him is to go fuck himself and stay for the second set. But it's late, and I'm tired of arguing with him. If I stayed, it would be a fight for sure.

"What the fuck? Cami, you can't be serious about this guy."

"Tucker, please don't," I plead, hiding my face in my hands. I had such high hopes for this night, but I should've seen this coming a mile away. Tristan and Tucker are nothing alike, oil and water. I should've known it would be a disaster. "He's complicated, and this isn't his scene, and it's just been a weird night, okay?"

"Don't make excuses for him." He shakes his head, eyes still trained on the door Tristan walked out of.

"He's not as bad as he seems," I tell Tucker, trying to smooth the waters.

Finally, he lets out a pent-up breath, pinching the bridge of his nose. "I don't like it."

"You've never liked anyone I've been with," I tell him.

"You haven't *been* with many people," he shoots back.

I huff, not wanting the night to end like this. I don't know when I'll see Tucker again, and I'm sure as hell not going to let an argument be how we leave things. I love my brother. He's overbearing and overprotective, but he means well, and I know he only wants what's best for me.

"Hey," I tell him, grabbing his arm so he'll look at me. "You know me. If I didn't want to be with him, I wouldn't."

"The Cami I know wouldn't *want* to be with him."

I start to say more, to argue with him and try to make him see things my way, but I decide to let it go. Hopefully, the next time Tucker and Tristan meet, it'll be better. But for tonight, I just want to cut my losses and go home.

"I love you," I say, reaching up and giving him a hug. "Don't be a stranger."

"I love you too," he says, hugging me tightly back. "Don't hesitate to call me if you need someone to kick his ass."

CHAPTER Twenty-One

Camille

Present

$\mathcal{A}$S WE WALK DOWN THE long, stark white corridor, I have to remind my feet not to run. Everything in me is saying faster, quicker. I need to get to Deacon, and now that he's in a room, I can't get there fast enough.

When Annie's hand touches my back and she begins to rub, I say a silent prayer that Deacon looks better than he did the last time I saw him. No mother wants or needs to see their baby, no matter how old they are, in that state.

Stopping in front of the door, Sam looks over at me, and we make eye contact for a brief moment, both of us probably praying for the same thing. I see him take a deep breath before he pushes the door open, quietly, so he doesn't disturb Deacon.

The four of us—me, Sam, Annie, and Micah—walk in single file.

I let out a sigh of relief when I see his beautiful face. It's soot-free and peaceful. The ventilator is still doing its job, but he looks so much better.

While Annie, Sam, and Micah stand by Deacon's head, whispering to him through their tears and sniffles, I stay by the foot of his bed. From this vantage point, I can look over his entire body, and I take my time scanning for injuries. I don't doubt any of the information we've been given by the doctor; I just want to see everything for myself.

Just like the doctor said, Deacon has a few scattered bandages on his body that, I assume, are covering his minor burns, but it's his leg that makes my breath catch in my throat. It's not covered by a blanket, so it's easy to see the long strips of gauze covering the stitches he just received. All of this will heal, though, and I say a quick prayer of thanks that things didn't turn out any worse than they are.

"Cami, we'll let you have some time alone with Deacon. We'll be in the waiting room when you're done," Sam says. I nod my head and watch them walk out of the room. Already they seem much lighter, not as burdened as they were just ten minutes ago, and I even notice a hint of a smile on Annie's face before the door closes behind her.

I pull up a chair right next to Deacon's head but, before I sit, I gently kiss his forehead.

"Hey, Deke," I whisper softly. "You're gonna be just fine; you hear me?" My voice starts to tremble, so I clear my throat. If he can hear me right now, I don't want him to know how scared I am. I have to be strong . . . strong for both of us. "I need you to wake up, though, okay? Carter, your parents, Micah, Tucker . . . everyone who loves you, we're all waiting for you to wake up."

I grab his hand, sliding my fingers through his, and bring it up to my mouth so I can kiss it. I hold his hand against my cheek and revel in the feeling of his skin against mine. Feeling his strong pulse beat against my arm reassures me that he'll wake up soon.

This is just another trial for us, another test for us to pass. Deacon was there for me during one of the darkest, hardest times of my life, and I'm more than happy to do the same for him.

CHAPTER Twenty-Two

Camille

Past

RESTING MY ARMS ON THE white marble countertop of Tristan's pristine bathroom, I fill my hand with water and bring it to my mouth. It's been five days since I threw up the first time, and I've dry heaved at least once a day since then. I've ruled out food poisoning, a twenty-four-hour bug, and the stomach flu because I'm not running a fever.

I was on WebMd yesterday but quickly closed that out. According to them, I'm dying.

After I gargle the warm water, I spit it back out into the sink and pat my mouth dry with a towel, examining my face in the mirror.

I can't be pregnant.

That's what I keep telling myself.

There's just no way.

But if I am, what then?

That's not exactly in my plan, not that I have one.

But, if I had to guess, many babies probably aren't.

Well, I was.

My mama told me. She wanted a girl so badly; she convinced my daddy it was better to have your babies all at once, so they can grow up together. My daddy agreed because he didn't think they'd get pregnant so fast, but they did . . . and there I was. So, see . . . I was planned, and I still surprised them.

I've heard Annie say time and time again over the years how babies are never a bad thing.

I think I feel the same way, but that still doesn't mean I'm ready to have one.

I can't be pregnant.

"Camille," Tristan calls through the door, exasperation thick in his tone.

"Yeah," I reply, cracking the door to talk to him.

"We're receiving the Langley pieces today. I need you to be on time."

"Right, I'll be there."

He gives me a tight smile and then turns to walk away. "If you're still sick, you really should go see a doctor."

"Yeah," I reply, quietly shutting the door and turning the lock.

Bending down, I pull out the large stack of fluffy towels and reach into the back where I stash my tampons. Inside the tampon box is the small package I hid there after my trip to the drugstore. There's only one way to find out what kind of doctor I need. I might as well put on my big girl panties and figure it out.

Sitting down on the toilet, I read the small directions printed on the foil package, and they look pretty straight forward: open, pee, wait.

And that's what I do.

I put the stick on the counter because I figure it'll be better, more accurate, if it's on an even surface. After only a few seconds, it starts to change—the white fading into a pale pink plus sign.

I grab the package out of the trash and piece it back together, my hands shaking, as I search for the picture that showed an example of what it'd look like if the test is positive.

A pink plus sign.

I look back at the stick to make sure it didn't change, but it's still there.

My heart is racing as I stand up. I look toward the door and then back at the stick. And then down at my stomach and then back at the stick. And then I shake the stick. I don't know why, but I do . . . because maybe it needed more time to process, like a polaroid picture. When my hand stops moving, I look back at the teeny tiny window, and the pink plus is still there, possibly more vibrant than a few seconds ago.

Stumbling over to the mirror, I look at myself again. Or maybe for the first time. I don't know. But my cheeks are kinda pink for someone who's been throwing up a lot. Is that normal?

Oh, my God.

Have I eaten anything I'm not supposed to?

Have I drank anything I'm not supposed to?

Don't I need vitamins?

I should tell someone.

I open the door and Tristan is still standing in the living room, fixing his sleeves like he does right before he leaves.

Should I tell him?

I mean, of course, I should tell him, but now?

My blood is pumping through my body so fast I feel light-headed, and I brace myself on the wall.

"Camille?" he asks, hearing me and turning around. The frown on his face could be mistaken for concern, but it's not, it's annoyance. I know that frown.

"Sorry," I say, "I was just, uh, goin' to get dressed and got dizzy."

"You need to have that checked out," he says, sighing as he picks up his suit coat. "I'll see you at the gallery."

As I watch him leave, my hand flutters to my stomach and I stand there quietly.

Tonight.

I'll tell him tonight.

TRISTAN AND I HAVE ORBITED around each other all day. I've stayed out of his way, and he seems to be avoiding me. My stomach is in knots, and I don't know if it's because of my nerves or the baby.

I'm still trying to come to terms with that.

I guess I better get used to it, because if my calculations are right, and I think they are, I'm almost two months along . . . or more. But from what I read online, it says most morning sickness usually happens in the first trimester, or in my case all day sickness. The waves of nausea hit me at random. The only good thing is that I also read morning sickness is a positive thing. It means your pregnancy hormones are high, which is good.

I honestly don't know how I missed the signs. When I didn't have a period last month, I didn't think much about it. I chalked it up to a crazy schedule and lack of sleep. That's happened to me before, so I didn't worry . . . and honestly, I kinda forgot about it.

When I see Tristan pack up his messenger bag, I know it's about that time. Part of me wants to make up an excuse to stay here a little longer, avoiding the inevitable, but the other part of me wants to go back to his apartment and get it over with.

That thought makes it sound like I'm telling him bad news, but I don't feel like this is bad news.

A baby is never a bad thing.

I keep telling myself that and hope that if I stay positive about it, Tristan will be too.

"Are you ready?" he asks, flipping off a few lights on his way to my desk.

"Uh, yeah, just let me grab my bag," I tell him.

"Sushi?" he asks.

My eyes grow wide, and I freeze as I'm bending over.

That was the first thing I looked up this morning, the dos and don'ts of pregnancy. Sushi is one of the things you're not supposed to eat.

"Uh," I say, delaying. "I'm still not feeling well. Sushi probably wouldn't be a good choice."

Tristan lets out a frustrated sigh like I just ruined his whole evening.

"Fine," he says, "what sounds good to you, Camille?" His tone is so condescending, I'd like to shove my knee right in his balls, but I don't want the evening to start out with a fight.

"You know what, sushi is fine. I'll just get some soup or something."

"No, it's fine, Mon Cheri," he concedes, a change in his tone. "How about a muffuletta from Cochon Butcher? You like those, right?" His voice has turned sweet as he walks up to me and wraps his arm around my waist, pulling me to him. This is Tristan; he's a complete ass one minute, and then he tries to make up for it the next.

"That sounds amazing," I tell him, leaning into his chest. I really could use a soft place to land right now, and I hope Tristan can be that. He has to be.

We're going to be parents.

Panic rises inside me for the hundredth time today, but I tamp it down and put a smile on my face.

Everything is going to be fine.

Later, when Tristan heads into the bathroom to brush his teeth before bed, I begin to pace. There's no way I can go to sleep without telling him. The anxiety from it all about killed me today. Anxiety can't be good for a growing baby. I can't go through that again tomorrow.

Besides, I desperately want to call Annie. I need a woman to talk to, but I can't call anyone until Tristan knows. So, it has to happen now.

"Are you okay?" he asks, walking out of the bathroom and catching me mid-pace.

"Can we talk?" I ask, clasping my hands together in front of me to keep myself from worrying them to death.

"Camille, if this is about my mood lately, I'm just really stressed with work right now," he says with a huff.

Of course, because it's always about Tristan.

"It's not about that," I assure him.

"Then, what is it?"

"I . . . well," I say, trying to think of the right words and the perfect way to say them. Finally, I just square my shoulders, remind myself of Annie's words—babies are never a bad thing—and spit it out. "I'm pregnant."

There, that's wasn't so hard. Simple. Two little words—I'm pregnant.

But those two little words hang in the air like a weighted-down balloon.

Tristan's focus is on the floor. He's yet to make eye contact with me or move. His hand is frozen in his hair, and I almost say something, anything, to get him out of the trance, but then he snaps.

"What the fuck, Camille?"

The way his face is turning a vibrant shade of red reminds me of a day not long ago when he showed up at my apartment after one of our monumental fights. He scared me that day and today is no different, but there's even more on the line now. Even in the dim light of the bedroom, I can see the veins popping out of his neck as he screams my name. Everyone in a two- block radius probably heard him.

His hand comes down swiftly on the dresser, and the loud bang makes me jump.

I think about apologizing, but for what? For carrying a life inside of me, one that is part me and part him? I can't apologize for that. The last time I checked, it takes two people to make a baby.

Instead, I stand there as still as a statue and wait for him to calm down and think clearly.

But that doesn't happen.

His hand, the one he slammed down just a few seconds ago, swipes across the polished wood and clearing the contents of the dresser.

The box he keeps all of his watches in flies across the room, barely missing my head before making contact with the wall. The rest of the stuff falls to the floor in disarray. Thank goodness for carpet, or most of it would've shattered, including the picture of us he had framed. It was taken a year after we started dating. I remember feeling so happy that day, like maybe he was someone I could spend the rest of my life with. But like that picture, I'm now displaced and on the verge of breaking.

"It's a baby. Babies are supposed to be—" I start, hoping I can somehow make him see things clearly, make him want this life inside me . . . make him want me, but he cuts me off.

"What, Camille? Babies are supposed to be what?" he asks, grabbing my arms and pushing me back.

The tears start flowing immediately, partially from pain and partially from fear—fear of the unknown, fear for my baby, fear of him.

"Let go," I plead, unable to stop crying.

"What did you think my reaction would be?" he asks, loosening his grip just a little and I think for a moment that maybe, just maybe he'll come around. "You just graduated and finally started your career. This is no time for a baby!"

"It's not like I planned it."

"You better hope to God I never find out you planned it," he says, the ice in his voice chilling me to the bone.

"I—I didn't. I would never do anything like that behind your back," I sob.

"Well, then how did this happen?" he asks, accusation dripping from his words.

"I don't know. I take my pill every day," I promise. "It just happened. Sometimes things just happen." My voice rises and I sound a bit desperate . . . desperate for him to believe me . . . to understand and accept this baby, our baby.

I want to say that maybe this happened for a reason and that sometimes God has a different plan than we do, but I don't say that because that would only piss him off more.

"I need some air," he says abruptly, dropping my arms and walking to his closet.

I stand there, trying to figure out how this all went so wrong, but I can't.

A few minutes later, he walks back out wearing slacks and a sweater. He grabs his wallet and keys and walks out the door. Just like that. No more words. Not even a backward glance.

When he's gone, the tears start falling. I feel alone and scared. The only thing I can think of right now is home.

I want to go *home* home, but my apartment will have to do for now.

After I slip on my shoes and grab my bag, I head out the door, wiping my face on my shirt. I'm sure I look like a hot mess, but I don't care. I just want out of here.

Tucker is the first person who comes to mind after I get inside my apartment; he's always up late. I'm not sure where he is right now, but I know he's only a phone call away. I don't know how much I'm willing to tell him over the phone, but hearing his voice will hopefully be enough. Sometimes, you just need your big brother.

I dial Tucker's number, and it rings five times, then goes to voicemail.

I don't leave a message, but I do listen to his recorded one.

"Hey, this is Tucker. If you leave me a message, I'll call you soon. If you leave me a sexy message, I'll call you sooner."

His crazy ass makes me half smile. If I wasn't so upset, it would be a full one, but I just can't manage that right now.

All of Tristan's hateful words and actions are playing on repeat in my mind—the way his face gets red when he's mad, his icy glare and rough hands. I've never been afraid of Tristan, but I was tonight. Maybe not for me, but definitely for the innocent life inside me.

When my phone rings in my hand, I answer it without looking.

"Hey."

"Cam?" he asks, practically yelling into the phone over the noise in the background.

"Yeah, I'm here."

"What's up?" he asks, the voices and music fading.

"Nothing, I just . . . I just wanted to say hey," I tell him, trying to keep from crying.

"What's wrong?" His voice takes a more serious tone.

"Nothing."

"Bullshit. Since when do you call me on a random Tuesday night at midnight?"

"I just miss you," I tell him, and that's the truth. I miss him right now more than I ever have in my life.

"Cami, what's wrong? You know you can tell me."

I close my eyes and shake my head, and a few unshed tears roll down my cheek.

I can't tell him.

How am I going to tell him?

"Are you crying?" he asks.

"No," I say, sniffling and not sounding very convincing. "I'm fine. I promise."

I will be.

I'll be fine.

I can handle this.

"Is it that fuckin' asshole?" Tucker asks with fire in his voice. "I swear to God . . ."

"No," I lie, because it is. It's all Tristan. If he'd have just been happy about the baby, or at least civil, I wouldn't be having a near-breakdown right now. I feel my hands start to shake as my whole body trembles from a sob I'm trying to hold inside.

"I wish there were somethin' I could do," he says solemnly. "I hate not bein' there."

"Come get me?" I ask out of the blue, not even thinking. I don't want to put him out, but I know I'm in no shape to drive myself. And I just want to go home. Not here. Not this apartment. I want *home*.

"I would," he says followed by a deep, frustrated sigh, "but I can't. I'm in fuckin' California."

California?

Of course.

The tour.

"It's fine," I say, sucking up my tears as my heart drops. "Really, it's fine. I'll be fine. I'm sorry I called you while you're out on the road. I know you have enough stuff to worry about," I say, feeling even worse now.

"Don't ever apologize for callin' me," he says sternly, sounding a lot like Daddy.

Oh, God.

I can't tell Daddy.

"I'm gonna go to bed," I say. "It'll look better in the mornin', right?"

That's what Daddy would say.

"Yeah," Tucker sighs, but I can tell he's not convinced. "Get some rest. I'll call you in the mornin'."

"Love you," I tell him.

"Love you too."

When he hangs up, I stand up and walk to the door, checking the deadbolt on my front door. And with the last bit of energy I have left, I crawl into my bed and pull my pillow close, hugging it to me.

Maybe a good night's sleep will make all of this better.

It takes me awhile to go to sleep, but finally my mind unwillingly slows down enough. I'm deep in some crazy dream that doesn't make sense when a loud banging on my door startles me awake. At first, I think it's part of the dream, but then it continues.

BANG.

BANG.

BANG.

Slipping out of bed and tip-toeing to the door, I check the peephole. Tristan.

He's standing there, looking worse for wear under the pale light outside my door. My heart breaks a little for him, because he looks vulnerable and undone, and that's not him. I know how he's feeling—shocked, blindsided. Finding out you're having a baby is startling. Trust me, I know.

Even though I'm still pissed at how he acted earlier, I take pity on him and crack the door open.

"Hey," he says, at least having the decency to wince, because I'm sure he can tell I was sleeping. "I was worried when I got back to my apartment and you were gone."

"I figured you'd know where I went."

"Yeah," he says, shoving his hands down in his pockets and rocking back on his heels. "Can we talk?"

"Sure." I open the door wider, letting him inside.

He looks around my apartment and then spins on his heels back toward me.

"You dropped a bomb on me tonight," he says, crossing his arms over his chest. "I don't like being caught off guard like that."

I think he expects me to say something, maybe even apologize, but that's not going to happen. I cross my arms tighter over my chest, like a shield.

He laughs harshly and runs a hand through his hair. "Listen, Camille. I don't think either of us wants this. We," he pauses, gesturing between the two of us. "We're busy people. You have your art, and I have the gallery. A baby doesn't exactly fit into that kind of lifestyle."

I cock my head at him and try to figure out where this is going. I don't like him saying neither of us wants this. I might not have asked for this or planned this, but now that this is here, I don't want anything but *this*.

This needs me.

My hand instinctively goes to my flat stomach.

"We can take care of this and everything can go back to normal," he continues, sounding confident in his plan. "We'll forget it ever happened. And our lives can continue as planned."

"Take care?" I ask. "I don't think I understand."

"Abortion, Camille. I'm talking about an abortion." He says the words like I'm a child who might not understand them, but I do. I understand them completely.

"Get out," I seethe, standing back and opening the door. My blood is boiling. Fierceness rises within me, and it's all I can do to keep from physically harming him.

"What?" he asks incredulously.

"Get out!" I scream, my words coming out just as loud as his did earlier. I feel myself losing it. My hands are shaking, and the tears are threatening to make a reappearance.

"Mon Cheri," Tristan croons, walking closer, using that sickening tone he always does when he's screwed up and is trying to make me forget that he's an asshole. But the second his hand touches me, I jump back, bumping into the door.

"Don't call me that! Ever! I hate it!" I scream, losing what little control I had.

"Camille," he says with more force, grabbing my arms. "Calm down. You're being completely irrational."

"Get the fuck out of my apartment!" I cry, squeezing my eyes shut and willing him away.

I don't want him.

I don't want him to touch me or call me his stupid pet name or hear how he thinks we can take care of this situation.

I just want him out.

Out of everything.

My apartment.

My sight.

My life.

"Camille," he says again, acid dripping from my name. "If I leave here tonight, I'm not coming back. If you keep it, I'm not claiming it. I never wanted kids, and I won't let you ruin my fucking life. Do you understand me?" His face is furious and right in front of mine, our noses practically touching.

"Get your fuckin' hands off her." A low, menacing voice comes from outside my open door.

Tristan's grip loosens on my arms, and he takes a small step back to see who's speaking.

"Did you fuckin' hear me?" the voice rings out again, probably waking up any neighbors who were still sleeping.

I'd know that voice anywhere.

Deacon.

Deacon Landry is standing on my doorstep, staring Tristan down like he's the devil incarnate, and relief floods my body. I don't know why he's here, but I have a guess, and I've never been so happy to see him.

Tristan must get the message because he backs away.

"Who the fuck are you?" Tristan snarls.

"If I ever see you touch her like that again, you'll leave in a body bag." Deacon's voice is menacing, threatening and he completely ignores Tristan's question.

Tristan laughs, shaking his head. "I'm not afraid of empty threats," he says, bumping Deacon's shoulder as he walks past him.

"Deacon," I say, not wanting any more craziness for the night. I don't think I can handle it. He must see I'm at my breaking point because he gives Tristan a wide berth to let him pass.

When Tristan gets to the bottom of the steps, he turns around, pointing his finger at me. "I meant what I said, Camille."

"Don't worry," I tell him. "You'll never hear from me again."

And like that, he gets into his car and peels out, leaving me standing there with Deacon.

"What are you doin' here?" I ask, trying to keep from crying now because it's so good to see him.

"I'm here to get you. Pack your bag. We're goin' home," Deacon says, watching out the door, like he's worried Tristan will show back up.

I don't hesitate.

I walk into my bedroom and throw everything I can into a duffle bag and my backpack.

When Deacon and I get into the truck, the clock on the dashboard says it's just after three o'clock in the morning. I'm exhausted—emotionally and physically spent.

I feel Deacon's glances, but I keep my eyes on the road. I can't talk about it right now. Besides, I'm sure he overheard enough. I feel ashamed and embarrassed and grateful and thankful and like I just need to sleep for a few days.

"Thank you," I whisper, needing to at least say that much, even though it doesn't come close to expressing my gratitude. When I feel his hand reach across the seat for mine, I squeeze it tightly, never wanting to let go.

Leaning my head against the cool glass, I let more tears fall as I watch the city fade into the background.

Twenty-Three

DEACON

Present

I NOTICE THE BEEPING FIRST and then the smell.

It's clean—too clean—but not in a homey kind of way.

My brain feels foggy and everything's dark, but it's not until I try to clear my throat that panic sets in.

Because I can't. I can't cough. I can't talk. I can't do anything.

My hand flies to my face, and I find the tubes that are down my throat and up my nose. My heart races and I worry I'll suffocate until I somehow realize something is helping me breathe.

What the fuck happened to me?

Once I've calmed down, and my heart isn't drumming in my ears, I hear the beeping again. This time, it's louder than before, and I want to make it stop. I don't know if it's an alarm or what, but I'm certain that sound will drive me insane. I try to lift my left arm, so I can hit the machine or do something to make the beeping stop, but it feels like it weighs a ton. I can't move it.

Slowly, I look down and see the reason my arm won't move.

Cami.

Her arm is wrapped around mine, and her head is laying on top of them both. She's in a deep sleep, but I can see that her eyes are pink and swollen, like she's been crying.

But, why?

I try to think back to how I got here in this hospital and, after a few moments, it all comes flashing back to me.

The fire.

Pockets.

The excruciating pain in my leg.

Not breathing.

Then, nothing.

It's killing me that I can't talk to Cami right now. I want to tell her I'm okay and that I love her. I want to say I'm sorry for putting her and my family through whatever they've gone through since I've been here.

How long have I been here?

I was stupid to run into the restaurant, but I wasn't thinking; it was instinct. All I could think about was putting out the fire and saving everything Micah and I have worked so hard for. It wasn't until I was choking through the smoke that I realized how bad it was.

I'd take it all back not to have to see Cami like this. Seeing her cry breaks my heart, and I'm reminded of another time I watched her cry in her sleep.

My own tears start to fall as I think of what I could've lost. Cami, Carter, my family . . .

DEACON

Past

*A*FTER GETTING CAMI SETTLED INTO my bed, I wait to make sure she's fallen back to sleep before I walk out of the room. I had to wake her when we got here because she passed out about twenty minutes into our drive from her apartment in New Orleans. Before I close the door, I take one last look at her, still trying to wrap my brain around everything I heard and saw tonight and the fact that she's here, *in my bed*. It's a little surreal.

The anger that's still coursing through my body has me feeling like I could punch a wall or run a marathon. I'd love nothing more than to hop back in my truck and drive back to New Orleans and hunt that bastard down.

It wouldn't end pretty.

It would probably end with me in jail, and that wouldn't help anybody.

Instead, I make my way down the hall and into the kitchen and try to decide if I need a beer or coffee. I don't want to sleep, in case Cami needs me, but I know I could use some. So, instead of adding to my hype, I grab a beer from the fridge and hope it takes the edge off.

I don't stay here often, spending most of my time at mine and Micah's apartment in Baton Rouge, but I always make sure to keep the fridge stocked with beer. Usually, when I'm here, it's to escape the chaos that is my life these days.

I plop myself in the middle of my couch and stretch my limbs out, letting the events of the night play out in my mind. When I saw Tristan with his hands on her, it was everything I could do to keep myself from jumping the banister and removing his limbs.

And when I think about the news I overheard—Cami having a baby. *His* baby. I can hardly see straight.

Anyone who would treat her less than the amazing person she is, isn't worthy.

I pull at my hair in frustration and slam my empty beer bottle down on the table in front of me as different scenarios flash through my mind.

What would've happened had I not shown up?

Nope, not gonna go there. If I let myself go there, I'll go crazy, and that won't make this situation any better.

Instead, I grab a second beer and sit back down. Work kicked my ass today and, normally I'd be passed out already, but I doubt I sleep at all tonight. I want to be ready the second Cami wakes up.

Leaning back into the sofa, I text Micah and tell him I'm at the cottage and will be for the next few days. He immediately texts back, asking if something is wrong. He knows I usually only come here for some down time. And the fact that I'm here on a random weekday night is definitely out of the ordinary. I text him back, assuring him everything will be fine and that I'll talk to him about it tomorrow. I know for a fact, if I were to tell him about Cami, he'd be here within the hour, but I don't want to overwhelm her like that. However, when Tucker finds out, all hell will break loose, and I won't stop him from murdering Tristan. I'll help him bury the body. Or maybe I'll do it for him.

As I'm contemplating ways for the dick to die, my phone buzzes in my pocket and I look at the time before answering.

"Hey, Dad," I say cautiously. "Everything okay?"

"Well, I was about to ask you the same thing," he says, clearing his throat. "Are you home? I was getting a drink of water, and I noticed a light on down at your place."

"Yeah, I'm here. Sorry I didn't warn you."

"That's fine, son. Just wanted to make sure you were all right."

"Yeah, I'm fine. Cami's here, actually." I rub my face wearily, wishing I could keep it . . . her . . . to myself, but I can't. "She's, uh, sleeping . . . but I don't want to give any details without her permission. Just wanted to let you know." I'm not sure who else Tucker called, so just in case, I want them to know she's with me, and she's safe.

"Alright," my dad says matter-of-factly, a bit of concern in his voice. "I trust you to take care of whatever is going on, but if you need help, you come get me." That last sentence is said in a lower, hushed tone, unspoken understanding coming across thick.

"Yes, sir. I will. Thanks, Dad," I say, ending the call.

My whole family is fiercely protective of Cami, Tucker, and Clay, too, but especially Cami. We always have been, even when she didn't want us to be. I know, when we were all in school, she hated the way we hovered over her, but we couldn't help ourselves. She's special. She always has been, and she deserves to be treated with the utmost respect.

I must've dozed off because the next thing I know, my eyes fly open at the sound of my bedroom door. My cottage has been around since my dad was a kid and still has the original hardwood flooring that creaks when stepped on, but Cami is doing her best to be quiet. I don't want to startle her, so I remain still and watch her. She gently tiptoes a few steps into the hallway until something on the wall catches her eye.

It's the first time I've truly been able just to look at her in a long time. Her blonde hair is longer. Her legs are longer, or maybe it's the shorts she changed into that make them appear that way. Whatever it is, she's gorgeous. The Cami walking quietly down my hall is a woman, not the girl I spent my days with by the pond. She's older, wiser, and even more beautiful than she was then.

My heart races as I watch her inspect the paintings that are hung on the wall. *Her* paintings. They vary in shape and size and cover the space from one end of the hallway to the other. I can see her eyes squint when she tips her head to the side, almost like she's trying to solve a mystery and I guess she is. She has no idea that I've bought nearly every painting she's sold in French Settlement over the last few years.

I wish I knew what she's thinking right now.

She's so fucking beautiful, and I feel like such a creeper spying on her that I decide to make my presence known.

"Good morning," I say, clearing the sleep out of my throat. I try to speak softly, but she still jumps a little and covers her heart with her hand. Once she realizes I'm on the couch, she relaxes and smiles.

"How did you get all of these?" she asks, pointing to her works of art. She never was one for beating around the bush.

I stand and walk over to her, stretching a little to work the crick out of my neck. "I bought 'em," I say, admiring the one she's standing right in front of. It's one she painted of the barn, probably her senior year of high school. Sometimes, when I'm here, I look at it and imagine her in there painting her mural.

"Deacon, not once have I ever seen you at a craft show. I think I would've remembered sellin' you one of my paintings."

"Well, I didn't want you to know I was buyin' them, so I'd send friends in to say they were buyin' them for their moms or girlfriends. Sometimes I'd get ladies from the senior home to buy 'em, but that didn't always work out for me."

"How so?" She has a small smile on her face, but it doesn't quite reach her eyes. I have to change that.

"A few of the ladies liked 'em too much to give 'em back to me, so they'd keep 'em. They took my money *and* my paintings!" I tell her, laughing at the memory.

She's laughing now, too, and I feel like I can breathe again.

"Why on earth would you go to all that trouble? If you wanted a painting, all you had to do was ask."

I shrug, feeling a little embarrassed. "I wanted to support you, to show you that you can do anything you set your mind to. I have no doubt all your paintings would've been sold to others if I hadn't butted in, but I was selfish. I wanted as many as I could get."

"I can't believe you hung them, though. I mean, here in your cottage."

"This is where they belong. I love them, Cami, and every time I'm here, and I look at them, I think of you, and it's like you're here with me. And I love that, too."

Her eyes glance at me before she blushes and turns her head. "I'm gonna take a shower if that's okay?" she asks.

"Of course. Take your time. Everything you need should be in there."

She gives me a quick smile before she shuffles back down the hall and locks herself in the bathroom.

That was . . . interesting.

A few minutes later, there's a knock on my door. It's seven in the morning, so it can only be one of two people, and I talked to my dad last night.

I open the door to find my mother standing on the porch with a basket in her hands and a frantic look in her eyes.

"Hey, Mama," I say, stepping out of the way to let her inside. She walks straight to the kitchen and puts the basket down before turning to me.

"Where is she?"

"I don't—"

"Deacon Samuel, you let me see my girl right this instant, you hear me?" Her eyes are watery, and it breaks my heart to see her so worried. Cami is like a daughter to my mom; I should've known she'd react like this.

I hold my hands up in a display of surrender. "She's in the shower. I know you're worried, but you're gonna have to be patient. She hasn't really spoken much since I went to get her last night and I don't want her to feel pressured to share anything with us if she's not ready. I mean, I know a little bit of what's going on, but she needs to be the one to tell you."

It's not often that I stand up to my mom or not give her what she wants, but I'm hoping she'll understand and not try to whip me.

"Just tell me one thing. Is she hurt?" Her voice cracks and I pull her into my arms.

"She's not hurt, at least not physically. Besides, you think I would've just walked away from that asshole if I knew he'd laid a hand on her?"

"Well, I hope you have bail money set aside, because if I find out he hurt her in any way, his ass is mine."

"You got it, tiger," I say with a laugh before kissing the top of her head. I know she means it, too, but right now we have to focus on Cami. Kicking the douchebag's ass will have to wait.

Mama steps back and wipes her face. "I know it's been awhile since you've stayed over here, so I brought you some coffee and breakfast. You make sure she eats enough; you hear me?"

"Yes, ma'am. Thank you."

She walks to the front door and opens it. "You take care of her, Deacon. She needs you."

"I will. I promise."

She blows me a kiss, then leaves.

By the time I have the coffee poured and my mama's biscuits and gravy plated, Cami walks into the kitchen.

"Oh, wow," Cami says with wide eyes. "Are those your mama's biscuits?"

Her hair is wet, and she's in a pair of sweats and a t-shirt and she's still beautiful.

"Yeah, she stopped by while you were in the shower."

Cami's eyes question me, but she doesn't say anything. She just sits down at the small table in my kitchen and pulls a plate to her. I follow suit and dig in because it's been awhile since I ate last. When I look up, Cami is practically inhaling her food, and I have to laugh. She's never been a girl who doesn't eat in front of boys, but I don't think I've ever seen her like this.

"Hungry?" I ask when she looks up at me.

"Starving." She smiles with a mouth full of food. "Sorry, it's just that this is the first morning I haven't been sick right off the bat. And I've really missed Annie's cookin'."

"You've been sick?" I ask.

"Well, pregnant."

She cuts her eyes away from me, and we both sit there for a minute in silence. It's the first time she's said anything about last night and the baby.

"About that," she finally says. "How much did you hear?"

"All of it," I tell her, leaning back in my chair and crossing my arms over my chest. Just thinking about it makes me feel like punching a wall. "Enough."

Cami bites on the corner of her mouth while she's thinking and I want to walk around the table and hug her because I can't imagine how scary the last day or so has been for her. I don't like to see her hurting, never have. I'd take it away in a heartbeat if I could. Well, not the baby, but the douchebag boyfriend and everything else she's been through.

"I don't know what I'm going to do," she says, taking another bite of her breakfast, slower this time.

"About the baby?" I ask.

"No," she says adamantly. "Not about the baby, just about every-thing else. Like, telling my dad . . . and Tucker." She pauses and takes a deep breath, closing her eyes. "My daddy is going to be disappointed in me."

"No, he's not."

"And Tucker is going to want to kill Tristan," she continues.

"Now, that I can believe. And I plan on assisting."

She laughs, but there's little humor there. "Honestly, I'd be fine if I never saw him again . . . or heard his name. If I could tell people I had some sort of immaculate conception, that'd be great." This time, when she laughs, it's real, and I can see the old Cami—the carefree, dream chaser.

"You can stay here as long as you want," I tell her. "I'm hardly ever here, and if I'm in town, I'll just sleep at the big house."

She pauses with her fork in mid-air. "Serious?" she asks.

"Of course."

"That would be . . . well, it'd be great. I didn't really want to stay at Daddy's. With Kay there, it feels different. Good, but different."

"You okay with all that?" I ask, realizing we haven't had a chance to talk about Clay and Kay getting married.

"Yeah, I'm happy for them. They're good together."

I can tell by the way she smiles that she means it.

"I won't stay here forever," she says. "I'll figure everything out and find a place to live."

"I meant it when I said you could stay here as long as you want or need."

"Well, this is *your* house. I'm sure there will come a day when you and Micah are tired of sharing an apartment, and you'll want to be here more permanently."

"Yeah, someday," I tell her. I've always thought I'd settle down here one day, but I can't imagine Janie living here. She'd never want to move to French Settlement, let alone this place. I brought her here once to show her around, but she wasn't impressed.

"What about you and Janie?" Cami asks, like she can read my mind. "I'm surprised y'all don't live together."

"Nah," I say, shaking my head. "Janie likes her space and so do I. We also have completely different schedules. I'm up late at the restaurant, and she's more of an early to bed kind of girl. Being in med school takes a lot of dedication."

"Med school?" Cami asks, her blue eyes widening. "Wow. I didn't realize she was going to be a doctor."

"Yeah, her whole family is in the medical field in one way or another. She was kinda born into it."

"Are y'all serious?" she asks, and I can tell she shocked herself with that question. "Sorry, none of my business. I guess it's just been so long since we've been able to sit down and talk, just the two of us. I feel like I need to know everything." She laughs at herself and blushes a little. It's adorable. I've missed her.

"Don't apologize. I've missed talking to you."

"Me, too."

"I'm here if you need anything, Cami," I tell her, wanting her to know that I'm serious.

"Thank you," she says, her eyes never leaving mine. "Really, I can't thank you enough for coming to get me last night. Yesterday was probably the worst day of my life, besides the day my mama died, and all I wanted was to come home."

"I'm sorry about all of that."

"Don't be, it's not your fault," she says and the shine that was in her eyes moments ago fades. "I should've seen his true colors a long time ago. I don't . . . I feel so stupid." Her attention is focused on her hands in her lap, and the way her voice cracked, I wouldn't be surprised if she's crying.

I hate this.

I don't know what to say or do or how to feel. I can only imagine how she's feeling right now.

"Please don't say anything to anybody," she whispers, her voice trembling now. "I've gotta tell my daddy, and then I'll tell Tucker. I just need a day to process."

"Take all the time you need," I tell her, standing from my chair and walking around the table. I kneel down beside her and force her to look at me. "You're not stupid. He is. Got it?"

She nods her head as a few more tears slide down her cheek. I wrap my arms around her shoulders and pull her to me. If I could protect her from everything coming her way, I would. I'd take bullets for this girl—or bury a body—whatever I needed to do.

"A baby is never a bad thing," I tell her, repeating words I've heard my mama say. Besides, this baby will be part Cami and nothing that is part Cami can be bad.

Twenty-Five

Camille

Present

THE FEEL OF FINGERS LIGHTLY stroking my cheek rouses me, but I can't force my eyes open. It's been the longest twenty-four hours of my life, and all I want is sleep. But there's something comforting and familiar about the touch, and I don't want it to stop. It reminds me of how Deacon wakes me in the morning—his beautiful face hovering above me—just before he kisses me.

Oh, my God, Deacon!

I sit up in my chair so quickly, it scrapes against the floor before knocking into the bedside table. My back aches from sleeping in the awkward position I was in before, but I don't care because Deacon is awake.

He's awake, and he's staring at me with tears pouring from his eyes. My heart doesn't know whether to heal itself or break even more at the site of him. I'm thrilled he's finally awake, but I've never seen him cry like this. It dawns on me that he could be in pain and I spring into action.

"Deacon, you're okay. I promise everything's gonna be alright." I grab some tissues from the bedside table and gently dab at his face, wiping away his tears. "Are you hurtin' anywhere?" I ask.

He shakes his head, but I can see the worry in his eyes. I can't imagine what it must've felt like waking up attached to tubes and not knowing where he was. I'm furious with myself for falling asleep. If I'd stayed awake, I'd have been able to reassure him sooner.

In between soothing words, I place kisses all over his face. I can't help myself. The relief I'm feeling is exhilarating, and I know I need to get a nurse in here, but I just want him to myself a little while longer.

Deacon's strong hands grab the tops of my arms and he pulls me away so that we are face to face.

"Baby, what's wrong? Am I hurtin' you?"

He closes his eyes tightly for a moment, and when he opens them again, I'm struck by the amount of sorrow I see. I've never seen Deacon like this, and it worries me greatly.

"Shh, I'll go get the nurse, okay?"

His grip on my arms tighten, and I give him a smile. "I'll be right back, I promise. I love you."

He smiles back the best he can and lets me go. Before closing the door on my way out, I turn back to look at him again, partly to reassure him, but also to reassure myself that he really is awake and he's going to be okay.

Chapter Twenty-Six

Camille

Past

SITTING OUT IN THE SUN, I roll my jeans up so my legs can be exposed. It might be winter, but here in Louisiana, it's still possible to get a tan now and then. Besides that, the warmth feels good.

Deacon has these ridiculously comfortable wooden chairs on his porch. Who would've thought a simple wooden chair would be so comfortable? But they are. I might steal them when I leave . . . or borrow them. Normally, I camp out on the front porch for an hour or two in the afternoon or morning, depending on my shift at the restaurant, but today, the sun was too inviting. So, I drug the ridiculously comfortable chair as close as I could get to the pond.

It's different sitting on this side. The same, but different. When I was younger, and I'd lay out by the pond, my back would be to the big house. But from this vantage point, I can see the big house and the pond and even the barn off in the distance going the other way toward Micah's cottage.

Like his brother, Micah hardly uses his cottage. They both spend most of their days in Baton Rouge. Mostly because they recently opened their new restaurant. It's just getting off the ground, but already drawing quite the crowd, or so they say. I haven't been yet, but I'm planning on going tonight for the grand opening. My brother's band is playing, so I'll get to see him, which is good. It's been a month or so since he's been home.

I'm also in my second trimester as of today, so it'll be a sort of celebration for me. I'm hoping the baby books Annie bought me are right, and I'll be rid of this "morning sickness" soon. It's amazing how something the size of a pea can wreak such havoc in your body.

Seeing the restaurant will be fun. I haven't been there since the party they had when they got their loan. I had thought about asking Deacon for a job there, something to pay the bills until the baby comes and I can figure everything out, but decided against it. The drive is long for minimum wage. I'd probably end up spending half my wages in gas. So, I got a job waiting tables at Sally's Diner instead. Deacon doesn't think it's a good job for me, but I beg to differ. The hourly wage sucks, but the tips aren't bad. I still know how to use my girlish charms, and I'm not showing yet, so that isn't a deterrent.

Surprisingly enough, there are still a few people in French Settlement who don't know I'm pregnant yet.

A few.

News travels fast in a small town. News about a girl like me, who's never made the news before, travels at lightning speed. I've been the talk of the town since I moved back.

And so has Deacon.

His first mistake was letting me live in his cottage.

His second mistake was hovering over me like a mama bear.

So, people are gossiping.

They should know better by now that Deacon and I are just friends.

I mean, it's been years since we were anything but, and even then, most people didn't know. And by most people, I mean no one. No one ever knew that there was anything between us, except Stacey, and she didn't find out until long after the fact.

But people have always stuck the two of us together because we've always been so close. Of course, they're gonna talk and speculate. It's what they do best.

If they only knew who the real daddy of my baby is. Boy, that'd give them something to talk about. People in this town would probably rip him to shreds. He's just the kind of person that would rub 90% of the people in French Settlement the wrong way.

Thinking of Tristan doesn't make me mad anymore. I've resolved to being in this on my own, and I'm okay with that. I think deep down I always knew that nothing long term would come out of our relationship.

I got the best of him, anyway.

I'm not sure everyone feels the same way, though.

Tucker and Deacon went to New Orleans to get my beat up truck and clean out my apartment. They took a drive by Tristan's to collect a few of my things. I don't know what happened that day, but Deacon and Tucker both seem to have gotten over their need to kill him on my behalf. Now, whether that means they did the deed or had a nice talk with him, I don't know. They won't tell me. All they'll say is that it's taken care of, and Tristan won't ever bother me again. And that's enough for me.

I haven't seen a missing person ad for him, so I'm assuming he's still in one piece, but I couldn't care less either way.

The second Tristan wanted to do away with my baby, I was done with him. It was like a switch flipped, and it was no longer me and Tristan or me and anybody else, it was my baby and me.

I want him or her to grow up knowing what it feels like to put your toes in the green grass and run through the sugarcane fields.

I want them to enjoy Annie's cooking and ride around the fields with my daddy.

I want Sam to teach them how to throw a baseball.

I want them to learn how to play the guitar from Tucker.

I want them to have the life I had and then some.

And I don't know what I'll say when the day comes, and I have to tell him or her about their dad, but I hope by then, I'll have something good to say.

I know what it's like growing up with one parent, and I hate that they'll start this life out like that, but I also know that one parent can do the job of two. It's not easy, and there will be days I mess it all up, but it's okay. We'll make it.

"You still come out here and chase castles?" Deacon's voice comes from too dang close. I never heard him walk up, and it literally scared the piss out of me.

"You should not scare a pregnant lady like that," I tell him, one hand clutching my chest and the other covering my eyes so I can see him in the bright sunlight.

He's doubled over laughing, always the jokester.

"It's not funny," I warn.

"I'm sorry," he says when he finally gains his composure. "I thought you were gonna jump out of that seat."

"I felt like it," I say, laughing. "And I mighta peed my pants a little."

"Okay, too much information," he says, waving a hand in the air, still laughing.

"What the heck are you doin' sneakin' up on me like that anyway?" I ask, settling back into my chair again.

"I'm sorry," he says, finally curtailing the laughter. "I thought you heard me comin'."

"No, too deep in thought I guess."

He sits down on the grass beside me and leans back on his elbows, so reminiscent of our days lying by the pond.

"So, do you still chase castles?" he asks again.

"I guess so," I tell him, feeling a wave of nostalgia hit me so strong that it almost takes my breath away. How does time go by so fast? And how can things change so quickly? Looking back, I never would've thought we'd end up like this. When I looked into the future, I saw Deacon. I thought, somewhere down the road, we'd end up together. But I didn't see this. I didn't see me sitting here, on the other side of the pond, pregnant and living in Deacon's cottage. I had a dream about living in Deacon's cottage, but that always included him living here too.

"I'm not sure I even know what I'm chasin' these days." I say it without thinking. "Life is so strange."

"Yeah," Deacon agrees, lying on his back with his muscular arms tucked behind his head. "If you try to predict how things are gonna go, you're gonna be wrong." He sucks in a deep breath and lets it out. "I think we end up right where we're supposed to be, anyway. Sometimes, we might take a different route, but in the end, we're where we're supposed to be."

"I guess so," I agree, looking up at the clouds.

"I think that one looks like an arrow," Deacon says, pointing straight above his head.

Falling into our familiar game, I play along.

"And that one over there kinda looks like Bugs Bunny," I tell him, pointing to the right.

We bounce back and forth for a while, spotting different objects. Deacon claims to see Ozzy Osbourne, but I never see it. I let him have that one, though. I'm sure there've been times over the years when I've seen something that wasn't really there and he did the same for me.

"Hey, Cam," Deacon says after a while, rolling onto his side and facing me.

"Yeah?"

"Don't stop chasin' castles, okay?"

I don't say anything for a second. I just look down at him. He's still so achingly beautiful, inside and out. And it makes my chest hurt, just like it did when I was fifteen and wanted him so bad. It might hurt worse now because I know what it feels like to have him and lose him.

"Okay," I finally tell him.

"I know right now your dreams might seem like they're on the back burner, but it doesn't mean you have to leave them there."

I nod my reply because I'm not sure what to say to that. I do feel like everything's changed in a few short months and I know so much more change is coming, but I don't plan on giving up on the things I love—my dreams, my castles in the sky.

I don't give up that easy.

But hearing Deacon say that makes me want everything, even things I know I can't have.

"You're still planning on coming to the Grand Opening tonight, right?" he asks, changing the subject and I feel the atmosphere shift, allowing me to breathe a little easier.

"Yeah, I wouldn't miss it."

"Cool," he says, standing from his spot. "Do you need a ride? I'm sure Mom and Dad wouldn't mind if you ride with them. Unless you're planning on riding with your dad and Kay."

"Nah, I don't want to make people leave early if I need to come home before they're ready. I'm planning on just driving myself."

He looks at me for a second. His beautiful face telling me he doesn't approve of me driving by myself. "Okay. You sure?"

"Positive. I'll see ya tonight."

"Okay."

"Call if you need anything," he calls back as he walks away.

Like I would call him for anything on a night like tonight, but just the fact that he offers makes my heart flutter, feeling things it shouldn't.

Later that evening, after a shower and a change of clothes, I pull on a denim dress that does a good job of hiding my bump, and I hit the road to Baton Rouge. It feels good to be out and about. I haven't done much of anything since the night Deacon drove me home from New Orleans. Two doctor visits and work at the diner has been my extent of fun.

I'm ready to think about something else and get my mind off of things, even if it's just for a few hours.

Pulling up in front of the rustic building, my stomach flutters. It's not the baby. It's excitement.

I couldn't be happier for Deacon and Micah. They've both worked so hard to open this restaurant, putting hours upon hours of blood, sweat, and tears into it. Most people probably think Sam and Annie footed the bill, but that couldn't be farther from the truth. Deacon secured the loan by putting up his cottage for collateral. If things go badly, that's a lot to have at stake, but the good news is that things have been going great.

Deacon said that business has been steady and getting better by the day. Their hopes are that with this grand opening, they'll be able to bring in new customers and give people a real glance at what they can expect every time they come in the door—a unique atmosphere with great food and great music.

Tucker's band, Hard Limits, is playing tonight, and I have to admit, I'm almost as excited about seeing my brother and watching his band play than I am the grand opening.

As I walk in, my mouth drops. I haven't seen this place in a long time, and I'm floored by the transformation. The exposed brick walls give it a vintage feel, and the subtle lighting makes it inviting. The bar is tucked back underneath the second-floor loft, and a good-sized stage is at the other end, leaving a wide open area for tables and a dance floor.

It's amazing.

"There you are," Deacon says, catching me off guard.

I whirl around and clutch my chest, partially in shock. That's twice he's nearly scared the pee out of me, but I'm going to let it slide this time.

"Deacon," I say, with praise. "This place is so amazing!"

"You think so?" he asks, looking around at his restaurant. *His* restaurant.

I watch as the proud smile widens on his face, his blue-green eyes sparkling with happiness and his adorable dimples shining through the scruff on his face.

"Yes. I couldn't believe my eyes when I walked in. It looks so different from when I was here last time."

"I was hopin' you'd think so," he says, still beaming.

"Yeah, I'm so proud of you," I tell him.

"Thank you."

"Way to chase your castles," I say with a wink.

"Learned from the best," he says pulling me into a side hug.

"Deacon," a voice calls out from behind him, interrupting our moment.

When Deacon turns, I see Janie walking in the door.

I almost forgot about her. Almost.

"Hey," Deacon says, bending down to kiss her. "I was wonderin' when you'd show up."

I pretend like everything else in the room is so much more interesting than the two of them, but I can't help eavesdropping on their conversation.

"Sorry," she says. "I thought I was never going to get out of the lab tonight."

"It's fine. I'm just glad you're here," Deacon replies.

I look closer around the room, trying to find someone else I know. It seems as though I'm here before everyone. I thought Tucker would at least be here by now.

"Cami," Deacon says as he touches my arm to get my attention. "You remember Janie, right?"

"Yeah, I do." I plaster a smile on my face and give her a stiff one-handed wave. "Hello."

"Hey," she says, smiling in return, but I don't miss the way her eyes travel from my head to my toes. And I wonder if she knows . . . about the baby? I'm sure Deacon's told her and it makes me self-conscious.

A shuffle of people coming through the door is my saving grace, and thankfully, it's Annie and Sam, followed by my daddy and Kay. A flood of relief rushes through me, and I take sanctuary in one of Annie's hugs.

"You should've waited and rode with us," she chides.

"I didn't want to impose," I tell her, leaning over to accept a kiss on my cheek from Sam.

"We stopped by to check on you, and you were already gone," Kay adds in.

"I'm fine, guys. Really. I just thought I'd drive myself in case I need-ed to go home early or stay late," I say, shrugging. Last time I checked, I'm twenty-two, not twelve. That's what I want to add, but I don't, be-cause they're just their overprotective selves, and they can't help it.

"Hey, Cam," my dad says, pulling me into a hug. "How're you feelin'?" He pulls back and looks at me with the eye of a skilled doctor.

"Feelin' fine, Daddy," I assure him.

Deacon shows us to a large booth he has saved for us, and it gives us a great view of the stage.

"Tucker is supposed to set up in about ten minutes," he says. "I'm gonna go check to see where his ass is at."

Annie swats at him, telling him to be nice.

I smile at him, loving that some things never change, like Deacon and Tucker getting on each other's nerves.

Janie didn't sit with us, and I see her sitting at a pub-style table closer to the stage. I watch her for a minute, wondering what she's really like. I've only ever seen her when she's with Deacon, and we've never talked much. I wonder how serious the two of them are, and when I think about that my chest aches.

She looks around the room until she spots Deacon and then her eyes follow him around. She doesn't seem clingy, just like she wants to be where he's at, and I get that. Deacon is like sunshine on a warm summer's day. Everyone wants to be in his presence. I don't blame her. But I don't like her. And I have no idea where that thought just came from.

I clear my throat and sit up a little taller in the booth, trying to listen in on the conversations going on around me and get my mind off the pretty girl across the room.

She's who Deacon wants.

She's who Deacon deserves.

She's a successful student who was accepted to medical school.

She's beautiful and mature.

She's everything I'm not.

When my brother's boisterous voice comes over the sound system, my attention snaps to the stage, and I can't help the smile on my face. He's crazy and a little over the top sometimes and the perfect distraction to my downward spiraling thoughts.

I look around the restaurant and notice that the place has filled up since we sat down.

Tucker welcomes everyone and introduces himself, giving Micah and Deacon a hard time in the process, and then the music starts and the dance floor fills up.

I spend the next hour enjoying the atmosphere, the good food, and laughing at the crazy people I call family. It's exactly what I needed. But by nine o'clock, I'm practically passing out at the table.

Before the party's even getting started, I start telling everyone goodnight.

My daddy and Kay promise they'll be right behind me. Annie tries to talk me into waiting on them, but I seriously can't wait another minute. Lately, when I get tired, I just have to go to bed. There're no two ways around it.

On my way out of the restaurant, I spot Micah in a back corner, taking in the crowd with a proud smile on his face. As I walk over, he smiles wider.

"I was just getting ready to come over and join the table," he says, motioning behind me.

"I know. I'm a party pooper," I tell him, laughing. "But I'm *so* tired."

"Understandable," he says, giving me a hug and kissing the top of my head.

"This place is great," I tell him. "You and Deacon did such a good job."

"Thanks, Cam."

"Tell Deacon I said bye, okay?"

"I will. Drive safe and call someone when you get home," he says with a pointed look.

"Yes, sir," I reply with a salute. "Oh, tell Tucker I'll see him tomorrow, or he can always come crash at the cottage with me tonight."

"I'll tell him," he says, smiling. "I'm glad you're home, Cam."

"Me too," I tell him.

It's under circumstances I never could've predicted, but I'm happy. At least, I'm trying to be. I have to be because someone else is counting on me now.

CHAPTER
Twenty-Seven

DEACON

Present

"DEACON, DON'T RUSH. YOU DON'T have to talk right now. You just need to rest and let your throat heal," my mom tells me.

I shake my head again. I know I need to rest, but I also need to tell them what happened and get this part over with.

Cami, who is sitting in my bed with me, hands me a cup of water. When the nurse walked in a few minutes ago, she wasn't happy to see Cami in bed with me, but I don't give a damn. I want her as close to me as possible. The few feet between my bed and the chair is too far right now.

I swallow the water in small sips before giving the cup back to her. As she turns, I catch a glimpse of her solemn, but beautiful, face. I can see the worry still weighing on her. It's in the way her smile doesn't reach her cheeks and her eyes aren't their typical sky blue.

I give her a wink, hoping it will ease her worries and let her know I'm okay.

I don't want her to know how scared I was when shit got real in the restaurant. I don't want her to know that the last thing I thought about when I hit the ground was how much I hoped she knows I love her and that she's my whole fucking world. I don't want her to know, because then she might realize just how close I came to dying, and I don't want her to think about that.

All I've ever wanted was to make her happy.

This last day and a half wasn't part of the plan.

"When I got to Pockets, I could smell smoke from outside," I start. My throat is scratchy from the tube they had down it helping me breathe. "I didn't realize how bad it was until I went inside. I tried to find a fire extinguisher, but the smoke was so bad I couldn't see. That's when a shelf or somethin' fell on me. The next thing I remember is wakin' up here."

Cami lays her head on my shoulder and wraps her arm around my waist, comforting me with her warmth. She's always been there for me. Her presence has always calmed me and this moment is no different.

I look at my parents when I ask, "Is Pockets gone?"

Mama can't look me in the eyes, so my dad answers. "It's not a total loss, but it doesn't look good either. I'm sorry, son."

I lay back in the bed and close my eyes. This has to be the most I've cried in all my life. I know Pockets is only a restaurant, and we can rebuild, but Micah and I put our hearts and souls into that place, probably even more than we did Grinders, and it fucking hurts that all that hard work went up in flames.

The most important thing is that no one else was hurt. I wouldn't be able to live with myself if someone else got hurt in the fire. My injuries will heal, we'll build a bigger and better Pockets, and life will go on.

CHAPTER

Twenty-Eight

DEACON

Past

SPRING TIME IS UPON US, which means it's been raining a lot, but the clear skies today are giving us a much-needed respite. While I drive over to Janie's apartment to pick her up for our lunch date, I roll my window down and let the warm breeze blow in. It's exactly what I need to refresh me after a week of long nights at Grinders.

When we first opened, I'd stay up all night and do paperwork, then go home and stress about things just enough to keep me from sleeping. After a few weeks of putting up with my mood swings, Micah and Janie had an intervention and sent me home with strict orders to sleep for as long as it takes to get my shit back together.

I slept off and on for two days before I was bored out of my skull. I went to work that night and, after apologizing to Micah and the staff, I grabbed an apron and headed to the kitchen to help cook. I've never looked back.

Now, I make sure to schedule downtime so I won't get too stressed out. I just love it so much,—the job and the people—and I want us all to succeed. Running a restaurant takes the entire team, and I've learned I have to take better care of myself if I'm to be the best coach I can be.

Another thing I had to start scheduling is alone time with Janie. I know how awful that sounds, but if I didn't put our dates on my calendar, along with a few reminders, I'd let myself get too busy and forget. Janie is important to me, and she's been there for me through every stage of the restaurant. So, I'm trying to make it a priority to show her how much I appreciate her.

With her being in medical school, it gets harder and harder to set aside time for us. We're both so busy, but making lunch dates a couple of times a week seems to work well for us. With today being so beautiful outside, I decided to pick up some muffulettas and drinks before picking Janie up and taking her to a local park. Truth be told, it's not a lot of fun visiting restaurants when I spend so much time at Grinders. A picnic outside will be perfect.

I knock on Janie's door, and she pops her head out to let me know she needs to get her shoes.

As I wait for her outside, I hear Cami's ringtone coming from my phone.

"Hey, Cami. What's up?"

I immediately tense up, my blood running cold when I hear her crying hysterically.

"Cami, sweetheart, you gotta settle down. I don't know what you're sayin'. Take a deep breath and start over."

Without thinking, I walk back to my truck and get inside, firing up the engine.

"I . . . I'm on my way to the Women's Hospital . . . in Baton Rouge," she sobs.

"What? What's going on? Are you driving? Maybe you should pull over while you talk to me and calm down," I tell her. My mind is racing with worst-case scenarios, but I try to stay focused. If something were really bad, she'd be in an ambulance, right?"

Cami takes a deep, shuddering breath before she speaks again. "I'm okay, but I can't stop drivin'. I have to get to the hospital. I'm havin' contractions."

What? That can't be happening yet; it's too early.

"Cami, I'm gonna meet you at the ER, you hear me? I'll be there in about ten minutes," I promise her.

"Okay, I'm almost there. Thanks, Deke."

"You don't have to thank me, Cami. I'm glad you called. Just be safe, you hear?"

I put the truck in reverse and back out, but when I start to drive forward, I have to slam on my brakes because Janie is standing right in front of me.

Shit. I completely forgot where I was.

She walks up to me with her hands on her hips. This is not going to go over well.

"Hey, baby, I'm sorry, but I gotta go. Cami just called, and she's on her way to the hospital."

"And? What does that have to do with you?" she asks.

"You can't be serious right now? She's family and something's wrong with the baby. I have to be there for her. I *want* to be."

"Of course, you'd rather be with your *precious Camille* than with me."

I slam my fist on the steering wheel. I'm wasting time arguing with her when I should be on my way to Cami. And her shitty attitude is pissing me off. I grab the bags of food from the passenger seat and hand them to her.

"Look, I know the timin' sucks, but I'm not abandoning Cami."

"No, you're just abandoning *me*," Janie spits out, rejecting the food.

"Fuck," I groan, letting my head fall to the steering wheel. "Whatever. I've gotta go."

Carefully, I drive around her before speeding out of her apartment complex. I know I'll have to make this right later, but right now, the only thing I can focus on is getting to the hospital and being with Cami.

After finding a parking spot, I run inside the building just in time to see Cami being put in a wheelchair.

"Cami!" I yell out, getting the attention of her and the nurse pushing her.

The look of relief that covers Cami's face is more than enough to prove I made the right choice. Cami needs me, and I'll be damned if I'm going to let her down.

She reaches her hand out to me, and I take it, reassured by how strong her grip is.

I squeeze her hand and wink at her. "You're gonna be just fine."

She nods her head, and I don't know if she's agreeing with me or trying to reassure us both, but she manages to give me a small smile before the nurse ushers us down the hall.

With rushed precision, Cami is moved to a bed and hooked up to a monitor before I even sit down. Cami tells the nurse her personal information before explaining the symptoms she's experiencing. Nurse Patty, she introduces herself, checks the monitor and tells us the baby looks fine and that the doctor will be in soon before leaving the room.

I pull my chair to the side of her bed and grab her hand again. Her shoulders shake as she cries, rubbing her belly with her other hand.

"Shhh, baby." I kiss the top of her hand and leave my mouth there, speaking into her skin. "You're gonna be fine. Both of you."

"I'm so scared, Deacon," she whispers.

Her words tear at my heart, and I want nothing more than to make everything right. I fucking hate that this is out of my control.

I move her hair away from her face. "I know you are, Cami, but you have to stay strong, okay? Nurse Patty said the baby looks fine, so we're gonna focus on that. Can you tell me what started all of this?"

"I was workin' at the cafe when my stomach started feelin' . . . *tight* and uncomfortable. It was weird. It's not that it hurt, really, but it had never happened before, so I didn't know what to do. I went and sat down at an empty table, and it stopped briefly. When it started up again, I realized I was having contractions. I panicked and told Sally I had to leave before I jumped into my truck. I called my doctor while I was driving and they told me to go straight to the ER. I couldn't get ahold of Daddy or Kay or your parents, so I called you. I'm sorry if I'm keepin' you from somethin' important."

I try not to be hurt that she didn't call me first, because why would she? It makes perfect sense that she'd call her parents, then mine, but it still bothers me. I can't think about why right now, though.

We both stare at the monitor, the one that's attached to the band around her belly. The readings seem to be even. I think that's good. I've never been around anyone who's pregnant before.

"What if somethin's wrong?" she whispers, letting her fears out into the open.

"Don't think about that," I tell her, kissing her hand again. "Let's talk about something else while we wait."

"I got a check in the mail last week," she says. "I've meant to ask you about it."

"A check?" I ask, confused why she'd need to ask me about it.

"Yeah," she says, repositioning herself on the flimsy hospital pillow. "It was from Tristan. It didn't come with a note or any explanation. But in the memo line, it said payment in full for seven 18 x 24 canvases."

She looks at me like she expects me to say something, but I let her finish.

"That sounds a lot like the paintings from my exhibit," she says, a bit of hedging in her voice.

"I'm glad he followed through," I tell her, not wanting to offer up any more information than I have to. The truth is that Tucker and I went and had a *chat* with Tristan. Originally, we were going to get her paintings but then decided that he could do her one better than that. He could sell them and give Cami one hundred percent of the sales, no commission.

"Did you buy my paintings?" she asks. Her eyebrows are furrowed together like she's trying to solve a puzzle.

"No."

"Then who did?"

"Some lucky motherfucker," I tell her, smiling.

"So, Tristan sold my paintings?"

"Sounds like it."

"The check was for way more than what it should've been," she adds. "It's like he didn't take his commission. Tristan always gets his commission."

"Not this time. He already got more than he deserved." He never deserved Cami. He got more than he deserved the first day he met her. He didn't deserve to breathe the same air as her. If I have anything to do with it, he never will again. And he'll never touch this baby.

She relaxes and gives me a genuine smile.

A short while later, the doctor comes in and, after a brief examination, he tells Cami that she's experiencing something called Braxton Hicks contractions. It's not anything too serious, but she'll need to be careful not to overdo it for the remaining time of her pregnancy.

"Would you like to see your baby?" the doctor asks Camille.

"Sure. I'll never turn that down," she answers. Her excitement is contagious, and I find myself anxious to see the baby, too.

Once the ultrasound equipment is set up and the doctor has the wand-thing on her belly, I lean over to get a better look. I've never been in this situation before, so I'm curious, but I also don't want to intrude on Cami's moment.

"Deke, come here," she tells me.

"Are you sure?" I ask, wanting to be closer . . . always wanting to be closer to her.

"Of course, silly. Hurry." She reaches out for me, and I take her hand, coming to stand by her side. For some people this might seem weird, but for us, it feels natural. I can't imagine anyone else standing beside her. I wouldn't want anyone else standing beside her.

With my free hand, I massage the area of my chest over my heart, because thinking about someone else besides me standing here makes my chest ache. But I don't know what to do with that feeling, because while I'm here, with Cami, my girlfriend is pissed at me for ruining our lunch date.

Part of me feels like the biggest douchebag ever, but the other part of me feels like it has no other choice than to stand right here, holding Cami's hand.

I've felt so torn over Cami since as far back as I can remember. When I first started having feelings for her, way back before puberty hit, I thought it was wrong. She's always been close, like a sister, but I never thought of her that way. A best friend, yes, but never a sister. But she is Tucker's sister, and that was also a roadblock to my feelings for her. I knew Tucker would shit a brick and want to kick my ass if he knew how I felt about Cami back in high school. Shit, if he ever found out that the two of us had sex . . . I don't even want to think about it.

"Ready?" the doctor asks, pulling me out of my thoughts. I feel Cami's hand tighten around mine as my eyes try to adjust to the screen.

Eventually, I realize that it doesn't matter if my eyes adjust because I have no clue what I'm looking at. The doctor must recognize the confused look on my face because he starts pointing out body parts, helping me make sense of what's on the monitor.

Cami's hand squeezes mine. "Isn't he beautiful?"

"Sure, is. Just like his mama," I assure her.

Wait just a damn minute.

I don't remember being told that she's having a boy.

My eyes flash to hers, and she's looking like the cat who ate the canary. *"He?"* I ask.

She giggles. "Yep. No one else knows, so you better keep your mouth shut, Deacon Landry."

"Your secret is safe with me, Camille Benoit."

Her eyes are sparkling again, and I'm overcome with the desire to kiss her.

That cannot happen.

But I want it anyway, and I literally have to force myself not to move in closer and do it.

That would be wrong, on so many levels.

But right on so many more.

The struggle I feel inside has been building strength the last month or so, and I honestly don't know how much longer I can fight it off.

It doesn't help that Cami seems to be feeling the same way. Her gaze has traveled from my eyes to my mouth a couple of times now, making it even harder to resist her.

Get your shit together, Deacon.

"Your baby looks perfect, Camille. Everything is on track. I just need you to be mindful of these Braxton Hicks contractions. If you feel them again, get off your feet and drink some water. If they continue or increase in intensity, call us immediately."

"Yes, sir. I will. Thank you so much."

Now that the spell we were just under has fallen, I kiss her on her forehead and tell her I'm going outside to call everyone and give them the good news.

After getting my ass chewed out by everyone for not calling sooner, I make my way back to Cami's room. She's back in a wheelchair and looks like she's ready to leave.

"Is everything okay?" I ask.

"Everything's fine. I can go home now. I'm just waiting on the final paperwork, and I'll be on my way."

"Let me drive you home." The idea of her driving home after everything she's been through today has my stomach in knots.

"Don't be silly, Deacon. I can drive myself. Besides, don't you have to work tonight?"

"Micah already knows I'm here with you. I doubt he's expectin' me to show up." In fact, he already told me not to come back until Cami was safe and if he or Tucker found out I let her drive home, they'd both beat the shit out of me. Well, they'd try anyway.

"But what about my truck? I can't just leave it here."

"Sure, you can. Micah and some of the guys from Grinders will take care of it, I promise. Your job isn't to worry right now, it's to keep that little guy and his mama safe, got it?" I point to her small but rounded stomach.

She laughs before conceding. "Okay, fine. I have to admit I'm pretty tired. Sorry in advance for falling asleep on the way home."

A few minutes later, Cami is buckled into my truck, and we're on our way to French Settlement, but not before we drive through a fast food place and order almost everything on the menu. Neither one of us had lunch and didn't realize how hungry we were until we saw those golden arches.

"Thanks, again, for comin' to my rescue. I'm sorry you had to waste almost an entire day at the hospital," she tells me before shoving at least four fries into her mouth at the same time.

"Stop apologizin'. And, I didn't rescue you; I just kept you company for a little bit," I say before winking at her. "Besides, spendin' a day with you is never a waste."

"I bet Janie would disagree." I can tell she's surprised that she blurted her comment out which only makes me laugh harder.

"Yeah, you're probably right." I wipe my eyes on my shirt sleeve before taking a drink of my coke.

"Does she know where you've been all day?"

"Yep."

"Was she okay with you going to the hospital to see me?"

"Nope." I wish I could tell her differently, but I've never lied to Cami intentionally, and I don't plan on starting now.

"I'm sorry." She looks away from me and out of her window.

I grab her hand to get her attention. "Didn't I tell you to stop that? You don't need to worry about Janie. If she has a problem with you or with me seein' you, then she can take it up with me. She knows you're family and family comes first with me. Always."

"But she's your family, too, right? I mean, don't you think you'll get married eventually?"

I hate this. I have no desire to hurt her any more than I already have or throw my relationship with Janie in her face.

When did life get so fucking complicated?

"I don't know," I say, sighing because that's the truth. I feel like I don't know what the hell is going on in my life these days. "Usually, we're just easy, but lately, everything is a big fight. I'm tired of arguing with her, to be honest."

She sits quietly for a second, and I wonder if I've said too much, but I'm not ready for our conversation to be over.

"I'm an asshole, huh?" I ask, truly wanting her opinion.

"No, you're not. You're just confused or somethin'. But don't ask for romance advice from me. We both know that's not my forte," she says with a small laugh.

My blood still boils every time I think of that prick, Tristan.

"Let's not ruin this day by mentioning Mr. Douche," I say.

Her laugh is music to my ears. "Deal."

When we reach my cottage, I help her out of the truck and into the house. I'm so glad she's agreed to stay here until the baby is born. I'd worry myself sick if she lived in town by herself. I know she did it for years in New Orleans but, now that she's back home, I can't imagine her not being on this property.

"You sure you should be drivin' back to Baton Rouge tonight?"

"I probably should, but I think I'm gonna go see the folks for a bit. I might even spend the night over there."

"You really are tryin' to piss Janie off, aren't you?"

I laugh. "No, I'm really not. I just don't feel like leavin'."

"Well, this is your house, you know. You can stay here. I don't mind sleepin' on the couch."

All humor has left my face, and I give her a stern look. "I'm not even gonna acknowledge that comment. You've had a long day and need your rest, so I'm going to get out of your hair. But, if you need me for anything, you call or text me, okay?"

"Yes, sir," she says while saluting me.

Damn her for being so cute. Truth be told, I don't trust myself to stay here with her any longer than what's necessary. I'm not a cheater, but I can't handle any more temptation. Being with Cami in my cottage, in such close quarters, is pushing me to my limits. She's everywhere here. It used to be bad enough with her art on the walls and little touches that have always reminded me of her, like looking out my front window and seeing the pond. It's always been our pond in my mind. But since she's moved in here, her sweet smell permeates the walls and her shoes are by the door and her half-eaten peanut butter and jelly sandwich is in the refrigerator. And all of it is too much.

"I've gotta go," I tell her with my hand already on the door.

"Okay."

I hesitate for a split second because the slight disappointment on her face and in her tone is enough to make me want to stay. Forever. But I can't.

Damn it, if I don't want to.

"I'll talk to you later," I say, needing to assure her in some way that I'm here for her. I just can't be *here*. If I'm going to be here, then I can't be with Janie. And I don't know what to do about that right now. The torn feeling I have when I shut the door behind me is jarring.

Twenty-Nine

Camille

Present

WHILE THE NURSE IS TENDING to Deacon's wounds before bedtime, I walk Sam and Annie out to their truck. They'll leave Annie's car here until Micah and Dani can drive it back to the Settlement tomorrow.

I can't help but notice the difference in the way we're exiting the hospital compared to how we entered earlier today. I'm grateful for the change. Grateful and exhausted.

Annie loops her arm around mine and smiles at me. "How you doin', sugar?"

"I'm fine," I answer automatically. Annie quirks her eyebrow at me, and I laugh. "I am. I'm tired but, all things considered, I'm doin' great. Today could've been so much worse, you know?"

"I do know. Believe me; my mind has put me through all kinds of scenarios today. I'm looking forward to a quiet drive home followed by lots of Carter snuggles." It warms my heart the way her face lights up when she talks about my little boy. It's kinda crazy when you think about it, because he's not related to her by blood, but there's no doubting the bond those two share.

"Annie, you don't have to keep Carter tonight. I'm sure it's fine if he stays with Daddy and Kay. Besides, you and Sam need a restful night, and you know that won't happen with him there."

"You hush right now. I'm takin' that boy to my place and won't hear another word about it. Your daddy and Kay are leaving early to go fishin' anyway, so if he stays with us, he can sleep in."

It's a good thing we're now outside of the building because I let out a laugh so loud, I even surprise myself. I think it's the first time today I've laughed, and it feels good. "You know good and well my son doesn't know the meaning of sleepin' in."

Annie joins me in laughing. "True, but he naps like a pro."

We reach Sam's truck, both of us wiping our eyes, but this time it's happy tears instead of fearful tears. Annie turns to me with a serious look on her face. "Thank you, Camille."

It's not often she calls me by my given name, so it catches me off guard. "For what?" I ask. I can't imagine why she feels the need to thank me for anything.

"For bein' you and for lovin' my son like it's your sole purpose in life."

"It *is* my purpose, outside of Carter, of course. I was meant to love Deacon. There's no choice in the matter. But, even if I had the choice, I'd still choose him."

She hugs me tightly and whispers in my ear. "I love you so much, baby girl. Now, go take care of our guy, you hear?"

"Yes, ma'am."

I smile at Sam and wave goodbye before walking back toward the hospital.

CHAPTER
Thirty

Camille

Past

SITTING IN THE OLD BARN on a stool Annie let me borrow from her greenhouse, I close my eyes and take in a deep cleansing breath. Ever since my scare with the Braxton Hicks contractions, my doctor has given me strict instructions to take it easy. He wanted me to quit my job, but I told him that just wasn't possible. I needed to save as much money as possible, so I'll be able to provide for my baby. He understood even though he didn't like it. Kinda like Deacon. And everyone else, for that matter. They finally realized they were causing me more stress than good, so they've let me be and let me do my own thing.

Well, for the most part.

They still check up on me every day I'm at the diner. One of them will stop by. Usually, it's my daddy and Kay, or Sam on his way out of town. They play it off by ordering a piece of pie or a cup of coffee, but I know what they're up to.

Deacon calls me at least twice a day.

Tucker calls when Deacon doesn't.

Sometimes I wonder if they have some secret schedule.

But now, the watch has officially started.

As of yesterday, I'm in my 39th week of pregnancy. According to my doctor, this baby could come at any time, and I'm so ready.

Even sitting feels taxing these days.

I can't eat, because there's no room for food.

I can't sleep because the baby is pressing on every vital organ inside my body.

If it weren't for this glorious extra-large box fan that Sam installed in the barn, I would be pouring buckets of sweat.

I'm miserable.

And I feel like a tank.

Annie assures me that my motherly glow is in full swing, but I think she's just saying that to keep me from crying.

The tears. Oh, my God. The tears.

They come at less than a moment's notice. Just this week, I've cried over running out of Sprite and Oreo cookies. I cried when I saw a dead squirrel leading up to the cottage, sure that I was the one who killed it, and now a baby squirrel is somewhere without a mother.

Just thinking about it again has my eyes watering up, blurring the mostly-blue canvas in front of me.

I've taken the advice of my doctor, and I stopped waitressing four days ago. The week before that, Annie, Kay and I finished up all the pertinent shopping for the baby. Now, I'm just waiting. And what better way to pass the time that sitting in front of a canvas.

My dreams have been so vivid lately. I'm not sure if it's the extra hormones or the late night eating, but every morning I wake up with some new image burned into my brain, and I just have to put it on canvas. I've been finishing a painting every other day, which is the fastest I've turned out paintings since I was a starving college student in New Orleans.

For a brief moment, when I found out I was pregnant and everything went south with Tristan, I thought maybe this part of my life was over. How could I support myself and my baby *and* be a struggling artist? That just didn't add up in my mind.

Deacon is the one who made me realize I can't give up on my dreams. He's encouraged me to continue to chase my castles, and when I didn't believe in myself, he still believed in me.

So, here I am, finishing one of my most important pieces to date.

It's a painting for my baby's room.

Well, he doesn't technically have a room yet, but he will one day. And when he does, this will hang there. It'll be a reminder of everything important in life. It started from a dream I had a few days ago. In my dream, I was running through an open field. My long hair blew behind me like a cape, and my arms reached out to the sides. I seemed so care-free, so happy.

Usually, I'm an active participant in my dreams, but this time, it was like I was merely an observer. I watched myself get to the edge of the field and there, among the trees, waiting for me, was my mama. She was beautiful, just like I remember her. She stared at me for quite awhile, the two of us standing in silence, and then she reached out and touched my face . . . and then my protruding belly. A bright smile graced her features, and then she was gone. The wind picked up, and she drifted away like a flock of birds.

But I wasn't sad when I woke up. I was happy. I felt like I had been with her, and even though it was only a brief moment, she touched me . . . and my baby.

I knew I had to paint something that represented that dream and gave my mama a place in my baby's life.

The painting took on a life of its own once I sat down. Looking over the almost completed piece, I follow the swirls of blue and smile when I see the small castle I painted into the clouds. At the edge of the canvas is where the field ends and a forest of trees begin. In that forest, on a tree trunk, I painted a heart. That's my mama. She's there. She's watching over us. And I get the feeling she's already met this wiggly baby in my tummy.

I hope he looks like her.

I hope he has sparkling blue eyes and curly blond hair, just like her.

As I dip my brush in some dark green paint to finish up the shading on the large oak trees, I feel a slight popping sensation and then liquid seeping through my cut-off jean shorts.

Looking down, I'm worried that I peed myself. It wouldn't be the first time in the last nine months, but all of the times before, I at least sneezed or laughed beforehand. This came without warning.

When I stand up, more liquid runs down my leg and realization dawns on me.

My water broke.

Oh, *shit.*

I'm having a baby.

I drop the small palette and my brush and walk cautiously out of the barn. I feel like if I run or make any quick movements, the baby is going to come out, and as much as I love this barn, I do not want to have a baby here.

It's dirty, and there aren't any doctors.

As I walk a little quicker, I begin to pant as the first real pain hits me.

I felt a few contractions this morning but assumed they were stupid Braxton Hicks once again, because that's what they felt like and they weren't that close together.

Pausing to let it pass, I look up and feel like the big house is a million miles away, but I have no choice but to make it there. I didn't bring my phone with me to the barn. And the big house is closer than the cottage. So, I waddle my way down the path.

The sweat is starting to bead up on my forehead when I get close enough to the house to holler for some help.

"Annie!" I yell, not wanting to freak her out, but as another contraction hits me, I can't help it.

I need a hospital.

Stat.

"Annie!" I call again, taking a few more steps and almost making it to the patio when the back door flies open.

Sam is standing there in his three-piece suit looking like he's ready to go into a boardroom, but the panic in his eyes when he sees me is enough to make me start panicking.

"My water broke," I say, trying to sound calm, but feeling anything but.

"Are you sure?" he asks, grabbing at the tie around his neck and loosening it.

"I think. Or I peed myself, but I don't think—"

"Of course, your water broke," he says, beginning a ramble. "I'll, uh, call Annie and then we'll drive to the hospital. I've done this twice before. Don't worry."

One hand is in his hair as he holds the phone to his ear with the other. I watch as he mumbles to himself about no one ever answering their phone when he needs them and wondering why he pays so much money for phone service if no one is going to answer the *damn* things.

"Annie!" he yells into the phone when she finally picks up.

While they're talking, another contraction hits me full force, practically bringing me to my knees. I bend over and start breathing like the video I watched showed me. I felt stupid going to Lamaze classes by myself. So, my doctor gave me a video to watch at home. And they lied. They all lied because these stupid breathing exercises are *not* helping.

I scream out in pain and Sam whirls around to me, still talking on the phone.

Suddenly, he drops the phone to the ground and ushers me straight into the garage and then into the front seat of his SUV.

I realize when he jumps in and peels out of the gravel drive, that he's left his phone.

Annie's going to be pissed, but I can't think about that right now.

Right now, all I can think about is breathing.

Whooo whooo wheee.

Whooo whoo whee.

"Should we call your doctor?" Sam asks, and when I look up at him, I feel bad. He looks a wreck. Just five minutes ago, he popped his head out of the back door looking like a suave model for J Crew. And now, he looks like the hot version of Nick Nolte's mug shot. His eyes are a bit crazed, and the top button of his shirt is undone, leaving his tie hanging haphazardly. And his hair. His hair is all over the place. Kinda like Micah's, but worse.

"I don't have my phone," I tell him, squeezing my eyes together as I feel another contraction coming on.

He shoves a hand down into his suit coat pocket and then his pants pockets.

"Outside," I tell him, losing the ability to form complete sentences.

"What?" he asks, trying to keep both eyes on the road and me at the same time.

"Outside. You dropped . . . ahhhhh," I pause, breathing through clenched teeth. "You dropped it."

"Oh, fuck," he groans. "Sorry." His hand flies up like he's going to somehow protect my unborn baby from hearing his profanity.

"It's okay. He's heard worse," I joke, trying to lighten his mood as the pain subsides.

"I'm kinda out of practice," he admits as we fly down the road, making record time getting onto the highway.

"It's okay," I assure him. "I'm just glad you were home."

"Oh, God. Me too." He pauses and then reaches over to grab my hand. "It's gonna be fine . . . you're gonna be fine."

His normal, soothing tone is back, and it helps me relax.

Until the next contraction.

We continue in that cycle—Sam soothing me, me panting through contractions—until we finally reach the hospital.

He screeches to a halt under the canopy of the emergency room at the Woman's Hospital in Baton Rouge.

"This is it," he announces, and I think he means more than the fact that we've arrived at the hospital.

This is *it*.

This is the day that changes everything.

This the beginning of the rest of my life.

This is the day I become a mom.

I'm unusually calm as Sam runs through the doors and shows back up a minute later with a nurse and a wheelchair.

The rest of the events happen so quickly. It's a blur.

One second, I'm being wheeled down the familiar hallway, the same one I was in a couple of months ago when I got the scare of my life. The next second, I'm in a room, hooked up to every monitoring device available and waiting on my epidural.

When I got here, I was already four centimeters dilated. My nurse told me I've probably been in labor since this morning, but it picked up when my water broke.

An hour later, everything is calm, and my room is full of all the people I love, except Tucker. His plane is supposed to be in within the hour. Annie flew through the doors about thirty minutes behind us and cussed Sam a blue streak for dropping his phone.

My dad and Kay had been in Baton Rouge already, running a few errands, so when Annie got here, she called them.

Deacon and Micah showed up about fifteen minutes ago, and now we're all just sitting here, waiting on a baby.

"Guys," I say, and everyone turns their attention to me, thinking I'm going to make some grand announcement. "Y'all should go find a comfortable spot or take turns or somethin'. We could be here all night."

"We're fine here with you," Annie says, squeezing my hand from her spot right by my bed.

"Yeah, I'm not plannin' on going anywhere," Kay says. "You'll have to kick me out."

I smile at them. They've both been nothing short of amazing the last few months—fielding every question, quieting every concern, and giving me all the motherly advice I could ask for.

Kay's never had children of her own, but it's not because she didn't want them. She miscarried twice in her early twenties, and she and her late husband stopped trying, deciding to be happy with each other. But she loves getting to be in mine and Tucker's lives now. And she's even more excited about this baby getting ready to be born. She already has a name picked out for herself: KayMa.

I love it.

Annie wants to be called Nannie.

Get it? *nAnnie.*

Sam and my daddy both say they'll settle for whatever the "lil' guy" comes up with.

Speaking of the "lil' guy," as most of my family has resorted to calling him, I have to decide on a name. A few have been floating around, and I'm pretty sure I know what I want it to be, but I want to see him first, just to make sure.

Besides, I think it's kind of fun to torture them and keep it to myself.

"HEY." TUCKER'S VOICE COMES FROM the crack in the door as he slides quietly inside my room.

"Hey," I tell him, reaching a hand out for him. "I was wondering when you were gonna get here."

"I got here as fast as I could. I told the pilot to step on it."

I laugh lightly, but twinge as I feel a contraction, even through the epidural, but they're nothing like they were earlier.

"You okay?" Tucker asks, moving closer and being careful not to wake the two ladies sleeping on either side of my bed.

"Yeah, I'm fine."

"I can't believe you're havin' a baby," he says in a low whisper with a small smile creeping up on his handsome face. He looks tired but happy.

"You're tellin' me," I smile back and squeeze his hand. "I don't think there's any backin' out now."

"Nope, only one way out of this thing."

"Don't remind me."

Kay begins to stir when we laugh again, her eyes peeping open and catching a glimpse of Tucker.

"Hey, baby," she says in a tired voice. "Glad you made it in safely."

"Thanks," he says, leaning over and planting a kiss on her cheek. "Can I get you ladies anything?"

"I could use a cup of coffee," Kay says. "I bet Annie could too."

"I'm on it."

He slips back out of the room, and I close my eyes for a while longer. The doctor told me to rest up as much as possible because this baby will be here by midnight.

I hope he's right.

I doze off for a while, but even with the epidural, I can still feel the pressure from the contractions. So, when Deacon slips in the door quietly, I'm already awake but turned on my side to try to get some relief.

"Sleepin'?" he asks as the bed dips beside me.

"Tryin'," I tell him, slowly rolling over to face him.

He reaches up and brushes the hair out of my face.

"Shouldn't be long now," he says. "I overheard the nurse when she left, and she said just a little bit longer."

"Yeah," I say, unable to keep from admiring his beautiful eyes and the dimple in his cheek when he smiles down at me.

"You scared?" A look of concern takes over the smile as his eyebrows furrow.

"No," I say confidently. "I'm not. Just ready for this baby to be here."

"Good." He goes back to the easy smile as if he was waiting to find out how I felt before he could decide how to feel himself. "I'm gonna go get Mama. She's down in the waiting room with everybody, but she said to tell her when it was gettin' time."

"Okay," I tell him, hating it when he stops touching me. I'd ask him to stay, but that'd probably be a little weird.

"You're gonna do awesome," he says.

It makes me giggle because he sounds like he's giving a pep talk for a big game.

"Thanks, coach."

Annie comes back in, looking refreshed and happy. She always manages to be a pillar of strength in any situation. It's one of the many things I admire about her.

"Ready to have this baby?" she asks.

"So ready," I tell her, hearing the fatigue in my voice, but as she grips my hands, it's like some of her strength is transferred to me and I feel like I can do this.

Less than an hour later, my feet are in stirrups, and Annie's hand is planted firmly in mine.

"Push on three," the doctor says.

I squeeze Annie's hand while she pats down my forehead with a wet cloth.

"One, two, push," the doctor instructs and I do. I push with everything in me until I scream out in pain and determination.

"One more time, Cami," he assures me. "You're doing great."

I pant and catch my breath, gripping my knee with my free hand.

"One, two, push," he says once more.

At the end of the longest push of my life, a crying baby congratulates me on a job well done.

"It's a boy!" the doctor says happily.

"Ten toes and ten fingers," the nurse adds.

I look up to Annie, who is looking from me to the bundle of baby and back to me with tears in her eyes. "I'm so proud of you," she says, kissing my forehead.

The nurse brings the baby and lays him on my chest, and I feel like my heart is now living outside of my body.

He's perfect.

He's everything good in this world.

After they clean me up a little and my bundle is back in my arms; I ask to see my family. All of them. I want them here to witness this moment with me, because if it wasn't for each one of them, I'm not sure I would've had the strength to get to this point.

I watch as each of them walks into the room, one by one. Their eyes grow wide, but no one speaks. Each of them moves around the bed until they're standing in a semi-circle looking down at the baby in my arms with awe and adoration.

My eyes land on Deacon, and I watch as he rubs his palms roughly across his eyes. The look on his face, the way he's taking in my sweet baby, I know, deep down in my soul, that he'll always be there for him, just like he's always been there for me.

They all will.

It's all I could ask for.

Except for my mama. I feel her in this room. I know she's looking down on me and this little bundle in my arms, but I wish she was physically here. I feel like I need her more right this moment than I have in the past sixteen years. Leaning in, I kiss the soft sweet skin of my baby boy's head and breathe him in, silently promising to love him every day of his life.

This is what love at first sight must feel like.

The second he came into this world, my heart followed him.

"What's his name?" my daddy asks, emotion thick in his voice.

"Carter Matthew Benoit," I say confidently, looking down at his matted-down hair and his cherub cheeks. He cracks an eye open at the sound of his name and lets out a grunt.

"I think that's his stamp of approval," my brother says, reaching down and touching his little arm that flails up out of the blanket.

"Carter for my mama . . . ," I begin. My mama's maiden name was Carter—Jessie Anne Carter. "And Matthew for daddy and Tucker," I tell them, looking up at both of them with tears of joy in my eyes.

"I think it's the best damn name ever," Deacon adds.

"Language, Deacon," Annie chides as she wipes her eyes and nose, never taking her eyes off the baby.

"He's perfect," Micah says, leaning over to get a better look. "A little football player in the making."

"Baseball," Sam corrects. "I need a baseball player."

We all laugh . . . and cry.

And as I sit there, with my baby in my arms, I look down at him and hope he feels this much love every day of his life.

CHAPTER
Thirty-One

DEACON

Present

"HEY." CAMI'S VOICE IS SOFT and soothing, just like her hand stroking my arm.

"Hey." I can't help but smile. Her beautiful face is all I want to see every time I wake up.

"Did I wake you?"

"No, I think I've slept enough for a week."

"Not even," she says with a light laugh. "The doctor says your body is still healing. You need all the sleep you can get. Don't stay awake on my account. I'm perfectly happy watching you sleep."

The smile on her face is happy, but I can still see the worry. Her eyes look tired, and even though she's still as gorgeous as ever, I see the effects of the day. Her hair is a little unruly, and she's still in the clothes she normally wears when she paints. It's obvious that she left the gallery and ran to Pockets. That's when it dawns on me again how scared she must've been.

"What is it?" she asks. "Are you in pain? Does somethin' hurt?"

I shake my head.

"Then why the frown?" Her hand reaches up to my face, and she gently rubs her thumb between my eyes, making me relax.

"You were probably really scared." It's not a question. It's a statement. I can't imagine if I had been in Cami's shoes. If I was the one who drove up on a scene like that. How would I have felt if it was her life on the line? "I'm so sorry."

"It's okay."

She gets up from the chair beside my bed and crawls in beside me, burrowing into my side. When her arms are wrapped around my waist, she lets out a deep sigh.

"You wanna talk about it?" I ask.

"I just knew I couldn't lose you. I feel like it's taken us so long to get here, and all I could think was that I couldn't lose you now. I wouldn't."

Her voice is so determined that I believe her. I believe Cami's sheer determination was enough to keep me alive.

"You still want to marry me?" I ask, teasing and trying to lighten the mood a little. There's been too much heavy for one day. Actually, there's been enough to last a long time.

Her hold on me tightens. "I want to marry you even more than I did yesterday and I didn't think that was possible."

"I'm glad. I'd marry you tonight if Father Damon were available."

Cami laughs. "Your mama would kill us."

"And Kay."

"Yes, and Kay."

We lay there for a few minutes just holding each other. I'm glad it's my leg that's banged up and not my hands or arms.

"When the doctor finally came out to talk to us," she starts, her voice low as her fingers trace circles on my chest, "he asked for the Landry family, and it dawned on me that I legally wasn't a part of your family. I want to be attached to you in every way possible. I want to be yours, and I want you to be mine."

"I *am* yours. I always have been." I kiss the top of her head and breathe in her familiar sweet scent.

"I want Carter to be yours too," she says softly.

"I want that too. Next to marryin' you, there's nothing I want more."

"One week," she sighs.

"One week."

In one week, Cami will be a Landry, and I'll be the happiest man on the planet.

CHAPTER
Thirty-Two

DEACON

Past

SUNDAY MORNINGS AT GRINDERS ARE my favorite.

The restaurant is closed, but Micah and I still come in and work. Saturday nights are always crazy here, especially now that LSU football season is upon us, so we like to come in on Sundays to make sure everything is cleaned and restocked for when we open for lunch on Monday. It also gives us a chance to catch up on our paperwork in relative peace, which is practically impossible to do during the week.

Other restaurant owners I know around town told me I was crazy for keeping Grinders closed on Sundays, but that wasn't an option for Micah and me. We were raised believing Sundays are for the three big F's: Faith, Family, and Football, and even though we spend most of our time in Baton Rouge now, we're still expected to come home for church, lunch, and the game, as often as we can.

I'm in the office looking over the staff's timesheets when Micah sticks his head in.

"Hey, Janie is at the door. You want me to let her in?"

Even though Janie and I have been together for a few years now, she knows I don't like to be bothered by anyone when I'm in the office on Sunday mornings. I glance down at my phone and see that I've missed a few texts from her, warning me that she's on her way.

"Nah, I'll go talk to her," I say, getting up and stretching my arms over my head. "I could use a little break anyway."

Micah knows that my relationship with Janie hasn't been going well for a while now, and I appreciate him asking before allowing her in, even though I know she'll be pissed about it.

Micah goes back to restocking the bar while I unlock the door for Janie. She flashes me a glare before breezing past me and heading straight for the office.

Well, this should be fun.

"I don't know why you make me stand outside and wait every time I want to drop by. It's like I have to answer three riddles before the troll under the bridge lets me in," she pouts, sitting on the edge of the wooden desk.

"Who, exactly, is the troll in this scenario, me or Micah?"

She rolls her eyes at me. "You know what I mean, Deacon. I'm your girlfriend; it shouldn't take an act of Congress to see you."

I rub my hands over my eyes, feeling completely drained. It's too early for this shit.

"You know Sundays are my time to catch up on everything here at work. I don't know why you're making such a big deal of it today."

"Believe me; I know how important your Sundays are." She crosses her arms over her chest and juts out her chin. "Lemme guess, when you're done here, you're going to go to your parents' house and watch football, right? And, then what? Have dessert with Cami? I know you can't leave French Settlement without seeing her. So, I guess the reason I'm making such a big deal about it is that I'm wondering when is it my turn? When do I get to spend time with my boyfriend?"

"Leave Cami out of this," I warn. I feel like the biggest asshole, but I can't let her bring Cami into this conversation. The argument needs to stay with us . . . me.

"Don't deny it. You haven't been the same since she moved back home," she says calmly, but I can see the fight brewing in her eyes.

"I know I've been spendin' a lot of time with Cami," I say, trying to keep my tone even, "but she's one of my best friends. I get that you don't like that, but it's nothing different than I would do for Micah or Tucker."

I pause, giving her a chance to say something, but when she doesn't, I continue, deciding it's better to just go ahead and have all the cards on the table. "So, I'm gonna continue to spend time with her. If you can't handle that, then maybe we should be having a different kind of conversation."

I've obviously made things worse with that statement because her eyes are full of fury now, but I'm not backing down. No way in hell am I going to let her, or anyone else, dictate how much time I spend with Cami or my family.

Fuck that.

We stare at each other for a minute, neither of us willing to budge, until she lets out a frustrated sigh and throws her hands in the air dramatically. This isn't like her, she's normally calm, cool, and collected. What's always made Janie and me work is our ability to be casual, and flexible, and forgiving of the other's schedule. The fact that she's recently started acting like some crazy, jealous girlfriend is starting to piss me off.

"Fine," she huffs. "Do what you have to do. You can come to my place tonight when you're back in town. Just make sure you take a shower first," she sneers, hopping off the desk as her dig fuels my anger.

"Go home, Janie." My voice is low, and I'm about three seconds from losing my shit.

She walks through the doorway but turns back to say, "That baby isn't yours. Maybe you should remember that."

I flip her off as she leaves, but she doesn't see it.

Needing a beer in the worst way, I stomp into the bar where Micah is still working.

"She's not wrong, you know."

"What the fuck, Micah?" I pop the top off my beer bottle and throw the cap at him.

"I don't mean about the baby. That was a pure bitch move on her part." He leans down and picks the cap off the floor and throws it away.

"I'm talking about how you've changed since Cami moved back."

I close my eyes and guzzle the cold liquid, hoping it will cool my temper.

When the bottle is empty, I toss it into the trash can.

"I know I have, but I can't help it. I didn't think she'd ever come back, but now that she has . . ." I don't know how to explain how I'm feeling.

"You need to suck it up and admit that you're in love with her," Micah advises. I want to wipe that smug grin off his face. With my fist.

"You don't know shit. Like I'm going to take relationship advice from the Cajun Casanova."

He laughs and wipes the bar down with a towel. "Take it or leave it, I'll still be ready to say I told you so when you finally pull your head outta your ass."

"Janie was right about one thing, though. You *are* a fuckin' troll."

"COME ON, SAINTS! GET YOUR head in the game!" My dad is pacing in front of the TV, yelling, and it's only the first quarter.

After leaving Micah at Grinders, I drove to the Settlement and met my parents at church. He has a date this afternoon, but he promised Mama he'd be home next weekend. Once Mass was over, we came home and grilled steaks, hanging out until the game started.

I love spending time with my parents, and I admire how their relationship has only gotten stronger over the years. I want that one of these days. There was a time I thought I might want that with Janie, but now I'm not so sure. The more I think about it, the more I think I've been forcing my relationship with Janie this whole time. It's not that I don't care for her, I do, and we've had some great times over the years. I just don't think she's the one.

What am I saying?

I know she's not.

"Knock, knock," a female voice rings out as the front door opens.

Cami.

It feels like all of my senses immediately go on high alert just knowing she's here.

"Oh! Give me that baby!" My mama squeals while running to the foyer. She leans down to where Cami has placed Carter's baby carrier and has him unbuckled and in her arms within seconds.

"It's true what they say. Once you have a baby, you become invisible," Cami says, jokingly. "My parents ignore me, too."

Mama swats at her as they walk into the living room. "Oh, hush. You get to love on this angel all the time. It's my turn now." She holds Carter up in the air and inspects him like he's a piece of fruit at the grocery store. "Now, let Nannie look at you. I do believe you've grown a foot since I saw you last."

Every time I see my mom and dad with Carter, I feel a weird twinge in my chest. I love it, don't get me wrong. It's just different, something I've never felt before, or at least not this strong. It's like a deep want or need. I've never been one to give much thought about kids or having them, even though I knew eventually I would. But with Carter in the picture, I think about it a lot.

Cami laughs. "Not quite, but he's definitely goin' through a growth spurt. He eats all the time." She looks at me and, if I'm not mistaken, her smile gets even bigger. "Hey, Deke."

I stand up and walk over to hug her. "Hey, why don't you go sit down and I'll fix you a plate."

"Thank you, but I just ate over at Daddy's house, and I'm stuffed. I'll take a water, though."

"You got it." When I come back from the kitchen and hand her the bottle, her fingers brush against mine as she grabs it. For so long, I've tried to ignore the feeling I get whenever our skin touches, but I don't know if I can do it anymore.

Is Micah right?

Is it finally time for me to admit that I have feelings for her?

Am I ready for that?

Is she?

She has my brain such a jumbled mess half the time, and she doesn't even realize it. I mean, like right now, for instance. She's just sitting there, looking amazing, and she's as calm as can be, cooing at her baby, while I'm on the other side of the couch breaking out into a sweat just because I'm in the same room with her.

What the hell is wrong with me?

It's all Micah's fault. Him and his big fucking mouth.

I walk back into the kitchen to give myself a chance to breathe and put a little distance between Cami and me. I'm not surprised when my dad walks in right behind me. I haven't missed his speculative stare.

"Alright, spill it. What's got you so spooked?" My dad was never one to beat around the bush.

"I'm not spooked," I say, rolling my eyes. "Tired and stressed, maybe, but not spooked. Why? Do I seem spooked?" I think I'm now spooked by how many times I've said the word 'spooked.' Between him and Micah, they're making me paranoid.

"Settle down," he chuckles. "I just noticed that you were over there sweatin' buckets, and it can't be because of the game. The Saints aren't that far behind."

"No, it's not the game," I tell him, letting out a laugh and leaning against the kitchen counter.

"Everything okay with Grinders?" he asks, grabbing another beer out of the fridge.

"Yeah, work is great." I pause, wondering if I want to tell my dad about Janie and me. He's always been great with advice, and I know he'll be honest with me, so I decide to be truthful. "Janie and I aren't doin' so well, though."

"Ahhh" is all I get from him as he pops the cap off his beer and offers me one, but I shake my head in refusal. I don't need alcohol to make me feel even weirder than I already do.

After a few sips, he's finally ready to talk.

"Do you love her? Janie, I mean." His mouth twitches like he's in on some joke, but I don't find any of this funny.

"I don't know. I mean, we've been together for a long time, and I do care for her."

"Well, damn, Deacon. If you don't love her by now, you think you ever will?" When I don't give him an answer, he continues. "It's understandable that you're questioning things. You're twenty-five, it's normal to be thinkin' about how you'd like the rest of your life to play out. Your professional life is going well; now's the time to figure out your personal life. But, remember, rushin' to fall in love makes as much sense as tits on a bull. When the time is right, you'll know it. And when the girl is right, you'll know it."

We walk back into the living room, and I take a seat on the couch opposite Cami. From this vantage point, I can still watch her and have a little distance to sort through my feelings. But mostly, I can watch her. Seeing her as a mom is fantastic. It's hard to explain, but it's like, I've always known Cami is caring, but seeing her sweetly talk to Carter or soothe him when he cries, it takes that caring nature I've always known and multiplies it. I could watch her all damn day.

When the game is over, I offer to follow Cami to her house. I make up an excuse that I want to talk more about the business plan I'm helping her with, but really, it's just an excuse to spend more time with her. Thankfully, she doesn't seem to mind.

I love being inside her house. It's small, like my cottage, but it's homey and comfortable. Cami offers to make us some coffee, and I accept, watching as she gracefully moves around the kitchen while still holding Carter. As our coffee brews, she sits down next to me on the couch and drapes a blanket over her and the baby, which seems weird until I realize that she's feeding him. Breastfeeding him.

Knowing Cami's breasts are exposed underneath that thin blanket while we're sitting next to each other has my mouth completely dry and my mind in places it shouldn't be, like her tits.

I cannot be getting turned on right now. She'll think I'm a pervert for sure. Hell, I think I'm a pervert, but I can't help it.

Deep breaths.

Think about dead puppies.

"So, tell me about this business plan you've drawn up for me," Cami says, completely oblivious to the torture she's putting me through.

I clear my throat, needing a second to recover from my highly inappropriate thoughts. "Um, let me get our coffee first." I get up and quickly walk to the kitchen. I take my time, fixing our mugs. When I walk back into the living room, I sit hers down and then promptly cover my lap with a throw pillow.

Problem solved.

I can do this.

When I start to speak again, finally feeling in control, my voice catches in my throat as I watch Cami switch Carter to her other breast.

For fuck's sake.

She keeps herself covered, but that doesn't mean my imagination isn't running wild. The thing is, I've seen her tits before, and I can only assume they've gotten even better now that she's older. Plus, she's had a baby.

Shit. I should not be thinking about that right now.

Somehow, in the haze of my obvious attraction to this incredible creature, I manage to begin to explain my ideas on how to make her business work. She's so interested in what I have to say that she never seems to notice my distress. Pretty soon, even I'm focusing more on our topic than on her bare breasts, because I'm so excited to be helping her with this.

She wants to open a place that's part gallery, part studio. Something she can, not only use for a place to create, but also offer lessons. It's perfect, and I think it'll fill a great void in the area—giving other aspiring artists the chance Cami never had.

Eventually, she places Carter over her shoulder and starts to burp him, mindful not to let the blanket fall and expose herself. She's such a natural at being a mother, and it warms my heart to see her like this. Carter lets out a couple of impressive burps and then starts to fuss.

"I don't know what's bothering him," she says. "I changed him, fed him, and burped him . . . usually he goes right to sleep by now."

"Want me to try?" I offer, without even thinking.

I'm great with kids, but I don't have a lot of experience with babies. How hard can it be, though, right?

"Sure, if you want." She doesn't sound very confident, but something inside me wants to show her I can do this.

I stand and gently take Carter from her shoulder, cradling him in my arms. Seeing him up close like this, I'm taken back by how beautiful he is. I've never really thought of babies as being beautiful, but Carter is. I can see Camille in every one of his features, and the selfish part of me is thrilled that Tristan isn't represented. He's still pretty wiggly and fussy and when I go to move him to another position, I end up holding him against my side with his tummy lying on my forearm.

"Uh, would you like some help?" Cami asks, sounding nervous. "You're kinda holdin' him like a football."

"Yeah, but I think he likes it. See?" I ask, kinda amazed that I'm doing this. "He stopped cryin'."

With a firm grip on him, while he's snuggled into my side, I slowly turn to face her. Instinctively, my body starts to bounce a little as I hold him, and I know I look ridiculous, but I don't care. I got the little guy to stop crying, and it feels like sweet victory, especially when I notice the look on Cami's face.

Is she turned on?

God, I hope so.

Her eyes are wide, and her mouth is turned up in a surprised smile, but it's her heavy breathing that's really got my attention. Thankfully, after I took Carter, she put herself back together, so at least I don't have her exposed boobs to distract me any longer. Or maybe I'm not so thankful.

Holy shit. Is it normal to be this turned on with a baby so close by?

I know nothing romantic will happen between Cami and me. Not tonight. That wouldn't be fair to her or to Janie, and I'm not a cheater, but I can't deny loving the fact that Cami is clearly checking me out and liking what she sees.

Maybe it wouldn't hurt to change poses . . . I mean positions, to see how they affect Cami. You know, for future reference. I make a show of carefully moving Carter to my chest and holding him up against my shoulder. I kiss the top of his head and take in a little whiff of his baby scent, surprised that he smells good, like really good. I think it's probably baby powder and lotion . . . and maybe a little of his mama. It's a bit intoxicating. Now I see why people always sniff their little heads.

I so got this baby thing down.

Because I'm a dumbass, I get a little smug with myself, while rubbing Carter's back. Just when I think I must be the baby whisperer, in rapid succession, he lets out a loud wail, burps, and then throws up an enormous amount of breastmilk down the front of my shirt, before falling swiftly back asleep.

How can he go from being so peaceful to full-on post-rager and back again in a matter of seconds?

I look to Cami for help, but she has her face planted in a pillow, trying not to disturb Carter with her laughter. And now I smell like rotten ass, but I don't care. I still consider this a win and proof that I can do this.

I can help take care of a baby.

I can be here for Cami.

And I'm exactly where I want to be.

CAMI WAS SWEET ENOUGH TO find me an old shirt of Tucker's to trade out for the one that was demoralized by spit-up. That shit is toxic, but oddly enough, it didn't make me want to give him up. After I got a clean shirt, albeit a size or two too small, Carter and I settled back on the couch while Cami and I finished our conversation about the art studio.

I told her I think it'd be best not to take out a loan for now. She still has some money in savings and all she needs is a small space to rent until the studio gets off the ground. Then, when she has a constant cash flow, she can invest in a building.

The passion she has for her art is tangible, and I know she's going to be successful. And beyond all of that, I'm so happy to know that she hasn't given up on her dreams . . . hasn't quit chasing her castles.

Before I even make the crossover onto Highway 16, my phone vibrates, signaling an incoming text message.

At the next stop sign, I check it and see it's Janie, reminding me to stop by her apartment before going home.

Sighing, I text her back before turning out on the highway. As much as I just want to go home and call it a night, I know I need to talk to her.

When I pull up at Janie's, forty minutes later, I park my truck and hop out. Before I even get to her door, I see the light from inside as she cracks it open and stands there with her arms folded across her chest.

Unlike earlier today, her expression is more solemn. I hate that this is what our relationship has come to. I always thought, if we ever quit dating, we'd at least still be friends. I'm not sure where everything went so wrong.

Well, I guess I do.

"I'm sorry," I tell her, without even thinking about what I want to say. First, I know I want to apologize.

"For what?" she asks, squaring her shoulders.

"For, I don't know . . . all of this," I say, waving my arms around in the air at invisible objects. "I know you're upset, and I hate seeing you that way. So, I'm sorry."

"Where do you see us going from here?" she asks.

I swallow, knowing what I want to say and what I need to say, but I'm having trouble forcing the words out.

"I don't know," I say, but it's not the whole truth. The whole truth is that I don't see us going anywhere. Janie is great. She's ambitious and smart and fun. But she's not who I see myself with in thirty years . . . or ten . . . or tomorrow.

"You'll never look at me the way you look at her," she says sadly, and it makes my head snap up, and my eyes find hers. "You look at her like she hung the moon and placed the stars. When she's in the room, she's all you see. But I want you to look at me like that." There are tears in her eyes and emotion thick in her voice.

"You deserve someone to look at you like that," I tell her with all the honesty and sincerity I can muster. Hearing her words makes my heart ache, but weirdly enough, it's not because I'm sad . . . it's because I know what she's saying is the truth. I've always thought that Cami is wonderful . . . because she is. She's my best friend, my first love, and I've suddenly realized she is the person I can see myself with fifty years down the road.

I don't know why it took me so long to see it, but I do. So clearly.

Janie pushes herself off the doorframe and takes a couple of steps toward me until we're standing toe to toe. Stretching up, using the front of my too small shirt to pull herself closer, she places a soft kiss on my cheek.

"I'm sorry," I tell her again.

"There's nothing to be sorry about. I've always known I could never compete with her. I saw it the first night at the restaurant, but I guess I thought maybe I still had a chance because you were with me. But some things just aren't meant to be."

And some things are.

Thirty-Three

Camille

Present

I WILL NEVER UNDERSTAND HOW a patient is supposed to rest while in a hospital when they're constantly being disturbed throughout the night. I know the medical staff are only doing their jobs, but it's frustrating, and I'm not even the patient.

The good news is that Deacon is expected to be discharged later today. The doctor wants to do another chest x-ray and, if that's clear, we can leave. I'm so ready to be in a real bed. I can only imagine how Deacon must feel.

"Hey, you think we can get a few of these hospital gowns to take home?" Deacon asks.

"Why on earth would you want that?"

"We could both use them. Just think about how interesting 'no pants day' would be with these things on! Talk about easy access," he says while waggling his eyebrows at me.

Yes, ladies and gentlemen, that's the man I'm gonna marry.

I take the small pillow given to me by the nurse last night and throw it at his face. "What am I gonna do with you, Deacon Landry?"

He leans over and grabs my hand, pulling me to him. "You're gonna marry me, that's what, Camille Benoit. Don't you forget it."

He kisses me, and it's almost as if we're home already and not still in this hospital room. That is until the door opens and we hear a throat clearing.

"Sorry, to interrupt. I just wanted to stop by and check on Deacon."

It's been a long time since I've heard that voice, and I can tell by the expression on Deacon's face he's just as surprised as I am.

"Hey, Janie. Come on in," he tells her. "I didn't realize you were workin' here."

When I go to move from Deacon's bed to the nearby chair, Deacon stops me and pulls me closer to him. I don't know if he's using me to protect himself or making sure Janie knows we're together but, either way, I don't mind.

Janie steps into the room but doesn't sit down. "Yeah, I'm doing my residency here. Sorry for just barging in like this. I saw your name on a medical file and wanted to make sure you were okay. I'm sorry to hear about your restaurant."

"Thanks. I'm lucky it wasn't worse—for me and for Pockets—but we'll both be fine."

I love the confidence in his voice. He's determined for the fire to only be a hiccup in his plans, nothing serious and, certainly, nothing long term.

"I also see that congratulations are in order," Janie says, nodding toward the engagement ring on my finger.

"Yep," Deacon beams, "we're gettin' married next week."

Janie looks a little surprised to hear about our wedding, but she plays it off well.

"Oh, even after the fire?" she asks. It's an honest question, even one we've discussed once or twice during the last twenty-four hours.

"Absolutely. I don't care if I have to wear shorts or walk with a cane, nothing is keeping me from marrying Cami next week just like we've planned." He's speaking to her but looking at me the entire time. I was the one who half-heartedly suggested we postpone the wedding, if only for another week, but Deacon adamantly refused.

"Well, that's great. I'm happy for you both." She walks back to the door and waves her clipboard in the air. "I have to get back to my rounds. It was good seeing you, Deacon. Take care."

Thirty-Four

Camille

Past

SOMETIMES, AT NIGHT, MY TINY house is too quiet.
And lonely.

But it especially is tonight because, for the first time since Carter was born, I'm spending the night alone. I went out with Stacey for a drink earlier since she's home for Thanksgiving and we ran into Deacon and Micah and my brother at the bar.

Seeing Deacon outside of my house or his parents' was different . . . good, but different. It's been a long time since I've hung out with him around other people and he was . . . different . . . good, but different. He watched me a lot. I didn't notice it at first, but Stacey pointed it out to me. I thought it was more of the protective bullshit that they used to pull in high school, but I don't know. He seemed intense, especially when I was dancing with a random guy from the bar. I thought Deacon was going to burn holes in the back of the poor man's head.

The pull I always feel when I'm around him was there, but I'm not sure if he feels it too. Sometimes, I want to ask, but things have been so good between us lately. Since he broke up with Janie, he spends a lot of time with me and Carter, even more than before the break-up and it's nice. I love it, actually. And I don't want to do anything to mess it up.

Sometimes, I'm afraid I'm relying on him too much. I don't know if he realizes the role he's beginning to fill, but I'm also afraid if I point it out to him, he may get spooked and bolt. Deacon and I used to talk about everything when we were younger. I know he wants children, but I don't know if he wants them now.

And I refuse to take his break-up with Janie at anything more than face value. I'm not going to jump to conclusions or take up wishful thinking. Those both sound like recipes for disaster and a broken heart. I don't have the luxury of taking those kind of chances these days. Carter needs me and Deacon turning me down or removing himself from our lives would crush me. So, for now, I'm good with how things are.

Standing at the kitchen sink, I watch the rain. I've always loved a good rain storm. Usually, I sleep like a baby, but tonight, I can't stop thinking about Deacon. I watch the drops hit the window over until the tea kettle I put on a few minutes ago starts whistling.

While I'm busy making my tea, I think I hear something outside.

It sounded like a car door.

But it could've been thunder.

I take my mug and walk back over to the window just in time to see a large figure running up the steps of my porch.

My heart pounds and I think about turning the kitchen light off and retreating to my bedroom, but then I see the face . . . and the rest of him.

He barely has a chance to get one knock in before I'm cracking the door open.

"Hey," Deacon says, and my heart drops out of my body. If I were able to peel my eyes off him and look at my feet, it'd probably be lying there in a heap, beating out of my chest.

He's always beautiful, but there's something about the way the water is dripping off him that emphasizes every feature, every strong line, and detail. His eyes aren't their usual blue-green abyss. They're darker. His shoulders are tense. His jaw is tight.

"Hey," I reply, using the half-open door for support.

"Can I come in?" he asks as his hand pulls at the now wet white T-shirt.

"Y—yes," I stutter over the reply and avert my eyes to keep from giving myself away. Deacon doesn't need to know the inward struggle I'm having. "Is everything okay?"

"No," he says as the door shuts closed behind him and my heart drops again, but for a different reason.

"What's wrong?" I ask begging him with my eyes to spit it out.

I'm about to reach back for the door when his hand comes out and rests on mine.

"We need to talk."

"About what?" I ask, deciding that if something were wrong with Carter or anyone else, he'd just come right out and say it. Instead of panicking, I try to take slow, deep breaths.

Deacon looks down at himself, and I jump into action as my brain catches up.

"Lemme get you a towel," I tell him, not waiting for his response before I retreat down the hall and into the bathroom to get him a towel and collect my thoughts.

When I flip the light on, I catch a glimpse of myself in the mirror and cringe. My hair's damp, twisted back at the nape of my neck, and I'm wearing a white T-shirt and no bra. I consider bee-lining it to my bedroom to throw on a sweatshirt, but I don't want to leave Deacon waiting, so I decide to deliver the towel first.

"Here," I tell him when I get back to the living room. "You want me to get you a dry T-shirt? I'm sure I have one of Tucker's around here somewhere. He just loves leavin' his dirty laundry for me to do." I chuckle, crossing my arms over my chest to cover myself, trying to make light of the situation that suddenly feels very heavy and dense.

"I'll pass," he says, crooking a smile and making his dimples go on full display.

Why, God?

Why must I be tortured?

I'm a good girl.

At least, I try to be.

"Uh, want some tea?" I ask, thinking of a way I can occupy myself and warm Deacon up.

I will not think about warming Deacon up.

"Sure," he says running the towel over his hair and down his face.

I walk back over to the stove and grab another mug and tea bag before pouring the hot water, using the methodical movements to calm myself.

"So," I say, turning around, ready to engage in casual conversation, but instead I'm completely caught off guard by the stare I'm met with. Deacon is standing on the other side of the table and he's looking at me like his life depends on it. "What did you want to talk about?" The words come out slow and low as I dip the tea bag a few times and then set it on the table in front of where he's standing.

"I can't do this anymore," he mumbles, but I hear him, and I don't know what that means, but I feel the atmosphere change.

"What?" I ask as I watch him ignore the hot mug on the table and take two steps toward me.

"I. Can't. Do. This. Anymore," he repeats, more pronounced with each word. "I don't want to."

For a second, just a split second, I think maybe he's talking about us . . . maybe our friendship, but I know, like deep down to the core of my being, Deacon will never leave me. He'll always be there for me. So, as I mentally pass by that option, I go on to the next . . . maybe he's talking about . . .

"I can't stay away from you," he says, interrupting my thought process. "I can't pretend that I don't want you. I can't watch other guys hit on you. I can't go another day without tellin' you how I feel."

His words come out sure and strong. With each statement, he takes a step closer, and my body responds.

First, it's my stupid heart that gives out.

Then, it's my breathing.

And then, my speech.

I just shake my head and watch him. I watch him as he walks to me like I'm his prize, and he's come to claim what's his.

And I don't know what to do.

I'm paralyzed.

Frozen.

"What?" I manage to squeak.

"I love you," he says so easily like he's saying the day of the week . . . like it's the most normal thing on earth. "I love you, and I need you to know that."

His damp hair is curled along his forehead, and he reminds me of the boy I fell in love with so long ago.

But when his hand reaches out and brushes my arm, I'm reminded of the man he's turned into.

The lump in my throat keeps me from responding.

I want to tell him that I love him too. I've always loved him. I loved him when he didn't see me for more than Tucker's little sister. I loved him when he knew me better than anyone on the planet. I loved him while I thought I loved someone else. And I loved him when I knew he did.

And I think, all along, deep down, I've always known that he loves me too.

He didn't have to say it.

He showed me in ways that can't be put into words.

He saved me when I needed it the most.

He understood me when I felt like no one else did.

He believed in me when I didn't believe in myself.

And he has no idea how long I've wanted to hear him say those words to me.

For the longest time, we've passed each other like ships on the sea. Our lives are always at different ports. I used to let myself dream that maybe one day we'd be on the same course, but that dream faded over time.

"I know this is out of the blue, and . . ."

"I love you," I blurt out, unable to let him stand there, with his heart exposed and not hear those words in return. "I've always loved you."

If he's ready to put all the cards out on the table, then so am I.

A second later, his hands are on my face, in my hair, and he's leaning into me—his damp body pressing into mine, and we're both breathing like we just ran a marathon.

"What are you doin'?" I ask, fighting with instinct and reason.

"What I've wanted to do for a long, long time," he drawls, his breath hot on my lips. "If you don't want this, you need to tell me now."

I use the half inch of space between us to look up, into his eyes, and it's over. Any lingering rational thought flies out of my mind with the brush of his thumb over my lip.

I don't know if I initiate it or if he does, but our mouths collide, and the world around us crumbles and the two of us are all that remain. His teeth graze my bottom lip and his tongue requests permission to delve further, and I give it to him. Everything.

Lost in his kiss and his touch, I barely register the feel of his hands on my hips. He lifts me up and places me on top of the kitchen counter. Something falls to the ground in a loud clatter, but I don't care. I eagerly spread my legs, giving him room to nestle between them.

In a fluid motion, Deacon grabs the bottom of my shirt and pulls it over my head, and I know I should care. I should feel exposed. I should want to cover myself, but I don't. I want him. And I want him to have all of me. I've wanted it for so long, and I'm so desperate for it that all I can muster is a pathetic whimper as I pull at his shirt and urge him to take it off.

Flashes of a time long, long ago flitter through my mind, like clips from an old movie. I see us, young and inexperienced, in the back of his truck. That night was so different from this. We knew what we wanted, but we didn't know what we were doing.

I didn't know Deacon was inexperienced back then, but I see the difference in him now.

Where once a young boy, with nervous hands and second-guesses once stood, now stands a man who is confident and knows exactly what he wants and how to get it.

I moan as his lips leave mine and make a hot trail down my neck. His hands take both of my full breasts, and he begins to rub and pull, teasing me into a panting mess.

Leaning into his touch, I silently beg for more, but then I find my voice, and I tell him.

"More, Deacon," I plead, removing my hands from his hair and reaching between us to find his belt buckle. "I want more."

"Are you sure?" he asks, his movements stopping for a second. "I didn't come over here just to . . ."

"I'm sure," I tell him, breathless. "I want this. I want you."

And those words are all he needs to hear.

He scoops me up off the counter and carries me down the hall. On the way to my bedroom, I wrap my arms around his neck and revel in the feel of his bare chest against mine. I revel in having him here with me like this. I almost fall apart right there in his arms, but somehow, I refrain.

Before he lays me down on the bed, I squeeze harder, wanting to say so much, but deciding it can wait when I pull back and see the hunger in his eyes.

No one has ever looked at me like that, and it sends a bolt of electricity straight to my core.

"You're beautiful," he whispers, hovering over me as he lowers me to the bed. "You're so fuckin' beautiful . . . so perfect." His words trail off as his fingers lightly move from my breasts to my stomach and down further to the waist of my pajama shorts.

My knees fall to the side, and everything after that happens in rapid succession.

My shorts are pulled off and tossed to the floor. I watch as Deacon makes fast work of his belt and jeans, his boxers meeting them in a heap. And then it's just me and him, and we both take each other in for a few seconds, unable to move or speak.

"I love you," I whisper, because now that I've said those words out loud, I don't think I'll ever be able to stop.

"Say it again," Deacon whispers back, crawling further onto the bed and hovering over me. His strong arms are caging me in.

"I love you."

He doesn't repeat it back to me, but he does show me.

His lips start at my mouth and work their way down to my stomach, leaving ashes in their wake. Before he dips below my waist, his eyes look up and find mine. I reach down and take his hands, grounding myself, readying myself for what's to come, because his gaze is enough to make me fall apart.

When his mouth is on my sensitive core, I buck into him, pressing my head into the pillows. The combination of his mouth and fingers are enough to bring me close to the edge in only a few short strokes.

Opening my eyes, I look down, and the sight of him, mixed with the feel of him is what eventually does me in.

I'm unable to contain the loud moan of pleasure that escapes, followed by God's name and his, almost used as one and the same.

I'm so blissed out; I barely notice when he sits up and kneels between my legs, pulling my hips and lining himself up. I vaguely remember him sliding a condom on and then my world shifts on its axis.

Deacon is on me, in me, consuming me.

It's everything and too much and not enough all in the same breath.

I push my hands against the headboard and force him further into me, seeking as much friction as possible.

"I want to see you," Deacon says, his voice is thick with demand and want. "Look at me."

I do as he says; I look at him. And I see him too.

He's so beautiful as he moves above me that I can hardly keep my emotions in check.

"I love you, Cami," he says. His jaw tightens and flexes, and my hands reach up to hold his face, keeping our eyes locked.

Our pace quickens, then slows, again and again, both of us desperately chasing what we've yearned for . . . needed for so long, but not wanting this moment to end.

This moment is everything I've dreamed about and so much more.

This is more than a night of passion.

It's more than three words I've never said to anyone this way before.

It's more than getting those three words back in return.

And that scares me, but I try not to overthink. I try just to feel.

Deacon's thrusts come fervently. My hands are on his chest and in his hair, that is now damp from the sweat beading on his forehead. His hips are angled just right, and I feel the coil in the pit of my stomach building.

His hand slipping between us and putting pressure where I need it, want it, is what sends me over the edge, falling to pieces beneath him.

"So. Beautiful." Deacon's voice comes out in short burst, mimicking his movements. "So. Fucking. Beautiful."

When his hips pump even faster, I grip his shoulders and hold on as he finds his release.

Both of us lie there, holding each other so tightly. Neither of us wanting to let go.

If I could, I'd stay right here, just like this.

Deacon's grip on me makes me think he might feel the same.

CHAPTER
Thirty-Five

DEACON

Present

"HOME, SWEET, HOME! FOR NOW, anyway," Cami announces as she opens the front door to her house.

This time next week, it'll be *our* house until we decide we're ready to add onto my cottage and move in. I feel like I've been a nomad for so long, going back and forth between Baton Rouge and French Settlement since I left for college. It feels good to finally put down some roots and settle down.

Of course, it's easy to settle down now that Cami is in my life in a more permanent way and having Carter is the icing on the cake. I can't wait for them both to have my last name. And, who knows, maybe we'll be adding to our family soon.

"What's causin' that cheesy grin on your face?" Camille asks.

"Just plannin' for the future, that's all." I limp over to where she's standing in the kitchen and wrap my arms around her.

"Oh, no. You brought home some of those hospital gowns, didn't you?" The look of horror on her face makes me double over in laughter, which, in turn, causes me to start coughing, but I don't care. That shit was funny.

"Of course, I did, but that's not what I was thinkin' about." I kiss Cami's face from her temple to her jaw and then down her neck until I reach her shoulder. "If you must know, I was thinkin' about us havin' another baby. Not right this second, but soon, maybe. Doesn't soon sound good to you?"

Her eyes are dazed when she looks up at me, but then she smiles and says, "Yeah, I'm good with soon."

That gets her a full kiss on the lips and gets me an erection the size of Texas.

The doctor suggested we take it easy in the bedroom until my leg heals more and, for some reason, that gave Cami the *brilliant* idea of us waiting to have sex until after we're married. I had to have been on some heavy pain pills to agree to that, but if it's what Cami wants then I'll give it to her. She's just gonna have to put up with a lot of boners for the next week.

I am more than surprised when I feel Cami's hand slip between our bodies and palm my dick through my shorts.

"Baby, you're not playin' fair. Remember what the doctor said?"

"He said to be *careful*, not celibate. Come on, let me take care of you." She wraps her arm around my waist and helps me walk into the bedroom.

"But, I thought you wanted to wait?" I'm not gonna pressure her in any way but, if she's offering what I hope she's offering, I'm not gonna say no.

"I thought I did, too, but then, I realized we have the house to ourselves for a few hours, and that doesn't happen very often and dammit, I missed you." Her hands are on her hips, and her cheeks are flushed, and I'm pretty sure I fall even more in love with her.

"Do you know how adorable you are when you're horny and ramblin'?"

"Shut up and take your shirt off," she commands with a grin.

"Yes, ma'am," I say before pulling her up next to me on the bed. *Our* bed. This bed will always have special memories for me, and I can't wait to make even more.

Thirty-Six

DEACON

Past

LYING HERE IN THE DARK, with Cami nestled against my chest, her leg thrown haphazardly over mine, I couldn't feel more content.

I do need to piss, though.

I've needed to for about the past hour, but I don't want to move.

I can't. I have an insatiable need to soak up as much of her as I possibly can.

Maybe I'm making up for lost time.

I don't know, but now that I have her in my arms, and I've told her I love her, something I've wanted to tell her for so long, I'm never going to let her go.

Honestly, I don't know what took me so long. I should've laid it all out on the table a long time ago. I should've manned up and told her how I feel—how I've felt for so long.

After Janie and I broke up, I wanted to tell her. Some days, when I'd stop by to see her and Carter, it'd be on the tip of my tongue, but then

I'd convince myself that the moment wasn't special enough. I felt like I needed a grand gesture.

And everything about us has always been slow and patient, so I didn't feel a need to rush things.

I just kept telling myself that we'd get our chance.

I've always held onto that thought, even when I knew I shouldn't.

Last night, at the bar, it was like a switch flipped . . . or the camel's back broke . . . I don't know. Whatever it was, something happened, and I couldn't stand it any longer. I couldn't stand seeing someone else look at her or touch her, even though it was just a dance.

I was so pissed at myself for waiting so long. And I felt sick at the idea that I might let her slip through my fingers a second time.

The first time I let her go, I thought I was doing what was right for both of us. There was a selfish part of me that wanted to see what college was all about. But more than that, I didn't want Cami to sit around and wait for me. I was scared I'd hurt her. I didn't trust myself with her heart.

Watching her live her life over the last six years has been part happiness and part torture.

I've watched her become a woman—a mom. I've watched her go after her dreams and achieve them. The graceful way she lives her life, even under extreme pressure, is addictive. I find myself wanting to be everywhere she is. I've always felt that way.

When we were young, if I had the choice of hanging with Micah and Tucker or hanging with Cami, I always wanted to choose Cami. I didn't always choose her, but it was only because I didn't want Tucker and Micah catching on or teasing me about it . . . or her.

It's always been about her.

What would make Cami happy.

What kept Cami safe.

What was best for Cami.

Because she deserves only the best things in life.

Her struggles nearly wrecked me. Watching her with Tristan was one of the hardest things I've ever had to do. The desire to wipe him off the planet was so real. I've never wanted to end someone like that before.

After I watched him scream at her and put his hands on her, all I could think about was making him pay.

And I wanted to blame myself. I thought a lot about the what-ifs. What if we'd made it work back in high school? What if I'd told her how I felt about her? Maybe she wouldn't have ended up with him.

But it was my mama who helped me see things clearly. She told me that we're not meant to see where our lives are headed for a reason. If we saw everything ahead of time, we wouldn't take risks. And without risks, we'd never learn how to pick ourselves up or try again. Without all of that, we'd never become the people we're intended to be.

When it all comes down to it, had Cami not met Tristan, there never would've been a Carter, and I can't even imagine that.

It's weird how something so small can change so much. For the better.

I've never seen my parents completely lose their shit like they do over him. He's bonded everyone together even stronger than we were before. As much as I wish I could've protected Cami, I know she wouldn't change the end result. And I wouldn't want her to.

I love Carter like he's my own and I don't even know what to do with that feeling.

Cami stirs beside me, her leg rubbing against mine.

"Are you awake?" she asks, sleep thick in her voice.

"Yeah," I mumble, rubbing slow circles down her back and then her arm.

She leans up and checks the clock beside her bed. "What are we gonna do?" she asks, settling back in beside me, her long blonde hair covering my arm that's wrapped around her.

"What do you mean?" I ask, not following her.

"They'll expect us to be at mass in a few hours," she sighs.

"And?" I ask, still not following.

She places her hand on my chest, right over my heart.

"I'm worried," she whispers, her lips landing on the bare skin of my chest.

"About what?"

"About what everyone's gonna think . . . what are they gonna say?"

I wrap my arms around her and pull her until she's nearly laying on top of me.

"It doesn't matter," I tell her, my eyes boring into hers. "It doesn't matter what anyone thinks. If they don't like it, they can take it up with me. Because now that I have you, I'm never letting you go. You're stuck with me."

A slow, small smile creeps up on her beautiful face, and she leans down to kiss my chest, her hair falling around her.

"I feel like I'm dreamin'," she says softly. "When I fell asleep, I was afraid you'd be gone when I woke up."

"Have I ever left you?" I ask her, tilting her head up so she'll look me in the eyes and know how serious I am.

"No." She shakes her head slowly, but I can see the worry on her face.

"I'm not goin' anywhere. It's you and me now. It always has been, but now more than ever."

"Okay," she says, pushing herself further up my body until her lips are hovering above mine. "It's just, I've dreamed about this for a long time, and I've wanted you for even longer," she admits. "It might take me a while to realize I get to keep you this time."

The *this time*, hangs in the air like a thick blanket of fog.

"You kept me then, too," I tell her. "I've always been yours; it just took us a while to get on the same page."

"Do you ever wonder what it would've been like if we'd tried to make it work back then?" she asks, her voice low and husky.

"Yeah," I admit. "It was all I thought about for a long time, but then I'd see you, and you'd be doing great—hanging out with your friends, enjoying life—doing all the things I hoped you'd do. And I felt like the sacrifice was worth it."

"And you were with Janie," she says, biting her lip like she'd like to take it back, but I don't want her to. I want her to know every-thing . . . anything she wants to ask, I'll gladly answer.

"I was," I tell her. "We were an easy fit. At first, we were just good friends, and that eventually turned into something else."

"Did you love her?" she asks.

"Yes, but I was never in love with her."

"Is that why y'all broke up?"

"Partly."

"And the other part?" she prompts.

"I loved you . . . I was *in love* with you, and she knew that. She told me she could tell by the way I looked at you. I think I'd been in love with you for so long, I didn't think it was obvious anymore. I'd denied myself for so long when it came to you, to loving you, I thought I was good at hiding it. But apparently, I wasn't."

She swallows hard and rests her chin on my chest.

"I thought you hung the moon back then," she says with a light laugh.

"And now?" I ask, needing the same reassurance she's looking for.

"I think you set the stars in place and the planets in motion."

I pull her up to me and kiss her so hard, tangling my hands in her hair and our bodies together. For a second time tonight, and the third time in my life, I make love to Camille Benoit. I pour everything I have into each touch and each caress, hoping I can somehow make up for lost time and prove to her that I'm here for the long haul.

After we're both spent, we drift back off to sleep.

There's nothing like being with Cami. I've always known that, but being inside her takes me to a whole new level. And waking up next to her just went to the top of my favorites list.

I can't help but watch her as she gradually wakes up. It takes her a minute to realize what, or who, she's laying on, and who's beside her. The smile that creeps up on her face is the most beautiful thing I've ever seen. I lean down and kiss her lips as a deep-seated longing takes root in my stomach.

This is right.

This is what life is all about.

Being with her.

Being inside her.

Being next to her.

I don't know what took me so long to make this happen, but I'm sure as hell not gonna let her go.

THE MORNING IS NICE, EASY. I can tell Cami misses Carter and is anxious to get to church to see him, but other than that, we're good.

"I'm nervous," Cami says, fidgeting in the seat beside me as we drive down the road. I grab her hands and hold them still, rubbing my thumb over hers.

"Don't be nervous. I swear, if anyone even looks at you wrong, I'll handle it."

"You don't have to do that," she says, shaking her head. "I'll be fine. I mean, I already got the prize and since when do I care what everyone thinks about me?" She laughs, and I can tell she's giving herself a pep talk.

When I look over at her, she gives me a beaming smile, and I have to fight the urge to turn my truck around and go back to her house and strip her out of her sundress. She can keep the red pumps. But the dress would have to go.

"What are you thinkin' about?" she asks with a knowing grin.

"You and how incredible it is to have you sitting here next to me," I lie, but it's not total bullshit. I do feel that way. I feel like the luckiest son of a bitch in the world.

There is a part of me, though, that would like to live in the bubble we've been in since last night for a while longer, but we can't. Our family is made up of a bunch of nosey asses. If we didn't show up to Sunday Mass, they'd be at Cami's house faster than you can shake a stick. And then they'd have seen my truck, and it all would've been over with anyway.

So, here we are. At church. And we're getting ready to walk into the devil's den, so to speak.

"Ready?" I ask her when I pull into one of the last parking spots and put the truck in park.

She takes a deep breath and exhales. "Yes," she says with sheer bravery written all over her face. "And I missed my baby, and he's in there. So, let's do this."

I laugh and hop out of the truck, running around to get her door.

When she steps out, I stop her for a second and tilt her chin up until our eyes meet. "I love you. It's you and me."

She nods and smiles.

"Okay."

I kiss her lips softly, and she leans in, deepening the kiss.

I moan in frustration as I reluctantly pull away.

"You're gonna kill me, woman."

She laughs, shaking her head.

"Let's get this over with."

When we walk through the heavy wooden doors, everyone else is already in their respective pews, and I think Cami and I both exhale a sigh of relief that maybe we'll go undetected for just a little while longer.

"I gotta see Carter," she whispers, pulling me down the hall toward the nursery.

"Okay," I tell her, following along. I want to tell her that I missed him too . . . that I miss him every time I don't get to see him for a day or two. But I don't know if that would sound weird, so I keep it to myself.

When we peek into the room where the babies are, I see him immediately, happily playing on the floor with another little dude about his age. I can't believe he can already sit up by himself. He's only seven months old, but I don't know what's normal. I haven't been around babies much.

Cami sighs and leans against the door. Mrs. Johnson, the lady who watches the babies, walks over and smiles. "You want me to get him for you?" she asks.

"No," Cami says softly, not wanting to disrupt his play time. "I just needed to see him."

"He's such a good baby," Mrs. Johnson says.

"Thanks," Cami says. "I think so too."

I kiss the side of Cami's head and get a knowing look from Mrs. Johnson, to which I just smile like this is the most normal thing on the planet.

And it is.

Loving Cami is like breathing. It's necessary and life preserving and what I was made to do.

As we walk in to find a seat, I grab Cami's hand, and she looks up at me. I can tell her nerves are back, but I don't care.

I want to shout it from the rooftops, but since we're in church and Father Damon has already started, I decide holding her hand will have to do for now.

The second we're seated, I feel a dozen set of eyes settle on us. Some of them are the people sitting on our pew, but the others are from a few rows ahead. My Mama, in particular, is looking at us with a raised eyebrow and a sly smile. She reminds me of a rubber-necker. One of those jackasses who can't drive past an accident without holding up traffic.

Just to clarify, I'm not calling my Mama a jackass.

I would never.

But she's still staring at us.

I smile at her, and when she still doesn't turn around, I take a page from her book and give her the universal hand gesture for "turn around and mind your own business."

She shakes her head and fights back a smile, but eventually turns back around. And I don't miss when she leans in and whispers something to my dad. The next person to gawk at us is Micah, with a smirk and a squint of his eyes. If he were able to send me a subliminal message right now, it would be *about fucking time*, or *I told you so*.

Cami's hand is still firmly in mine, and she leaves it there, even through the kneeling and praying. When her head leans against my shoulder while we listen to Father Damon, I let myself wonder, for a split second, if this is what we'll be doing in fifty years.

I hope so.

When the final prayer is finished, and the congregation begins to file out of the pews, Cami squeezes my hand and pulls me toward the back doors.

"Do you think we can hold them off until lunch?" she asks in a hushed tone as I clear a path for us, smiling and excusing my way to the back of the church.

"I don't know, but we can try."

We make a beeline for the nursery and retrieve Carter. It isn't until we're standing outside the nursery that Cami realizes we're at least going to have to talk to her dad because he and Kay have Carter's car seat.

"Why don't you go on to the house and I'll ride with them," she says, holding Carter close and placing a million soft kisses on his little head.

I lean in and get a few in for myself, loving the way he smells.

He smiles at her, and I know he missed his mama as much as she missed him.

"You sure?" I ask, worried about leaving her.

"I'm sure," she nods, giving me a smile.

I glance around the corner and see my parents shaking hands with Father Damon. My window of escape is narrowing.

"I'll meet you at the house," I tell her.

As I turn to walk away, I feel her tug on my shirt.

"Deke," she says with a bit of urgency.

Turning back around, I watch as she shifts Carter to her other hip and takes a step toward me.

"Thank you for comin' to my house in the pourin' rain," she says, her hand reaching out and pulling the front of my shirt to bring me closer.

"Thank you for lettin' me in," I tell her, reaching up to hold her face and pull her lips to mine.

Mrs. Johnson clearing her throat is what finally interrupts us and brings me back to reality.

We're going to the top of the short list for town gossip.

During the five-minute drive to the house, all I could think about was Cami. Now that we're all seated around the table, all I can think is telling everyone that Cami is mine, and they can all deal with it. But I'm trying to allow Cami to go at her own pace, so I'm doing my best to play it cool.

"Well," my Mama says, as she passes a bowl to my dad. "That was a lovely sermon today, don't y'all think?"

I know her. I know she's worming her way toward the two elephants in the room.

I feel Cami's hand brush against my leg, and I give her a small smile.

Maybe we should put everyone out of their misery and just spill the beans, but I'm having a little too much fun watching them squirm.

Except Micah. He's sitting on the opposite side of the table with that same damn smirk on his face. I'm tempted to kick him under the table. Such a smug bastard. Always thinking he knows everything.

"It was a lovely sermon," Kay chimes in, feeding Carter little bites of mashed potatoes. "Didn't you think so, handsome?" Carter gives a wide grin and slaps his hands down in a pile of peas. Everyone laughs, including me, because anything the kid does is the cutest damn thing I've ever seen.

"I liked the part where Father Damon was talkin' about the truth settin' you free," Micah says, cramming half a roll in his trap.

"I don't remember that part," Mama says, cocking her head in his direction.

"Oh, yeah. He also said," Micah pauses to finish his enormous bite of food. "It's always good to admit when you're wrong."

"Were we listenin' to the same sermon?" Dad asks.

I look at the opposite end of the table, and I see Tucker watching all of this, everyone. One second his eyes are on Micah and then me . . . and then Cami. I can't tell what he's thinking, and if I'm nervous about anyone finding out about Cami and me, it's him.

I don't want him to think I went behind his back or that I'm in this for anything less than forever.

I know he loves her and wants what's best for her.

I want that too.

"And you will know the truth," Micah's voice rings out like he's the one giving the sermon. "And the truth will set you free!" He bangs a hand on the table for added emphasis.

Everyone is staring at him when I feel Cami abruptly stand beside me.

"Deacon and I are together," she says, twisting her napkin between her fingers, nervously. "Like, together, together." She pauses and looks down at me for reassurance, and I give it to her by taking one of her hands and kissing it lightly. "So, if you have anything to say." She pauses and glares across the table at Micah. "Just say it. We're all adults here." When she says that last line, she looks down the table at her brother, but

I look the other way at her dad. It just dawned on me that Clay might not like the idea of me being with his daughter . . . in the biblical sense.

And now I'm nervous.

Clay chuckles as he takes a bite of chicken.

Kay sighs.

My mama looks like she's about to cry.

Micah is happily eating.

My dad looks . . . proud? Yeah, definitely proud. Like, the first time I rode a bike or the day I graduated from LSU. He smiles up at Cami and then back at me, giving me an approving wink.

Tucker's brows are furrowed and his mouth twists as he chews on the information he's just been given. I'm sure the conversation with him isn't over.

Cami calmly sits back down, and I lean over to kiss her cheek.

"Well said, babe."

"Oh, it's *babe* now?" Micah asks, quirking an eyebrow over his chicken leg.

"Shut up and eat your dinner," Mama says, swatting his shoulder, which gives me a sense of satisfaction. It's always warmed my heart to see Micah reprimanded, because, in my humble opinion, it didn't happen enough when we were kids.

And just like that, everyone goes back to normal.

Thirty-Seven

Camille

Present

PLEASE FIT. PLEASE FIT. PLEASE fit.

I suck in and wait for the zipper to be pulled. Holding my breath, I close my eyes and say a silent prayer. With the wedding in five days, I'm cutting it close. There's no time to order another dress. It's kind of crazy, waiting until the last minute like this, especially since I've wanted to marry Deacon my whole life.

Well, that's not entirely true.

If you asked me when I was six who I was going to marry, I would've told you my daddy.

If you asked me when I was eight who I was going to marry, I would've told you no one.

Boys were gross.

But, if you asked me when I was sixteen who I was going to marry, I would've told you Deacon Samuel Landry, or at least, I hoped . . . and prayed, and wished on every birthday candle and shooting star.

However, if you asked me when I was twenty-two who I was going to marry, I would've told you no one. At that age, I felt like I'd completely messed up—my life, my career, my relationship with Deacon . . . and the baby I was carrying. There were days I couldn't see more than an hour into the future. Everything felt so scary.

From then, until now, so much has happened. It feels like two lifetimes, but also like it all happened yesterday.

"There," Annie says, securing the zipper at the top and snapping a button into place.

I hear collective sighs behind me and then I turn, facing myself in the mirror in all my white satin and lace glory.

Dani's best friend, Piper, is with us today and she begins to frantically wave her hands in front of her face, letting out a deep breath. "I think I'm gonna cry."

"You're so crazy," Dani teases, nudging Piper with her elbow. "Weddings are happy, not sad. Save your tears for when someone dies."

I smile at their reflections in the mirror, catching Annie's tearful expression.

"Stop," I whisper, my voice catching in my throat.

"I'm sorry," she sniffles, dabbing under her eyes. "I just . . . you know."

I nod, biting the inside of my cheek to keep my emotions in check. I do. I know. She's thinking my mama would love to be here and that she'd be so proud. Annie's told me that a lot lately, how proud my mama would be of the woman I've become and how proud she'd be of the mama I am.

"Just wait until Deke sees you," Dani gushes.

Annie laughs and Piper hugs onto Dani's arm, and I stand there, staring at myself. The bridal magazines always say you'll just know when you've found the one—the guy, the dress. I knew the minute I put this dress on that it was what I wanted to walk down the aisle in . . . what I wanted to wear when I finally said I do to the love of my life.

Thirty-Eight

Camille

One month earlier

ONIGHT IS JUST YOUR AVERAGE Landry get together. There's a DJ and a dance floor and lots of food. Micah and his girlfriend, Dani, just got back from New York yesterday, and Annie wanted to welcome Dani to Louisiana. So, here we are.

But something about tonight has felt different.

Earlier, Deacon seemed a little nervous, and now, I can't find him anywhere.

Then, his voice comes through the speakers and the dance floor parts like the Red Sea.

"Cami," Deacon says my name so sweetly, his dimples on full display and his blue-green eyes dancing in the pale light. "My sweet Cami."

With those four words, tears start to blur my vision, and I don't even know why. I mean, I think I might know, but maybe I don't. Maybe this is something that only happens in my dreams, and maybe I'm afraid to blink because this vision in front of me might disappear.

"I have somethin' I'd like to give you," he says, nodding his head at Travis, the guy who helps Annie around the house with yard work. Travis walks up to me and hands me a small canvas. There's paint on it, but it's not a complete picture.

Then, Kay walks up and hands me another piece.

And then my daddy.

Annie, Sam, Micah, Dani, and even Piper . . . they all walk up and hand me pieces of canvas until I have too many to hold. Eventually, I set them down at my feet and spread them out, noticing a pattern with the shapes and shading. So, I begin to piece them together on the wooden dance floor, forgetting all about the people surrounding me.

Deacon stands quietly, watching me. Every once in a while, I glance up to see if he's still there, but he is. Just like always. He's still there, watching over me.

I get to a point where I know what the canvases make, but I'm missing a piece. That's when my brother kneels down and hands me the last one. It's the part of a castle where the princess usually stands. The window that's high up, where she can see the whole world, my favorite part.

I sit there, staring at the complete picture. Those tears I was trying to hold back earlier are trickling down my cheeks, and it's so quiet. The only sound is my occasional sniffle, but then I look up and see damp eyes all around me. So, maybe it's not just *my* sniffles.

Deacon kneels down in front of me, just on the other side of the painting and pulls out a black box, opening it up. His hand reaches across, showing it to me. It's simple, perfect.

"I know we've done things slowly," he begins, looking at me in that way that makes me forget everything and everyone, drawing me into our own little world. "But I've loved you since I knew what it meant to love someone."

I hiccup, trying to keep from falling completely apart.

"When I look into your eyes, I see everything—my past, my present, and my future. I see my best friend. I see the woman I want to wake up to every morning. And the one I want to kiss goodnight for the rest of my life. I still see the girl I fell so hard for so long ago, and the amazing woman she's turned into." He stops and laughs to himself. "I thought I loved the girl . . . and I did. But I didn't realize how much more I would love the woman. And tomorrow, I'll love you more than today."

I wipe at my face and sit back on my heels, letting out a deep breath.

"I want to grow old with you. I want to be Carter's dad. I want to have more babies."

And now I laugh, not because it's funny, but because I want all of that too.

"And I don't want to spend one more day than I have to where you're not Mrs. Deacon Landry. So, please, tell me you'll marry me."

The smile that splits my face makes my cheeks hurt.

The quiet gasps from around me pull me out of our bubble, and for the first time since he knelt down on one knee, I glance around. Everyone, my whole family—they're all waiting with baited breath like they wonder what I'm going to say, and that makes me laugh again . . . hard. Because I don't even have to think about it.

I stand up and Deacon joins me, still holding out the ring. And as beautiful as it is, it's not what I want.

In one leap, I jump over the paintings at my feet and into Deacon's embrace. My arms wrap tightly around his neck, and I kiss him so hard. His chest rumbles with a laugh, and I start kissing everywhere my lips can reach—his eyes, his cheeks, his nose.

"Is that a yes?" someone from the crowd yells. Maybe my brother? Or my daddy?

And I realize I haven't answered him or accepted his ring.

"Yes," I finally say. "Every day of my life. Yes."

Thirty-Nine

DEACON

Present

"CHEERS, MAN," TUCKER SAYS AS he clicks his glass of bourbon with mine. "We all know that I could've kicked your ass multiple times over the last ten years or so for bein' in love with my sister."

I nod my head in agreement. I don't think for a second that he could kick my ass, but if he ever knew the dirty thoughts I had about Cami while we were growing up or, hell, the thoughts I had of her just this morning, he'd have reason to try.

"But, now," he continues, "I'm reserving the right to kick your ass if you ever upset her in any way in the future."

"Duly noted, brother," I reply. I wouldn't expect anything less from Tucker.

He hugs me before clapping me on the back. "I know you and Cami are perfect for each other but, seriously, break her heart and I'll break you."

"Alright, alright. Damn, Tucker, I'm beginnin' to wonder if this is your way of flirtin' with me. You seem very preoccupied with my ass."

"Shut the fuck up, Landry. Finish your drink so you can finish getting dressed. The quicker you get hitched, the quicker I can score at your reception."

I finish my drink and hand the glass back to Tucker. Father Damon would be pissed to know Tucker brought booze into the church but, then again, he probably wouldn't be too surprised.

"Tucker, I bet you twenty dollars the only person you haven't hooked up with at our reception, besides family members, is Old Lady Johnson."

"Challenge accepted. I always did love the way she played the organ at church."

"You are one sick fuck, man. Hand me my bow tie, would ya?"

He tosses my tie, and I wrap it around my neck before slipping on my vest.

"So, how's your leg doin'?" he asks.

"It's good. The cut is still there, but the doctor says it's healin' well. The bruises are startin' to fade, too. I had to get my pants tailored a little on the loose side, though, so the fabric wouldn't get caught on the bandage."

"Aww, shit, man. I don't want to hear that." Tucker cringes before finishing his drink.

The last step to me being dressed for the ceremony is putting my jacket on, but I won't do that until it's time to walk to the altar with Father Damon. Now, we just have to sit here until we're told the ceremony is about to begin.

After a few minutes, Micah walks in.

"Hey, man, you nervous?" he asks.

"Hell, no. I'm ready to get this show on the road and make Cami my wife. How much longer until the girls get here?"

"Just a few more minutes, I think. Mama went over to make sure they were runnin' on time."

Moments later, Father Damon knocks on the door.

"Are you gentlemen ready to take your places?"

"Is Cami here?" I don't even try to hide the excitement in my voice.

"Not yet," Father Damon answers, "but she should be any minute now."

As we all walk to the small room in the back of the sanctuary, I try not to worry about why Cami isn't here yet. I mean, it's not that she's *late,* she's just not on time. I'm sure she just needs some extra help with her dress or hair or something.

Fifteen more minutes pass before my dad's pocket starts buzzing. I watch him as he takes his cell phone out and reads the incoming text. When he's finished, he looks up at me with an expression I can't name. Is he sad? Worried? Angry? All I can decipher is that he doesn't look happy, and that doesn't make me feel any better.

"What is it? Is Cami okay?" I ask, my voice full of desperation.

My dad takes in a deep breath and slowly lets it out. "Son, we might have a problem on our hands."

Forty

Camille

Present

TODAY IS THE DAY. THE day I'm marrying my best friend. The day I finally catch my ultimate castle—Deacon Samuel Landry.

Taking a deep breath, I look at myself one more time in the mirror of my childhood bedroom. I wanted to get ready here at home. I don't know why, but sitting at the same spot I got dressed in my entire life feels right. Plus, being here makes me feel closer to my mama, and I need that today. I always miss her more on important days, and I know today would've been a day she would've loved to see. I often wonder if she had any thoughts of who I'd eventually marry.

I think she'd be happy about me marrying Deacon. She loved him. And she loved me. So, I think she would've loved the two of us together.

I kiss the heart-shaped locket and lay it back against my chest. I think she'd love this dress, too. It's simple. I always thought I'd pick something worthy of a princess, but when I went to pick out a dress, this is the one that called to me. It reminds me of the one my mama wore the day she married my daddy. Maybe that's why I picked it. It's lacy and elegant, but understated. And it makes me feel beautiful.

"You ready?" Annie asks, sticking her head in the bedroom door.

"So ready," I tell her reflection in the mirror as she walks up beside me and squeezes my shoulders.

"You look beautiful."

"Thank you."

"You're gonna make my baby so happy."

"I hope so."

"No hopin' to it. You already do. And Sam and I are just glad we finally get to claim you legally."

We both laugh a little and try not to cry. I'm not going to cry today. It's the best day of my life, besides the day I had Carter. There's no need for tears.

Nothing could ruin this day.

As long as I'm Mrs. Deacon Landry by the end of it, that's all that matters.

"Gorgeous," Stacey says, fluffing my veil as I walk into the hallway.

"Oh, honey," is all Kay can muster with her white hankie held to her face. Kay is a crier. And she's a sucker for a good romance.

"Come on, guys," I say, like a coach to his team before a big game. "The goal is for me to make it to the church on time and with all of my makeup still intact."

Everyone smiles and nods as we begin to make our way to the front door.

"Just wait until your daddy sees you," Kay says from behind me.

"Kay," I warn, not needing to think about that just yet.

"Oh," I hear Annie say as she steps out onto the front porch and Stacey freezes in front of me.

"What?"

When I glance around Stacey, I see a sleek silver sports car parked in the driveway, and for a split-second, I wonder if I'm supposed to ride to the church in it. Maybe the place we rented the limo from got confused. But then I see *him*.

"Tristan?" I ask, confusion and shock making me practically trip over my floor-length dress.

"Camille." His voice is even, but unsure.

"What are you doin' here?"

"I—" he starts, but pauses, letting out a hard laugh and running a hand nervously through his hair. "I don't know."

I can hear the honesty in his voice and see it in his eyes when he finally allows himself to make eye contact with me.

"I was in a gallery last week, and I saw some of your work," he says. "It was . . . different, but the same. It made me think of you and wonder . . . I just had to come and see for myself. I needed to know what happened to you," he says, his hand dropping to his side. "I've missed you."

That confession makes my shock and confusion turn to anger. He's missed me? After all this time? Now? He chooses now to find me and say he's missed me?

"What?" I ask, trying to make sense of what's happening right now.

I feel Stacey's hand on my arm, and I hear Annie's grunt of disapproval.

"We were great together," he starts again, taking a step up on the porch.

"What?" I ask again, this time, my voice sounds a bit manic.

He takes another step toward me.

"No," I say, shaking my head. "No, you don't get to do this. You don't get to show up here." I stomp my foot on the wooden porch, and the sound travels over the fields and causes a few birds to take flight. "This is my house. This is my wedding day. And you," I say, pointing as I take a step toward him, years of anger boiling inside me, "you don't get to ruin this for me. You lost that right when you wanted to get rid of *my* baby. We weren't great together. We were toxic. You were toxic. I was blind, but that's the past. *You're* the past, and you can leave. *Now.*"

His face changes from soft and reminiscent to hard. He was always good at schooling his features, but he's failing miserably right now.

I guess the mention of *the baby* is a little too much for him to handle. I'm also guessing he's wondering about Carter about right now, and I'm daring him with my death stare to ask. I want him to. This is long overdue.

"Go ahead," I taunt as I feel a hand on my back, someone letting me know they're by my side. "Ask me."

"What?" He looks confused for a second before realization dawns on him. "The . . . the baby?"

"Is a boy and he's wonderful. The best thing that ever happened to me apart from the man I'm gettin' ready to marry. So, I guess I should say thank you. Thank you for giving me something I didn't even know I wanted or needed, and thank you for makin' it so easy to let you go. We were never gonna make it anyway."

"I have a son?" he asks, his brows furrowing at the thought.

"No," I say, with a harsh laugh as I bite my lip and shake my head. "No, you don't."

We stand there for a moment before Annie speaks up. "Now, if you'll excuse us. We have a wedding to get to, and we're late." The piss and vinegar in her tone are evident, and I believe she shoulder checks Tristan on her way by. "Oh," she says, turning around to face him. "If you ever step foot on this property or come near my daughter-in-law again, you'll be sorry. My husband happens to be one of the best lawyers this side of the Mississippi, and he'd love nothing more than to take you to the cleaners."

When I pass by Tristan, I look him square in the eyes. I want him to know that he didn't get any part of me and he never will. I don't know what possessed him to show up here today of all days, but I hope this is the last time I ever see his face.

As we pull away, I glance back just in time to see Tristan slide into the sleek sports car. My blood is still pumping feverishly through my veins, and the death grip I've had on my bouquet is making my hand ache. For a minute, I let him get to me. I let these last minutes overshadow the complete happiness I felt before I walked onto that porch.

"Hey." Annie touches my hand and makes me look at her. "Forget about that. Don't let him ruin this day. He doesn't get to do that."

I nod, taking a deep breath.

"What an asshole," Stacey mutters beside me.

"I'd like to kick his ass," Kay adds.

I glance up to see a scowl on her face, and it makes me laugh, like a full on belly laugh, because I can't imagine Kay hurting a fly. And all of this feels like an episode out of the Twilight Zone.

"We're goin' to get married," Annie reminds me.

"Yeah," I reply, nodding my head and clearing my mind of all of the mess I left behind.

"And we're runnin' a little late," Kay chimes in, looking at her watch. "Gonna need you to step on it, Tom." She leans forward yelling into the front seat.

Tom must get the message because the car lurches forward, and we all hold onto each other for dear life.

When we finally pull up in front of the familiar white church, I take a deep breath and then smile as I see my daddy jog over and open the door.

"Hey, baby. Finally decide to show up for your own weddin'?" He peeks into the car at the rest of the ladies and gives Kay a wink.

"We had a little delay," Annie says, fixing my dress as I step out and take my daddy's hand. "But we're here now."

"Cue the music," someone whisper-yells as I walk through the doors.

Stacey gives me a smile and a brief hug as she passes by me and begins her quick ascent up the aisle.

My dad pats my hand. "Nervous?"

"Nope."

"You got ants in your pants?"

"No," I laugh, trying to see into the church. "I just need to get to Deacon."

"Well, let's go," he says, and we start walking.

Everyone in the congregation is standing, and I can tell from the glances and whispers that they were wondering where I was. Maybe they thought I was a runaway bride? I laugh to myself at that thought. No way in hell. There's only one way I'm running, and it's straight toward the man staring down the aisle at me.

Deacon's big dimples are on display, and a tear is sliding down his cheek.

When we finally make it to the front, he clears his throat and rubs roughly at his eyes before taking my hand from my daddy.

"You okay?" he asks as his expression goes from adoring to

concerned.

"Yeah. Sorry, I didn't mean to make you wait." I don't want to even think about anything but promising forever to Deacon. When I smile up at him, he smiles my favorite smile back at me.

"Would've waited forever for you."

"I love you," I whisper, wanting to hurry and get to the kissing part because I need to kiss him so damn bad right now.

"I love you," he replies.

Epilogue

Camille

*I*T'S BEEN TWO WEEKS SINCE I became Mrs. Deacon Landry. Two weeks of wedded bliss.

Two weeks of pinching myself to make sure I'm not dreaming.

It might not have been the fairy tale I dreamed of, and it hasn't been perfect, but life isn't perfect. It's messy and unplanned.

Walking up to the bar in the old barn, I pour myself a drink and search the room for Deacon. He left me a while ago to find some extra chairs for his mama and never made it back.

I spot him standing on the opposite side of the barn, laughing with Micah and Tucker. When they're together like this, it's easy to forget all the years that have passed. They seem so young, like they don't have a care in the world. Granted, most of the time, the three of them don't.

Tucker breaks apart from the group and makes his way onto a makeshift stage. Not only are we still celebrating our newlywed status, but this also happens to be Sam and Annie's thirty-fifth wedding anniversary. Outside of our wedding two weeks ago, this is the biggest shindig French Settlement has probably ever seen.

As I look around the barn, it doesn't escape me how much has changed since the last big anniversary celebration. On their twenty-fifth wedding anniversary, I felt like Deacon and I were going our separate ways. It was the end of an era, the end of our childhood and us being attached at the hip. Everything changed after that night. But also, so much remained the same. Even though Deacon and I followed different paths for a while, we were still connected. He's always going to be the one boy I want. I'm always going to love the life I was given and the people in it. Those things will never change.

More people filter in through the doors, and I love watching their expression as they take in the transformation. The barn is decked out with a million tiny lights, making it feel more like a night sky than a dusty old building. Tables are set up all along the walls and out into the yard, past the double doors. And booze. There's lots of booze. Annie also has a spectacular buffet lined up with gumbo, jambalaya, and shrimp cooked three different ways.

These parties always start out as family and friends only, but tend to multiply quickly. All it takes is for someone to talk about it down at the Piggly Wiggly and word spreads like wildfire. Besides, everyone knows that a party at the Landry Plantation is *the* party, especially on a night like tonight.

"Cami!" I turn my head toward the familiar shriek coming from the large barn doors that are standing open, flanked by outdoor heaters. Stacey is walking through the door with a tall, handsome fellow on her arm.

Her new boyfriend Matt, I presume.

And I approve.

He's looking down at her like she's the belle of the ball, which she is, in her stunning white slacks and an off-the-shoulder sweater. Her hair is swept up in a sleek, yet messy bun. Everything about her screams grown-up, important, and put together, with a hint of edge, thanks to black heels.

She throws her arms around me and squeezes tightly. "I missed you."

"You just saw me less than two weeks ago," I tell her, smiling sweetly at the man standing behind her.

"I know, but I always miss you. And I'm not used to seeing you this often. It makes me miss you more," she says, ever the melodramatic.

"You must be Matt," I say, offering him my hand to shake, but instead he takes me from Stacey's arms and pulls me in for a hug. He was supposed to come to the wedding as Stacey's plus one, but something came up and he couldn't make it.

"You must be Cami."

"Sorry," Stacey says, clearing her throat. "Where are my manners? Matt, Cami. Cami, Matt. I talk so much about both of you to the other; I feel like you already know each other."

"It's really nice to finally meet you," I tell him.

"Likewise," he says, looking around the barn at all the people who keep filing inside.

Honestly, it's like they're coming out of the woodworks.

"You both need a drink," I tell them, motioning to the bar. "Annie and Sam have it well stocked and will be highly offended if you don't partake."

"I think we can handle that," Matt says with a wink.

"Hard Limits is the entertainment for the night?" Stacey asks, watching Tucker do his sound check.

"Yep, they're supposed to start playin' a little later."

"Cool," she says, smiling. "It's been awhile since I've been out here, but I don't remember it looking quite this pretty. Well, except for your paintings. Those are always pretty."

"You did those?" Matt asks, pointing at the walls.

"Yep, don't look too closely, or you'll see some of my earliest work, and trust me, it's not pretty."

He laughs, but shakes his head. "It's all beautiful. Really. You're seriously talented. I've seen some of your pieces that Stacey has in her condo, but this is probably my favorite."

"Well, thank you."

Yep, we'll be besties before the night's over.

I smile and send them to the bar as I go about trying to find Deacon . . . again because he's already moved from where he was standing just a few minutes ago.

"Hey, Cam," Dani says, sidling up next to me.

"Hey, Dani," I reply, giving her a little bump with my hip.

Having another girl around here is nice. When I was younger, it was always Annie and me against everyone. Then as I got older, I depended on Stacey a lot for girl stuff. Thankfully, my daddy eventually found Kay, and that helped balance out the testosterone, but having Dani here is just what we needed. She's perfect for Micah, and she fits in perfectly with our family. We've only known each other a few months, but she's already starting to feel more like a sister than a friend.

"Where's my little buddy?" Dani asks, her eyes roaming around the room.

"He's at the cottage with one of the girls from church. She's babysitting him there tonight. I figured since it's close by and I can check on him if I need to, it'd be fine," I tell her. "Besides, he'll have a lot more fun watching movies and playing games. Not to mention, he turns into a Gremlin after nine."

We both laugh because Dani has witnessed Carter past his bedtime. It's not pretty.

"Who's that?" Dani asks, pointing over to where Micah is standing talking to someone.

I bend my neck a little further to see around him, and a tall, blonde comes into focus.

"I think she's someone we went to school with," I say, thinking out loud. "I can't remember her name . . . Allie . . . Alex?" My voice drifts off, and I look over to Dani, who can't take her eyes off them.

"You okay?" I ask.

"Yeah, I'm fine," she says, but I can see she's not.

"You don't have anything to worry about," I assure her. "Micah only has eyes for you."

"Yeah," she replies, turning from them and offering me her best smile. "I just didn't like how she was touching him. It was too familiar." She frowns and it's adorable.

"Dani, sweetie," I say, gently. "Micah was *familiar* with quite a few people." I know no girl wants to hear that about the person they're in love with, but she deserves to know the truth.

"Oh, I know. I guess I just haven't had to interact with too many of them . . . yet."

"Like I said, you have nothing to worry about."

DEACON

"HEY, MAW, I PUT THE rest of the chairs out, like you asked. Anything else you need?"

My mama stands with her hands on her hips and looks around the barn. Her eyes squint as she takes in every detail, making sure everything is perfect. She's definitely in her element right now, party planning being one of her many talents, but I don't want her to stress out. She should be having fun along with everyone else and not worrying about keeping the stacks of napkins straight.

"No, I think we have everything we need. What do you think?" she asks.

"I think it's perfect and, if it's not, no one will notice or care. That's why we have booze, remember?" I wink at her and watch her shoulders relax while she laughs.

"Looks like the word got out we're havin' a party tonight," she says with a sigh.

"It's all good, Mama," I assure her. "Don't stress the small stuff, okay? All that matters is that you and Dad have fun. Thirty-five years is a long time to put up with his ass. Speak of the devil, I'm pretty sure that's him over there lookin' for someone to jitterbug with. You'd better get over there before he's snatched up by Ms. Devereaux."

"Oh, please, your daddy knows better than to dance with anyone else but me," she says, laughing. "I'll go, though." She kisses my cheek and looks up at me, smiling.

She starts to walk away but quickly turns back to me. "Shoot! I forgot to refill the ice chests. Would you mind going to the big freezer and grabbing a few bags of ice?"

"Consider it done. Now, shoo." I motion for her to keep walking then, head out to the big house.

Everywhere I look I see people smiling and having fun. Hearing their laughter as they eat and drink makes me extremely happy. It's the same feeling I get when I'm at one of my restaurants, but this is one hundred percent better because these are my people . . . people I've known and loved my entire life.

The freezer with the bags of ice is in my parents' garage but, since the garage door is closed, I have to walk through the house to get to it. I walk through the kitchen and down the hall toward the garage, stopping when I hear an odd sound, kinda like a moan.

The sound gets louder and louder, so I follow it until I'm standing in front of a bathroom. That explains the moaning. It's a little early in the evening for someone to be worshipping the porcelain god, but it's not unheard of. My people like to party hard.

I start to walk back down the hall but stop again when I hear a different sound coming from the bathroom. It's another moan, but the voice is different . . . deeper. Curiosity gets me, and I place my ear against the bathroom door. Various grunts and groans make me stifle my laughter, and I wrack my brain trying to figure out who's in there.

Oh, shit.

If it's my brother and Dani, I'll need some brain bleach. But I know I saw Dani talking to Cami outside, so it can't be them. And it can't be Micah with someone else. A year ago, maybe. But there's no fucking way Micah would cheat on Dani, and, if he did, he'd get the beat down of his life.

"Ugh, why do you drive me insane yet make me feel *so* good?" a voice growls from inside the bathroom.

Well, that's interesting.

The voices are muffled, so I press my ear harder against the door to hear better.

"Can you just shut up for a few minutes and let me fuck you? I'm so close, but your mouth is ruinin' it," the second voice replies.

Fuck. I know that voice.

"Shut up, Tucker Benoit. I don't need you to get off. I could walk out right now and leave you begging for more. Don't tempt me."

"Ha! That's not what you said last night, was it, Piper?"

Holy shit.

Tucker and Piper are fucking in my parents' bathroom and, apparently, it's not the first time. I don't even know what to do with this information, but it sounds like they're almost done in there. So, I'd better make a decision.

Do I bust them as soon as they walk out?

Do I tell Cami . . . or Micah and Dani?

Better yet, maybe I should keep it a secret.

I could always use this new information to bribe Tucker.

I step away from the door and walk quietly into the garage. After grabbing a couple of bags of ice, I open the garage door and leave that way, not wanting to run into the fuck buddies and blow my cover.

Once the ice chest is refilled, I grab myself a beer and start to mingle again. When I see my brother talking with someone from his past, it gets my hackles up a bit. Since I'm such a nosey motherfucker tonight, I decide to join in on their conversation.

"Hey, Micah, need another beer?" I ask as I walk up to him.

"Nah, I'm good. Alex, you want anything?" Micah asks.

"No, thanks." Alex turns and smiles at me. "Hi, Deacon. Congratulations on your wedding. Sorry, I crashed your party. I just couldn't pass up the opportunity to see everyone again. Oh, and I'm sorry about what happened to Pockets. I heard about the fire."

"Yeah, it's shitty, but we'll figure things out. It'll be back better than ever." I smile tightly at her and wish she'd never showed up here tonight. I've never liked her. Maybe because, unlike Micah, I've always seen her for exactly what she is, a manipulative bitch.

Back in school, she was always weaseling her way in with whoever would get her what she wanted and I doubt much has changed since then. "It's cool," I tell her. "It's been awhile. What has you back in these parts?"

"Alex was just telling me about a business opportunity we might be interested in."

I thought Micah had wised up to her ways, but apparently not.

"Oh, really?" I ask, quirking an eyebrow at my brother. "Well, I'm off the clock tonight, so you two have your little chat. Micah can fill me in later."

Micah gives me a strange look and shrugs. "All right."

Sometimes I could smack that boy upside his head. I don't know why he'd entertain any idea coming from Alex. With Dani in the picture, he's obviously not thinking with his dick, at least he better not be. But I'm not so sure he's thinking clearly. The last time Alex was in town, all she wanted was a piece of him, and he turned her down. Surely, he's not dumb enough to fall for her tricks this time, because I seriously doubt she has anything credible to offer.

Thankfully, the rest of the evening goes off without a hitch and Alex the bitch seems to disappear as fast as she showed up.

Cami and I sneak away around nine thirty and walk over to the cottage to tuck Carter in and tell him good night. On our way back to the barn, we detour by the pond, stealing a few quiet minutes alone.

"I love you, Mr. Landry," Cami says, stretching up on her tiptoes to reach my lips.

"I love you, Mrs. Landry," I tell her, leaning in for another kiss.

"We could stay here," she says. "No one would miss us."

"I doubt that. The second your brother takes that stage; he'll be hollerin' for us."

She laughs, and I love the way it sounds and feels as I hold her close.

"You're right. He's such a jackass."

"He is that, among other things," I snicker, thinking back about the bathroom festivities.

"Okay, let's head back." There's a reluctance in her voice, and I hold her to me for another minute. The fact that I get to leave with her, tonight and every night for the rest of my life, is the only way I'm able to let her go so we can walk back to the barn.

As we walk inside, the music starts up, as if on cue.

"Where are those newlyweds?" Tucker asks through the mic, squinting his eyes and searching the crowd. "Don't tell me they're still consummatin' the marriage."

Oh, I could ruin that asshole right now.

The joy that floods my soul with that knowledge is enough to keep my lips sealed.

This is gonna be fun.

I raise mine and Cami's joined hands and the crowd cheers.

"This one's for y'all," he says with a wink as he strums out the first chords of Marvin Gaye's *Let's Get It On*.

The people around us laugh and cheer and Tucker eats up every bit of it.

I hope he gets his fill, because he's so got it coming to him. Just wait.

Pulling Cami to me, we begin to sway, keeping our own rhythm. The second she's in my arms and my eyes are on hers, the world around us falls away, just like it always has.

THE END

About the Authors

S O, IN CASE YOU DIDN'T notice, there are two of us. We're both from the south, one just a little further than the other.

Jiff was born and raised in Louisiana. She's now living in Texas with her two teenagers and a bulldog named Georgia Rose. She loves purple and 80's movies and geeking out at Comic Cons.

Jenny Kate was born and raised in Oklahoma. She's raising a seventy-year-old in a twelve-year-olds body. She's also the mama to two Cavalier King Charles Spaniels, Wrigley and Oliver. She loves Kris Bryant and the Chicago Cubs and coffee.

Some people think we've been friends forever, but in reality, we've only known each other for five years. Four of those years, we've spent spinning tales and writing words. Our first published book, Finding Focus, was released in November 2015.

If you like romance set in the south, then you'll love our southern fried fiction with heart and soul.

CONNECT WITH US

www.jiffykate.com

or find us on

Facebook—*www.facebook.com/jiffykatewrites*
Twitter—*www.twitter.com/jiffykatewrites*
Instagram—*www.instagram.com/jiffykatewrites*
Goodreads—www.goodreads.com/jiffykate

Acknowledgements

FIRST AND FOREMOST, WE'D LIKE to thank our families. They're the ones who have to put up with our lack of domesticity while writing words. Thank you for being so understanding and willing to make yourselves meals and play hours of Minecraft and watch dozens of videos on YouTube while we write.

We'd also like to thank Lady Antebellum for their inspiring music. Practically every lyric they've ever wrote helped us through this story. We can't hear one of their songs on the radio without having all the feels for Cami and Deacon.

Our pre-reader and amazing friend, Pamela Stephenson, we're so thankful for your continuing support and encouragement. Thank you for being our fresh set of eyes when we needed it. You were there from the beginning to the very end, and we couldn't be more grateful!

And God bless our editor, Nichole. She's been with us through all the re-writes, two-hour phone calls, and weeks of editing. We couldn't have done this without you! We hope we didn't run you off with this one and we promise to never do a prequel again. *shifty eyes* Every time we say that, we feel like we're jinxing ourselves. But seriously, we're going to try really hard to keep it from happening.

And Nichole's counterpart, the other person who makes up the dynamic duo of Perfectly Publishable, Christine—you were a godsend from the very beginning. We're still in debt to Heather Maven for putting us in contact with you. Thank you for always being so generous with your time and for making our pages pretty.

Jada, thank you for another gorgeous cover!! We love working with you.

And vodka. Vodka has been there for us through the hardest parts.

Also, a shout-out to Amanda Daniel for being so willing to pre-read for us. You're awesome! Thank you so much for your feedback.

And there is no better pimp than Lynette Nichols! We're so happy that you're our friend and that you love our stories! We love you! Thanks for always being willing to help and read our words. Your input is invaluable.

If you've made it this far, bless you. We're so thankful for you. Writing is what we love to do, but having readers is what makes it worthwhile. If you loved this book or even liked it a little, we'd love to hear from you! Your reviews make our days.

Until next time,
Jiff and Jenny Kate